Windigr

By
Jim Erkiletian

© Copyright 2004, Jim Erkiletian

All Rights Reserved.

No part of this book may be reproduced, stored in a retrieval system, or transmitted by any means, electronic, mechanical, photocopying, recording, or otherwise, without written permission from the author.

ISBN: 1-59453-197-8

Dedication

To First Nations and Metis people everywhere.

The following manuscript was discovered inside an old cigar tin in a cabin in the Yukon Territory, said by locals to have been inhabited by a "mad and thoroughly confused prospector, sometime during the middle 1960s."

Contents

1. Out of the Frypan… 1
   Spacecase, his grandson, Yeuzor. The circus,
   Europe and Japan.
2. Into the Stewpot… 25
   Life on the road: Che'clavae's bargain, sheath,
   and eagle attack.
3. Rolling with the Haymaker's Daughters…......... 33
   Bierce, Bert, Harlin and Loralei.
4. Up the Creek Without… 55
   Molly and Loralei, Old man Wrangle, and
   Mickey.
5. The Sun's favourite children…............... 65
   The Poncas brothers and the Taratumara.
6. Perfume and Red Roses… 78
   The band takes shape at the party in the hotel
   room.
7. Deals off the Bottom… 93
   Wrangle and his goons, and the running escape.
8. No Man's Landing… 107
   The better part of valor: Escape into Loralei's
   desert.
9. Cactus Flowers and Sandstone Beads…........... 118
   Recuperation in the Apache country.
10. Heads I Win, Tails You Lose…........................ 129
    Bishop and the bounty.
11. Howling with Hunters: The Desert's Song…...... 139
    Return to the coast with Bishop.

12. The Wasp's New Stinger… 150
   The sting operation on Wrangle.
13. Crows on the Scarecrow… 160
   Investing the take, dividing equally.
14. The Singer Sleeps and the Ghost Floats… 174
   Songpoems and Landscapes.
15. Peter Pan Meets Robin Hood… 202
   Hiking Heads and Four-square Dancers.
16. Tunnels on Rails… 217
   Wobbling Folk and Wolves and Baboons.
17. Swinging in the Family Tree… 230
   Packs, Pods, Flocks and Families.
18. Snakebite Kits and Salmon Skins… 251
   Bears and Breathern.
19. Reversing the Tides… 270
   The Wind-up and the Pitch.

Cover design by Jim Erkiletian

1. Out of the Frypan…

war: n/v;
1. The beginning of politics and religion.
2. The end of politics and religion.
3. The en…

Grandpa, old Spacecase O'Toole, is wanted by the authorities in three provinces, twelve states and Mexico. He has some bad habits; writing checks on dead bank accounts, taking things that belong to rich people and getting married without bothering about divorces.

But he figured travel was good for his health, better for it than sitting around some grimy cell, so he'd never done any jail time. None of the powers-that-be had managed to score his prints, or even a solid I.D. He never had a real I.D. He sort of made them up as he went along. Like the rest of his life.

When I was eight my mother, Spacecase's daughter, decided to dump my father for a bright young gangster who seemed to have connections and qualifications that would assure him a solid career in creative arson. Unfortunately for her, the turkey turned out to be more competent with the fair sex than nitro. The night after Spacecase showed up at mom's place on West 12th in Vancouver's Kitselano, the gangster managed to blow off a couple of fingers botching a job. The mounties had his number, and mom was going to have to drive across the border with the possibility of gunplay at high speed. As grandpa was asleep on the sofa, I was left in his care.

Good thing, too. Mom and her boyfriend took the high side of an inside curve on the Barlow Canyon road to keep from barrelling head on into a twin-diesel semi. They rolled their '39 coupe down a hillside and burned in the wreckage. Tough way to go, but better than getting caught, I guess.

I was standing there studying him with the curiosity of an eight-year-old. I'd only seen grandpa a few times, but had heard stories and, worse, tantalizing bits of stories. Too many times I'd happened into the middle of adult conversation about grandpa O'Toole, only to have the participants clam up silent as a Huron scout in your pantry.

He was sleeping on his back on the couch with his parka tucked up around his chin, one leg dangling over the edge to the floor and the other propped on the arm rest. His snoring was even and low, causing the hairs of his mustache to flutter, but making very little noise. His long white hair curled over his ears and hung over the armrest in back.

I'd just come home from school, where I'd been given some kind of demerit and told I was going to be expelled next time they caught me cutting classes. I was down the basement rapping with the janitor and lost track of the time. You can't hear the bell from down there when the furnace is grumbling.

I decided to mosey on out to the kitchen to make a sandwich when the cops banged on the front door. "Open in the name of the King!" they used to say in those days. Grandpa came from the middle of a snore to full awake, had me bundled under an arm and was down the basement peeking out a window before the second knock.

"Shush," he said in a whisper. I wasn't planning on saying anything. We could see they had the back covered. The corner of a patrol car was visible behind the garage. Spacecase saw I wasn't going to do anything foolish, so he put me down and took his wallet out of his back pocket. He quickly rifled through several I.D. cards, took out all but one set, and shoved the others in behind some loose bricks in the corner.

At the same time he was telling me to go back up and answer the door. "You might want to tell them there isn't anyone home but you, and your folks told you never to let anyone in when you're home alone."

If they came in anyway, he suggested, I could tell them grandpa might be sleeping in the basement. He could verify my story by telling them he'd come in while I was at school.

I went back upstairs to the door, opened it a crack with the chain on, and told them I was the only one home. I also told them I'd like to ask them in, but that mom had told me never to let anyone in the house when I was home alone. For good measure I added it was illegal to enter a dwelling house if there's no one but a minor at home.

Someone called from behind the house that there is no car in the garage, and that someone had left in a hurry. Something about blood on the floor. They put two and two together and decided their man had split.

They asked me through the cracked door who my welfare worker was, and I told them we didn't have one. Then they left. Spacecase frowned at that, but then nodded his head indicating I had done the right thing.

"Nevertheless," he said around a mouthful of leftover meatloaf, "this place is too hot for us. We better think about moving to a cooler climate. How you feel about travelling?"

"I don't know," I told him. Mom was always moving from one place to another, but we'd never been out of Vancouver or the Lower Mainland before, as far back as I could remember. Most of my friends were here. On the other hand, I'd always wanted to get out and see some of the world. "What's in it for me?"

"I could leave you here and let the welfare find you a nice solid family."

"I'll pack my stuff," I went straight to my room and started stuffing clothes into my backpack.

He came to the door, said, "Don't pack more than you can carry easy," then stuck his head in and looked around. "Nice room to be leaving behind," he commented, then returned to the kitchen to rifle it for food.

An hour later we were out on the road, walking in the general direction of the interstate. He started right then telling me the story, an old Indian story he said, of the Wind Digger, a beast that lives in the bush and eats lonely travellers. It was a great way to start my new life away from home for the first time.

Windigr

That old windigr could be just about anywhere, could sneak up on you from behind and bite your whole head clean off. You'd never see a thing except the black of the inside of his mouth and then SNAP!, you'd be a goner. A goner was what you would be if you fell off a cliff or got hit by a car or slipped under a moving freight or got caught by a bear, or any number of other things I was to discover over the next few years.

Grandpa claimed to be on good terms with the windigr, said he had met up with the beast more than once. Although I learned to take most of what the old codger told me with a block of salt, his story of how he met and befriended the most terrifying beast to emerge from human imagination had a ring of truth to it. Somewhat louder than that school bell, fortunately.

"Uh, where are we going, by the way, grandpa?" I asked him, sort of to get him off that windigr rap.

He didn't answer right away, and the silence was starting to get to me when he said, "I suppose you're too smart to believe in the rock candy mountain, where the streams run with soda pop."

I smiled. "That's from a song," I remembered. "Good song, but it don't tell me much."

He kept on walking with those long strides that made me have to trot just to keep up. Finally he said, "We're going looking for your great-grandma's medicine bundle, which was stolen by some mean and powerful types. Pirates, we used to call them. But that's only part of it." Then he stopped and looked at me closely. "From now on you better start calling me

Buzzard, or Buzz. Some places we end up we might not want people knowing we're related."

"O.K." I said, feeling kind of hurt for no reason. "How come?"

He eyed me sidewise and said, "Cause if we meet up with any slave dealers, I could pretend to go along with them until we make our getaway. If they know we're related, they'd know I won't sell you for any price, would maybe just konk me on the head and hog-tie you, sell you to some rich pervert."

I thought that one over for a while.

It was a couple of months after that daring escape, the right combination of corn squeezings and homegrown Kentucky marijuana got old Spacecase into one of his best talkative moods. He was laying on his knapsack, blowing some slow blues on his harmonica, talking in between rifts. I had learned to listened real closely by that time.

He'd start by rambling on for a bit, muttering about politics in general, then kind of stumble into a story. That night it was about the circus he'd worked with in Europe back before the war. He'd made his way there on a tramp steamer, stoking coal, had jumped ship in Italy to go hiking and biking around France and Belgium, when he'd smelled the war coming.

He always called it the Great War to End War, which was his way of indicating his contempt for the powers-that-be, all of which participated in the former to a greater or lesser extent. "People aren't stupid. The goons have to use every trick in the book to get us to kill each other," he'd say. "The worse ones use our own idealism."

He described in some detail the circus of the day, owned by the Ringling's, and a European version of the one that operated in the United States and Canada before they sold out to P.T. Barnum. He first discovered it wintering on the Italian Riviera in early 1913.

"Back then in Europe, even a blind and deaf man with his nostrils full of snuff could smell a war coming," he said. "There were all these little countries with troops sitting on the borders, just waiting for the signal. Lots of places they could see each other across creeks or highways."

"Sounds like the whole world today," I said.

He nodded slowly, looked at me with a curious expression. "It made you feel kind of weird to be cutting across some farmer's pasture, between a couple of Guernseys chewing their cuds, and see soldiers waiting for someone to tell them to start killing each other off to either side."

He didn't say anything for a few minutes, then added, "You're right. It is like the world today. Except today they can't see each other's faces."

Being of a sensible frame of mind, Spacecase was busily looking for some way to get his butt back to the nice safe USA, or Canada. He preferred Canada. He'd been born and raised there. But he figured the British would drag Canadian boys into the conflict for cannon fodder. "British generals have a habit of using Canucks and Aussies, and Yanks when they can get them, to do the hard work like killing other soldiers. And saving their own troops for the easy jobs, like mopping up survivors, raping the women and pillaging the countryside."

"We won, anyway," I said.

"The guys who lost chunks of themselves at Gallipoli sure didn't win," he said quietly.

The Ringling's circus was getting ready for a move when he met up with it again in southern France. They were scheduled to play cities throughout France, England and Germany, some of the Baltic countries and Central Europe, winding up in Sweden before making their way back to warmer climes through Russia, the Ukraine and Rumania. He travelled with them through most of 1913 and back south to winter again on the Riviera.

As they were ending their tour, a young Japanese prince in Italy, introduced himself to the Ringmaster, under the mistaken assumption he was the man in charge of the show. He had a deal. He was willing to underwrite transportation costs of the whole show if they would be interested in wintering in Japan that year.

The winds of war were blowing strong through lots of noses, and a good part of the troupe expressed interest in such a plan. As the season drew to a close, and the winter of 1913-14 moved in on them, a major part of the circus shipped out for The Japans.

Spacecase, or rather Buzzard as he was known then, was a pretty good jack-of-all-trades, and a good enough roustabout to be running errands and helping put up tents and so on. He got to know most of the people in the show, and eventually put together a pretty good clown act, juggling clubs and doing simple magic tricks. He was easily accepted as a part of the troupe even though he wasn't particularly skilled at any one thing.

He figured he could maybe get passage on a steamer to Hawaii or the South Seas from The Japans. So he signed on with the Japan contingent.

Japan was just emerging into the so-called modern world. The Emperor was interested in anything Western. The Japanese explorer very rightly presumed a circus would delight the emperor and his family, and would give them much information about the Western world. A circus can do that, for those with a perceptive eye. The emperor, and his generals and advisors too, found enough glimmer to blind a stone eyeball with that one.

The Japanese prince, one Taka Nakamura by name, arranged for a barge and two large tugs to tow them all across the Mediterranean. On arrival in Egypt, the troupe was transferred aboard a Japanese man-of-war that had been dispatched to convey them to the islands, after a short train ride.

The Japanese navy of the time was quite modern, steam driven and luxurious even by today's standards. They had demolished the Russian navy in a short war nine years before, in 1905, and their post-Samurai nobility understood the importance to an island nation of having a strong navy.

The language barrier and naval discipline prevented most interaction between the Japanese sailors and the troupe. But Spacecase had picked up an international pidgin lingo that most of the sailors used. Taka was able to translate pretty well into English and pidgin, so some late-night bull sessions developed on the afterdeck.

Taka was also interested in games of chance, and wished to learn to play cards, with betting involved. Spacecase obliged him and they set up a game with some of the crew, him teaching them all how to play blackjack and various types of poker.

He taught them so well that he had a few yen in his pocket when they disembarked at Tokyo six weeks later. He claimed to have made some good friends in this activity, too. The sailors he fleeced recouped their losses by teaching others of their countrymen these Western games of chance. Taka, who'd lost money to the sailors on board the ship, was cleaning up pretty well before the troupe had played three gigs on the Japanese mainland.

After playing in several cities on the main island, the circus was invited directly to the imperial palace to provide a private show for the emperor, his family, and a few families of the Japanese nobility.

Being primarily a children's show, for the child in all of us, a circus can be disarmingly simplistic. Anyone interested in dance, martial arts, and sparkling entertainment amid an atmosphere of how much can we get away with, runs a risk of finding himself inside a circus. Carnys are like that, experimenting with balance while juggling as many irregular objects as possible. Working on the edge without a safety net. It was an especially good hideout for someone like Spacecase O'Toole.

Emperors who retain their scalp for any length of time usually display an interest in these same talents as techniques of survival. Any and all skills can become important where you are balanced precariously at the pinnacle of the heap and everybody wants to play king-of-the-mountain. Even emperors like to have fun while they learn.

Taka had arranged for the troupe to pitch their tents in a big lot outside the Imperial Gardens. But as they were setting up, a captain of the guards arrived to tell them that "His Majestry" was not able to leave the castle at the present time. The captain didn't explain. As they discovered later, there was reason to believe an attempt was to be made on the emperor's life. It had something to do with why they were in Osaka instead of the seat of government, which was at Tokyo.

There were a couple of rooms inside Osaka Castle big enough for the entire circus to perform and have a roof over their heads at the same time. So they moved inside, elephants, trapeze frames and all.

Their shows were a great success, of course. Afterwards, they were told they would be welcome to remain for the night and that the emperor would very much enjoy another show the following day. Since it was raining a monsoon outside, they stayed over.

Spacecase and Karl, one of the strong men' of the sideshow, were in charge of pitching hay to the elephants from out of a big wooden ox cart. They were working with their shirts off, trying to keep up with the hungry elephants, when they noticed two young women among the crowd of Japanese observers. Most were watching the elephants. Those two were paying more attention to the two workers.

Kind of flattering,' he thought. Them elephants, picking up big trunk-fulls of hay and stuffing it in their mouths, is a mighty interesting sight.' He concluded the two girls must have excellent taste in men.

Their second show played to a much larger audience. It was enjoyed more than the first had been, from both the performer's and the audience's viewpoint. The entire nobility, and much of the staff of the castle, had invited their families. There were more kids.

The circus cut right across cultural or national boundaries like good boogie music or maple sugar candies. This one had representatives of every continent, and most European countries. The elephants and their trainers were Indian and Malay. The acrobats were Romanian and Latin American. The ringmaster was Italian, the lion tamer English, the wire-walker Greek, and so forth. It was a normal circus conglomerate of languages and races. The most common talk was a combination pidgin and sign language, backed up by facial expressions and gestures.

By the second day some amount of friendship had built up between the circus people and the Japanese nobility, especially the young people of both sets.

Most of these people had been cooped up inside their castle for months. From Taka the performers learned some political nonsense was in the wind that made it dangerous for members of the nobility to roam around where they might be kidnapped or killed by some rival faction. It was strongly recommended that the performers stay within the great hall', and not wander around the castle without an approved escort.

After the second show Spacecase again noticed the same two young women watching him and Karl fork hay to the elephants. He nudged the Norwegian. "Looks like those two are interested in our muscles," he said.

"Yah," the big man replied. "I seen 'em, uh, before."

"Yesterday," Spacecase said. "I'll go ask Taka to invite them to a party."

He didn't know it, but they were daughters of very high noble birth. Taka, when he saw who they were, was totally opposed to any plan regarding those two girls. He described in graphic detail what would happen to Spacecase and Karl if they should be caught by either girl's father.

He owed Spacecase, however, for having taught him to play poker. In fact, by that time he had won a large amount more than he had lost, and was doubly indebted. The rules of karma are very strict on that score.

Spacecase and Karl managed to get him to gulp down just enough saki to build up his courage, then sent him into the castle on a mission, to set up a liaison with those two girls.

All developing relationships among Japanese nobility were very closely watched. Chaperons were expected to accompany young people everywhere. As in other societies that follow such rules of conduct, the more tight the constrictions, the more creative the methods developed by the young to circumvent them. With Spacecase and Karl it took the form of substituting a servant for the actual lady.

Along about dusk, after the last show was finished, Spacecase was able to slide into a warm pallet underneath and between the lion and tiger cages with a giggling and curious lady. It must have been rather a romantic spot for cuddling a young woman of noble birth, as one of her servants slept in her own warm bed. The knowledge that her Samurai father would be honour-bound to castrate and slowly disembowel him should they be discovered lent a definite air of adventure to the whole affair.

Karl and his equally curious new friend were similarly bedded down on a pallet just behind the lion cages.

Karl was one of two strong men of the show. He and his twin brother, Kurt, were big strapping blond giants who had grown up in Norway on a farm that was mostly rocks and gnarled pine trees. Used to hard, back-breaking labor from childhood making that land produce enough to feed themselves and their parents, they had grown into huge strong men. After their father and mother died, they had worked their way south and met up with the circus just as it was starting to swing south that year.

The strong man with the troupe at the time, a lumberjack from Canada, was looking to retire. When he saw the two giants ambling around in the crowd, and found out they were looking for work, he invited them to try out for his position. The next day he was able to recommend them to the boss, claiming, with many witnesses, that Karl and Kurt had both beat him arm wrestling.

"The lumberjack made a pile of money betting against himself on that one," Spacecase claimed. "I held some of the bets for him and my cut was over a hundred bucks. He could have had four or five other guys holding, I don't know."

"Those two ladies must not have got much sleep, under a tiger cage for the first time," I said.

He nodded. "None of us did, actually. The night with that young lady was as close to heaven as I'd yet managed, up to that time," he hesitated, "which should have told me something big and heavy and mean was coming barrelling down the road lickety-split."

In the wee hours of the morning, with a little edge on because of the possibility of the girl's father discovering her missing, and since he was, as I've mentioned, a light sleeper, something made him peek out from under the wagons. By the dim light of the gas-powered torches he could see several shadowy figures moving just inside the doorway at the end of the great hall. The emperor's men looking for seducers,' he thought. Holy shit!

Inside the doorway three juggler/clowns were sleeping on pallets on the stone floor. They were brothers who had been with the circus since childhood, a bit simple, but quite good at their trade. One of them came sleepily awake and looked up at the black-clad figures silently filtering into the room.

He probably would have rolled over and gone back to sleep. But these Ninja hadn't been informed a circus was residing in the great hall, right across their route to the emperor's quarters. Not wishing to take any chances, they killed him.

Spacecase caught a glimpse of spinning steel as a heavy four-bladed throwing star buried itself in the side of the man's head.

And them guys are sacked out alone, Spacecase thought. What will they do when they get to me and Karl!?

The other two clowns awoke, and the Ninja battle leader gave the order to kill them as well. But they were awake by that time, and they were carnies.

We tend to think of clowns as uncoordinated buffoons. Yet, they are often the most practiced artists of the circus. Hours on top of hours throwing balls, knives, clubs and torches in the air, and catching them without knocking out a tooth or grabbing the burning end, adds up to training, training and more training. These men slept with the tools of their trade within arm's reach.

Two more throwing stars were sent spinning through the air. Both ended up sticking in a wooden club that seemed to appear in their flight path by magic, shattering it but damaging no one. Then the two jugglers were throwing balls, clubs, blankets, anything they could get their hands on, at the dozen or so Ninja fighters clustered just inside the doorway.

And they were screaming, at the top of their voices, the short phrase guaranteed to bring carnies running from all directions, "Hey Rube!"

A few yards to the left of the three clowns, Kurt, the other strong man, was bedded down on some straw bales beside the elephants. He stood up to see what all the commotion was about just as the two clowns scrambled over the bales for cover.

It must have been quite a sight for that Ninja battle leader, to see this big giant suddenly looming up, and to realize he was going to have to fight his way through a whole circus. His schedule called for him to make it across this room in seconds. He estimated the time it would take moving his force along the wall instead, and sent the information back to his commander.

But now he was on unfamiliar ground. The circus was beginning to wake up. A lion, smelling blood and death, growled low in its throat in the cage behind Spacecase and his girlfriend. And Kurt, jumping up on the top of the bales, felt a throwing star graze his left arm and heard it clatter to the floor behind him.

Good thing that sucker didn't hit an elephant, he thought. Then he bellowed "Hey Rube!" at the top of his voice and jumped down off the bales to face his attackers.

The Ninja battle leader was thinking on his feet. But he was faced with a giant and some apparently well-trained opposition, certainly better trained than the imperial troops he had been expecting. And lions and elephants.

He made a quick decision to split his forces, sent ten fighters against the circus with orders to create a diversion. Then he took a handful of his best and began an end-run along the wall in an attempt to gain entrance to the emperor's quarters before the palace guard could be alerted. He was confident he could still make it in the new time-frame he had estimated.

Karl, on a similar bed of straw below the lion cage behind grandpa, heard his brother's yell, rolled out from under that wagon like a avalanche and ran to help. His girlfriend came jumping in with Spacecase and the other girl, her eyes as big as flying saucers.

"She sure had enough on her plate," Spacecase observed, "what with the Ninja on one side and the possibility of her father finding out she was gone from her room on the other. Plus it looked like her big blond boyfriend was maybe gonna get himself killed."

It was she who spotted the Ninja moving like shadows along the far wall, already nearly halfway across the great hall. She realized if they made it through the doors at the end they would not only be inside the emperor's quarters, they would cut off her escape. She grabbed the other girl by the arm, and throwing caution to the winds, they pulled their skirts up, ran to the doors and sailed through to safety, (and/or their respective fathers' wrath).

Once inside, they alerted the imperial troops. Several soldiers came through the doors, to be cut down by throwing stars almost before they could recognize their attackers. Those on the inside managed to pull the doors closed and held them secure.

The Ninja battle leader realized his move was hopeless; in seconds those doors would open again, vomiting imperial troopers who would destroy anyone in their path. He cursed briefly the intelligence that had not informed him of this circus, and ordered a retreat.

Taka, who had been awake all night worrying and trying to make sure all bases were covered, was the first to question the two girls. He alerted the captain of the Japanese imperial guard, on learning there were Ninja assassins inside the palace. They realized the circus was not responsible and told their men to be careful.

Knowing the castle, the guardsman also realized what way the Ninja must have entered to have come this far without being detected, and that there was one place where he could cut off their escape, if he moved fast. Instructing his men to hold the doors until more troops arrived, he took two of his best and made his way to the passageway that would intersect the Ninja retreat, soon joined by other troopers.

When imperial troops arrived at the door to the great hall in sufficient numbers, they cautiously opened them to come to the aid of the circus. But they found themselves on the opposite side of the action from the now retreating Ninja. Kurt and Karl were throwing bales of hay at their now-retreating attackers, scattering them like bowling pins and keeping them on the defensive. But what really caused the Ninja to reconsider their position was Spacecase. He had pulled the pin on the door of the tiger's cage.

The first instant when Spacecase had seen the tiger, back in Italy, he'd known that this was someone he wanted to be on the good side of. He asked around until he found out what the big striped cat liked to eat, got him some and singed it lightly over glowing charcoal. Then he brought it to the tiger's cage on a big silver tray he'd borrowed from the cook, wearing a maitre d's jacket, with a white towel draped over his right forearm. And a pillowcase full of catnip, tucked under his other arm. One of the burgers he'd met on his earlier trek through Germany was a herb farmer. On first meeting the tiger, Spacecase had sent for the farmer's entire crop of catnip. A good investment, as it turned out.

The tiger stood and stretched, then leisurely sniffed Spacecase, the meat, and the catnip through the bars of the cage. Then he sat back down and yawned a couple of times, looked off in the distance ignoring grandpa.

Spacecase opened the door to the cage, and waited respectfully to be invited inside. After making him wait a reasonable amount of time, the tiger sat up on its haunches with a groan, looked across the room, yawned and stood up. He went to the other side of the cage and took a leak through the bars, then padded back to the middle and sat back down and started licking his claws with his tongue.

Spacecase decided this must be an invitation. He stepped inside the cage and carefully slid the platter with the steak over to the big cat. The tiger, without seeming to look in that direction, suddenly speared the steak with a single claw, deftly swung it into his mouth, chewed very briefly and thoroughly, and swallowed.

Then he almost as quickly extricated the pillowcase from under Spacecase's arm with the same paw.

He tossed the pillow in the air, caught it with a front paw, claws retracted, and plunked it on the floor of the cage. A cloud of catnip pollen puffed out of the case. His eyes lit right up, and he lightly plunked it again.

Spacecase and the tiger became good friends. They managed to find time to dine together once or twice a week on average.

The tiger didn't actually get into the action. The sight of the beast bounding down the steps of the wagon, however, caused the Ninja to take notice. It was definitely time for a strategic retreat. By the time the imperial troops were able to secure the hall, the last Ninja was a brief whiff of black shadow down a dark corridor.

Both Kurt and Karl had been injured slightly, and the surviving two clowns were loudly lamenting the loss of their brother as several performers coaxed and cajoled the tiger back into its cage.

The Ninja contingent, some forty fighters in all, had kept their escape route open as well as possible. They used a signalling system of codes, with candles and mirrors, that allowed them to keep their leader informed of the progress of the forward attack group. Because of the quick thinking of the imperial officer, their escape route was intercepted and the forward group was forced to battle the imperial troops who, through sheer weight of numbers, managed to wipe them out. None were taken alive. The Ninja are paid assassins, and professionals. Should one be captured alive, information on the location of the Ninja stronghold might be tortured out of him or her. Surrounded by troops and half dead from fighting and running, the battle leader beheaded his last two lieutenants and fell on his own sword.

At the outer wall of Osaka Castle, the Ninja battle commander saw troops appearing on the wall above. Less than half his remaining forces were on the ground, the rest suspended from ropes on the wall and the cliff face. He allowed a brief flash of hatred for the nobleman who had hired them, but had either not provided proper information, or had been too stingy to hire enough Ninja to get the job done. He would be dealt with later. He gave the order to jump.

The Ninja lower on the face bounced and rolled to their feet. Most of the ones who jumped from higher levels managed to survive. Some had broken ankles and feet.

The commander methodically decapitated the ones who could not travel. Then, with the last of his fighters in tight formation around him, faded into the forest of the moonless night.

Spacecase saw the evidence of that grisly retreat in the morning, cautiously viewing the cleanup operation from the top of the wall. Needless to say, he was some spooked being surrounded by all that silent and lightning-quick death. From that moment he was looking for ways to get the heck out of that castle as soon as possible. And right out of Japan, for that matter.

Windigr

The emperor, although he was suitably thankful for the role they had played in diverting the attack, was not interested in keeping the circus troupe around for much longer. They were rather more expensive to feed and house than a like number of guards, and there were rumors of young aristocratic women becoming too friendly with some members of the troupe. He also thought it would only be a matter of time before his enemies infiltrated the circus. He suggested they should tour the rest of Japan, and provided a contingent of royal guards to accompany them for the next few days.

As soon as they reached a seaport, Spacecase began asking about boats heading in the direction of Hawaii or Australia. By that time war had indeed broken out on the European scene, so he was careful to reject any offers going in that direction.

He finally managed to hook in with a tramp steamer loading a cargo of silk and oranges, bound for Prince Rupert, B.C. He made it back to the Canadian shore before Christmas of 1914. Almost as soon as he stepped off the boat, however, he was requested by a local constable to report for training with the Royal Canadian Armed Forces. So he swapped his Japanese trinkets and money for a dugout canoe with a sail, and began a slow trip down the West Coast of British Columbia, camping out on the beaches and visiting the fishing villages and native camps along the way.

Once in a while he'd stop and work for a day or two, once for as long as a week. When there was no work, he relied on the good nature and hospitality of the folks he met.

"Did you see the windiger that time?" I remember asking him.

"Yep," he replied right away. "Saw him across a bay, one night, pick up a bull moose by the hind leg and bash it against a rock. Then he ate it, bones and all. Big sucker." "Some are smaller than others?"

He considered that, finally said, "I never thought about it before, but there must be little windigrs too, I guess."

2. Into the Stewpot...

Travelling with Spacecase, for an eight-year-old, was kind of like every kid's dream come true. Real dreams, where you never can tell what is going to happen next, how much of it is fantasy, and where the dream ends and the nightmare begins. I learned fast there isn't anything called home more dependable than the one that ends with your skin. I also picked up the code of the road, that you always share what you have with your fellow travellers. Even kids have to learn that one.

Eventually I learned the best way out of trouble is to not get in it in the first place, which means leaving yourself a good escape route before you close your eyes or relax. But nothing is foolproof, and once you're in the soup, the shortest way out ain't necessarily the best way.

Sometimes the only decision you got to make is when to turn loose of the tiger's tail. It helps if you're on good terms with the tiger, but most times you're not. If you let go too soon, you can't get away. Too late, you land right in his mouth like a popcorn tossed in the air.

Spacecase carried two things that I've learned to respect as pretty good primary tools of the hobo trade. In the top left-hand pocket of his Mackinaw he always had a harmonica. In the inside left pocket, a sheathed knife, honed to an edge that would split a hair. I saw him shave a six-inch strip off a human hair with it, just to remind me that I'd better handle it the right way if I was gonna use it.

Up the coast, about a week after he had picked me up, he decided he needed a new sheath for the knife. As a result I was fortunate to meet one of the wisest and most competent people of the Pacific Northwest. Henriette North was her white name, but Spacecase called her by her Kwagwilth nickname, Chi'klavea, or something like that. She said it means "wild rhubarb."

It was a typical cloudy coastal day, and pretty dark inside the log cabin where we met up with her. Spacecase chatted her up pretty good, and finally she said to him, "You want me do something for you. I can tell because you talk lots all around." Then she winked at me sitting on the mat by the door.

Spacecase said he did have something he needed, that it was real polite of her to mention it, and that he knew she was the best person hereabouts with quills and leather. Then he showed her the tattered condition of his knife sheath.

She took it and turned it over a couple of times, said "tsk, tsk" and handed it back to him. "You need new one," she said.

Then there was a considerable amount of haggling over what the price of a new one was, and whether or not he could make the old one do much longer, and how long it would be before he accidentally cut his thumb off if he kept the old one, and so forth.

Finally she ascertained about how much money Spacecase was claiming to be carrying, doubled it, let him haggle her down by a third, and told him he could owe her the rest.

Then she started putting the new sheath together, first pressing the blade against various strips of tanned leather she'd taken from several cedar boxes, and fitting the strips to the knife. She had to shape it just right, so it would hold the blade like a tight glove. Tight against the sides to protect the edge.

She did the whole trip in about an hour, told him her relatives up north who hunt seals have sharper blades, but that his was "pretty good, though", and that she wanted him to tell her a story as she sewed. She said she'd be willing to knock a couple bucks off the price if it was a good story.

Spacecase crossed his legs and settled in to watch her work. She truly was lightning, with those quills. She put a whole bunch of them in her mouth, sticking out from between her lips in a little row like pin tail ducks following their mother. Then she took the piece of moose hide she'd selected, with the outline of the knife still pressed into it, and started sticking the quills through the hide just where she wanted to put the thread through. The porcupine quill is about the only thing in the world that, because it's hollow, goes through hard leather and leaves a little hole all in one go.

Spacecase told her about the time he got jumped by an eagle. "Dang near took my head clean off, Chi'klavea," he swore solemnly. She nodded, already beginning to smile.

"I was floating out on the Yukon River, back in nineteen ought-eight or nine. I was sixteen, so it must have been ought-eight. I figured there might be some gold left in them hills up around Dawson City, in the Klondyke River country. The main rush was over. That was back in 1898. But there was still quite a bustling bunch of activity going on in that country, railroad building and big dredges working the creeks.

"I'd just got myself run out of California by my girlfriend's ogre of a father. Can't hardly blame him, looking back on it. I wouldn't want any of my daughters taking her clothes off with someone like me around.

"Anybody still up there that long after the rush was probably tough enough, ornery enough, and rich enough to be worth getting to know, I figured, even if they had played out most of the gold."

He'd bought an old canoe, fourteen-foot Metis-built cedar strip unit, down at Caribou Crossing on the Bennett Lake, and was having a typical Tom Sawyer trip, most of the time laying back looking at the sky, trees and abundant wildlife that lives out there. Salmon fisher people gave him food sometimes, and the berries were ripening all along the bank anyway. He was feeling no pain.

Some of the people he'd met in California the year before had made him a present of some of those bitter cactus seeds that make you see colours and hallucinations. He'd decided to eat them out on LaBarge, that big lake where Bob Service's lady friend had cremated her previous boyfriend in an old riverboat boiler.

That Yukon River coasts along over two thousand miles to the Bering Sea at a steady four miles an hour, and only speeds up at two places, the Whitehorse Rapids and the Five Fingers Rapids. The former is a lake today, feeding electricity to Whitehorse. Downstream from the Five Fingers, it goes steady, is wider than a half-dozen football fields, and flatter on top. Tends to make a man kinda woozy, watching that river for hours on end, especially downstream from the White River, which carries so much dirt that you can hear the noise of the little pieces of silt scraping together. Sounds like a cross between the gods grinding their teeth at the frustration of not being able to pull your boat under, and giant fingernails on a continuous blackboard.

Tends to get on your nerves after a while.

There was a long stretch, with the river running straight as an arrow and lots of time before the sun went down completely. Just starting to get dark, actually, with long shadows out on the water. The eagle was sitting on a snag, about twenty feet up and maybe three or four yards out over the water. Fishing most likely. He'd probably spotted grandpa, cause eagles can see quite a distance.

He was busy concentrating on his fishing, or something, because suddenly Spacecase was too close, and just below him, looking up and opening his eyes.

That eagle made his choice and jumped, straight at grandpa, coming on like gangbusters. "He couldn't have been more than fifteen feet away, when I first noticed him, and smack dab above me. Aiming right for my head."

Grandpa came out of his doze to the whoosh-whoosh sound of those big wings. The first thing he saw was that great feathered shape approaching on a trajectory that could have taken his head right off at the neck, if it had been a blade. An image of curved talons, sharp enough to spear a fish right through the scales, flashed through his brain. He threw his arms crosswise over his face and jumped about a foot straight up in the air just from the contraction of his back muscles.

He came back down pretty quick, but the canoe was still going with the current, so he was a little off centre and more toward the back. The bow popped up in the air and he grabbed the gunwales on each side to steady her as she tipped right, then back left. By the time he'd steadied the canoe and collected his wits, the eagle was half-way across the river, pumping to beat the band. And laughing so hard his wing feathers were fluttering.

Spacecase stopped to admire the work Chi'clavea was doing on his knife sheath. She let him look at it for a minute, then told him to get on with the story.

I remember I thought it was over already. Good story, I'd thought.

Spacecase settled back down and resumed his tale. "That seemed like a sign to me," he said. "And not a good one, neither. So I thought back over it real careful. Now that eagle was sitting there, watching the river for fish, just like you or I do when we're out there on the water."

Eagle was probably just about as mesmerized as grandpa. He'd have probably glanced upriver when the canoe came around the bend. But since grandpa was obviously sleeping or maybe dead, there wasn't any real need to give up his fishing spot just yet.

Then he got interested in fishing again, misjudged the current, or maybe lost track of the time, and all of a sudden there was this canoe right under his beak, and the guy on board starting to wake up or something. At any rate, the bozo wasn't dead.

There came a point of no return when eagle figured he'd have to get out of there. He was way inside arrow range. Might as well go for broke. So he jumped out over the water, spread his wings, and was onto the air, pumping hard, heading right for grandpa's head. Nothing to lose at that point. If the man was going to shoot him, he'd only have second crack. And eagle had the one thing that can make you or break you. The element of surprise.

"If I'd had time to think, and really thought he was attacking me, I'd have gone over the side anyway," Spacecase said. "But I knew he wasn't, because I could hear him out over the river, just laughing to beat the devil at the way I must have looked bouncing around in that little canoe. He's probably laughing yet today at the cheechako he nearly dunked in the Yukon River.

"Now if I hadn't heard him laugh, I wouldn't be so quick to believe he wasn't really trying to get me. But I had a good, wide brimmed cowhide hat on at the time and, by golly, if I hadn't of woke up right when I did, he would have got it for sure."

Chi'klavea had finished the sheath and was smiling real big. She said she guessed that would be good for a couple bucks. He admired the work, tossed it to me, and told me to look real close, that it was the best sheath I'd probably ever see, except for the ones Loralei made.

Come to think of it, he was right, I've never seen a better one.

We left after sampling some of Chi'clavea's stick bread spread with blueberry jelly, and some kind of tea that makes your poop turn black, but really cleans you out. At the door, Spacecase asked her if she had any news of the windigr in that part of the country.

She looked at him very carefully, scrutinizing him for signs of something only she understood.

"I'd like to avoid him if I can," he said. "I still owe him a fiver."

She laughed and waved us out the door...

3. Rolling with the Haymaker's Daughters...

Natural: n/adj. What one wants to do.

 Spacecase was really proud of his new sheath. When we got the rest of the money he owed on it, later that month in some little fish-packing town that liked his ability to tell jokes and play that harmonica, he sent it straight-away to her. Via Moccasin Express. A trapper who goes by her place on the way to his line. Spacecase always said it was a whole lot faster than the Canadian mail, and there was a lot less chance of it getting lost or ripped-off en route. One of the benefits of being Canadian that hasn't changed. Yet.
 We were sitting by the fire in the little longhouse at Kingcome, up the inlet, but not as far as the village, or even the ranch down-river from the village. Just off Simoon Sound. There wasn't anyone around, and we didn't know if anybody was actually living there. Nobody had put up any Keep Out signs, so we decided to bed down in there for the night.
 He was carving a little husky dog out of yellow cedar. It was about as big as his thumb, with its tail arched over its back and its tongue lolling out of its mouth in the gap between the teeth in the side of its jaw. He was a good carver. Always left his carvings for the next guy to find, someplace prominent. Except for the ones he made for someone in particular.

Jim Erkiletian

He'd made his way to San Francisco after getting back from Europe and finding out Canadians were being whipped into a passion to go fight the Kaiser. It must have been a swinging city in those days, full of Pacific Rim shipping and trade, and all kinds of sharpies and grifters and ladies of fortune and so forth. The Panama Canal had just started putting Atlantic shipping through in 1914.

South of Portland, he met a man on the train name of Traven, who had been a friend of Ambrose Bierce, the writer. Bierce and grandpa had known each other some time after Bierce had compiled his dictionary, what they later called The Devil's Dictionary.

Bierce had spent some time in the town where Spacecase's father had tried to make a go of it in 1906 and 07, Topika Springs, California. He'd fixed up one of the abandoned miner's shacks as a sort of combination retreat-hideout, where he could write with a minimum of disturbance.

Most of the kids around Topika Springs were scared of the old bird, but Spacecase took a liking to him for some reason. He started running errands for Bierce, until he was eventually invited into the man's house, treated to some tea and cakes, and some stories.

Spacecase had never done well in school. The classroom was all squares and rows while he was all paisleys and corkscrews. It was way too structured for him to get his mind into books. Bierce had a more relaxed attitude toward learning. He and grandpa would sit around for hours drinking Chinese green tea and occasionally taking a drag off a big hookah Bierce had picked up in Istanbul, making up definitions and discussing anything that might be of interest to a fifteen year old kid and a sixty-five year old man.

"Bierce had a good collection of what he called Sam's stuff," Spacecase said. "Mark Twain's writings. He let me read his dime novels. Plus some Dostoevsky and Wells. And Jules Verne."

Bierce, he learned from Traven, had headed down to Mexico the summer before, in 1914. He'd heard Pancho Villa was riding again, wanted to get into that sort of combination bandit/revolutionary lifestyle that gets the old juices flowing. He must have been a tough old bird, in his seventies but still able to ride a horse for days at a time. That's how you'd have to be if you were riding with Villa, at any rate.

The guy on the train was a writer, too, it turned out. He was heading for Mexico as well, but taking his time to get a feel for as much country as possible. "It's a dynamic and revolutionary country, still," he told grandpa. "Not like the States, which is a whole lot more decadent and fat than the Romans ever tried to be."

He should see it today.

Spacecase decided he might as well head down Mexico way when he heard Bierce was down there. It gave him an opportunity to go back through cactus country, to repay the kindness he'd been shown there some years earlier.

But first he decided to stop in at Topika Springs, up in the mountains above San Francisco, and look up a friend, lady friend actually, whose father had presented him with a healthy memory of how rock salt feels fired into your rear end from a modified buffalo hunter's rifle. "Not nice," he said, shaking his head.

Her name was Molly Wrangle, like the Alaska Wrangles. Her father had some outstanding warrants back East on his real name, whatever that might have been. He would have had his face on the post office wall, if they had managed to get a picture of him.

Grandpa hadn't seen Molly for nearly six years, when she'd been fourteen and fresh off the trail from Colorado. He figured she'd be twenty, and probably never been kissed since, if her grizzly of a papa was still alive and kicking.

"She could ride like a Comanche," he mused, "with her long reddish blond hair blowing in the wind."

In fact she'd learned to ride from the Pawnee. Her father had spent some time in Colorado swapping fat cows for skinny ones, trading one-for-ten to the homesteaders passing through. He had made California with enough of a herd to buy a hacienda, and run it until he made another fortune.

In California, Spacecase slipped off the train at the last stop before Frisco and hitched a ride on a hay wagon to the nearest roadhouse. His luck was holding. He discovered a poker game in the back room of the tavern. It was straight seven card stud with a revolving deal, and was open for some new money.

A half-drunk rancher was playing, in between bragging about the great quantities of women and cows he'd manipulated. He had some big bucks to throw around, and was totally oblivious to the fact that every time he tried to bluff, he'd absentmindedly stroke his mustache.

It wasn't long before Spacecase was starting to clean up.

The rancher got mad, after a particularly big pot turned over, and there were some guns on the table. But the owner of the joint was there with a double-barrelled scattergun, so the rancher had to back down. After a quick retreat, doubling back a couple of times to throw off the pursuit, Spacecase was able to return to Topika Springs with over $600 in his money belt.

Topika Springs was a burnt out gold town that had boomed very briefly in the 1850s, then settled down into fruit-growing country with some little cattle and sheep ranching. It had started with a bunch of Kansas dirt farmers who discovered the hard way 160 acres of Kansas won't support a family, had moved west looking for the big strike.

It was still a town when Spacecase had first moved there with his father, who had survived the coal mines of Nanaimo on Vancouver Island long enough to make a stake, then lost it all in the San Francisco earthquake and fire. They'd managed to make it as far as Topika Springs, and set up shop in an abandoned miner's shack. Then his old man had taken off for the prairies to try cattle ranching.

Spacecase had been left behind with his dad's girlfriend, who was nice, but not really interested in motherhood. He was fourteen, and was pretty well making his own way by then anyhow.

Jim Erkiletian

At the crossroads, in the mountains above Topika Springs, he remembered there was a roadhouse-hotel called the Eldorado. It had a good stage in the saloon, and was far enough from town to make the sheriff have to work overtime to investigate anything out that way.

Spacecase figured he might get a line on Molly there. It was just below where the trail forks, and anyone from Topika Springs was bound to ride by now and again. It was up near the springs, so had first access to the best water in that part of the valley.

He knew the Eldorado a little. He'd made deliveries up there for various businesses in town when he was a kid. But he'd never been inside the bar.

There was a singer working in the Eldorado who did everything from arias to show tunes and ballads. "To make a long story short," he said, "I made the super-colossal mistake of falling stark-raving in love with two women at the same time on that trip." He stared silent into his metal coffee cup for a long time, musing, then repeated, "super-colossal," just so I would get the point.

I figured he must be thinking I'm too young to want to hear any old love story, so I'd better play dumb if I'm going to get it out of him.

"Girls are a hassle, all right," I said cautiously. "Especially when they like you."

"That's true," he replied quickly, running his fingers back through his long white hair. "It gets even worst if they like each other, and still like you."

I told him I didn't know what he was getting at.

"When I pulled into Frisco, as we used to call it in them days, (Don't call it that today, he cautioned me. It means you don't know San Francisco if you call it that today) I was looking to contact Molly. Just to say hello, friendly like, and see what kind of woman she'd become."

He didn't mention it, but he was probably as horny as a hoot owl and figured Molly might be willing to take up where they'd left off some six years before.

The trick, as before, was going to be getting past her father. Presumably the old boy was just as ornery as ever, but this time Spacecase figured he could expect more help from Molly, since she would be an adult. That's assuming she wasn't already married to some California big shot or hacienda owner. Not that it would have made any difference to Spacecase.

The Eldorado was a good place to stop, to catch up on the local gossip and find out who you could expect to meet up with in Topika Springs. Or who you might wish to not meet up with, like old man Wrangle in this case.

"Topika Springs was fast becoming a ghost town even before I got there the first time, because the gold had all been mined out. Last time I was there, in the 1930s, wasn't anybody but old Mrs. Delbert, living in one of the miner's shacks."

The floor show in the main saloon had four cancan girls kicking up their heels and flashing their ankles from under big full skirts. There was a black dude with garters on his sleeves playing hot rinky-tink piano for the show, and some old geezer with a beaver skin top hat strumming a long-necked banjo.

At the break, Spacecase asked them if he could sit in for a couple of tunes with his harmonica. The piano man asked him to blow a few rifts, and he was accepted as one of the group for the next set.

At the break, the piano man told him there was a singer scheduled to play in the evening, so he'd have to sit out and wait for the late-night jam session they had just before closing if he wanted to keep playing with them.

Spacecase ambled over to the bar to talk with the bartender and see if he could get a line on where Molly might be hanging her hat. Sure enough, the bartender knew right away who he was talking about, but acted like he'd never heard of her.

Spacecase changed his tactics and asked after the health of Molly's father instead. The bartender pretended a flicker of interest, and Spacecase rubbed his butt to indicate he had some previous knowledge of the wrath of old man Wrangle.

The bartender smiled. "She comes in once and a while," he said, "but not her old man." The way he said it indicated he thought the old boy was a snob, but a powerful snob. "I hear he's a real Dead-eye Dick with a buffalo gun."

"Used to be, six years ago," Spacecase said.

He learned that Molly was still single, although she was often seen in the company of one or another officers of the Dragoons, and sometimes the captain of one of the cargo ships that operated up the coast into

Alaska. Old man Wrangle was a judge now, just as quick with a gun as before, but with a bunch of goons to do his dirty work for him.

Then the singer came out of the back room.

She was tall and statuesque, in a long black gown, with frizzy black hair down to her waist. Very dark brown, almost as dark as the piano man, but with smoother skin. Her eyes were large with big black pupils that seemed to reach right into a man's soul and massage the pain away.

"Loralei is one hell of a singer, too, spacing out the notes and controlling her voice like she's petting a hungry cougar." When she sang, all the conversation and, unfortunately for her, all the gambling in the bar stopped dead. Even hard-bitten old gunslingers, who would put a bullet in a man for an insulting remark or a silver dollar, stopped what they were doing and listened, as often as not with tears in their eyes after the first song.

She couldn't get a job in any of the well-paying clubs because the last thing those places wanted was an entertainer so good she stopped the gambling. Spacecase forgot about Molly for the moment. After all, he hadn't seen her for years, she was probably married or engaged to some rich rancher, or she more than likely wouldn't want anything to do with him after the rock salt incident anyway.

After her set, he sauntered over to the piano and let the musicians introduce him to her, as a harmonica player and fellow musician. He told her he would be mighty pleased to play some back-up to her singing.

Jim Erkiletian

With his poker winnings, he'd bought himself a new white suit and one of those shirts with ruffles down the front, so he was posing as a prosperous dude of some kind. Hence, he was some taken aback when she looked him over with a practiced eye, and asked him straight out, "You a gambler?"

He shook his head slowly, looking her carefully in the eye. She appeared to be about twenty-five, but it was hard to tell. Women are so much more aware of the art of appearance, and can shapeshift from innocent little girl to ancient wisewoman and back with a few simple cosmetic and mannerism changes. She might even be one of those mind-readers he had read about in the dime novels.

"I play a little cards, now and then," he said evenly. "But only for fun, cause I'm not much good at it."

"My father was a gambler," she said. "You have that look about you."

"You mean the harried look of the guy always looking over his shoulder," he asked with a grin, "or a man who has just met a beautiful woman?"

According to Spacecase, Diamond Jim Brady used to say there was no big secret to being successful with women. You just had to treat the ladies like whores, and the whores like ladies. That may have made it easy for Diamond Jim, who indeed had lots of women friends before one of them blew him away with a derringer. But it tells you absolutely nothing about dealings with women, who are often able to assume whichever mantle happens to suit their goals. And just under an infinite number of others besides. Plus there are some who are neither.

"You see, grandson," Spacecase was always fond of laying down good lines, "the questions are really a lot more complicated than we think. Beware of reducing things to simple solutions. Especially where humans are concerned."

"How did you get the drop on the windigr," I asked him then.

He looked at me like an old wolf who's just had a pup grab him by the tail and give a good hard jerk. "What makes you think I got the drop on him?" he asked.

"From what you said, he's mean enough to eat a kid. I figured you must'a lured him into a elephant trap or something."

"I'll tell you about it some time." He scratched the back of his neck. With his left hand, not his hind leg. "But let me tell you, a gambler's daughter can be either, or neither, or both, if it suits her mood and connects with what she's aiming to do to you. Or use you for."

Loralei invited Spacecase up to her room to work out some tunes with harmonica accompaniment, and their relationship started up that spiral staircase that often as not can end at the top of a precipice. Something was making the hairs prickle on the back of his neck as he followed her to the top floor of the old hotel.

They worked for about an hour on some tunes in her room, when a kid knocked on the door and informed Loralei she was on in five minutes. So Spacecase joined her for the rest of her performance and, with the practiced eye of a man who honestly loves women, convinced her that his money belt was really flat, he was putting on a show with the new suit, and couldn't afford a room for the night.

It was a warm night, and he'd been planning to sleep out anyway, had already stashed his gear down by the creek. But he let his smooth tongue take a stab at getting her to let him stay the night with her. She didn't exactly say no, so he followed her up to her room after the show.

It was kind of intimidating, I guess, for grandpa to be there in that hotel, on a sort of mission to look up old friend and potential roll-in-the-hay, Molly, and here getting mighty attached to this lady singer and independent woman-of-the-world, Loralei. But then, he hadn't seen Molly in over six years. It was easy for him to convince himself, stair by stair, that she probably wouldn't be happy to see him anyway, had probably forgotten all about him, had lots of rich guys courting her, had maybe run off with a gambler. And so forth.

Loralei stopped at the door to her room and waited for Spacecase to catch up to her. But she didn't open it right away.

"You have to tell me something," she said, looking straight down at the floor, "or I'm not going to let you come in my room." Before he could open his mouth, she looked up at him from under fine lashes, said seriously, "And you must tell me the truth."

His first thought was she hadn't known him long enough to be able to tell if he was lying or not. "Medium Safe bet, grandson," he'd decided. That was the best kind, in his opinion. There is Very Safe, but it's kind of anticlimactic when you win, and a real bummer when you lose. And there is the Sure Thing, which means you control all the variables, and pick up the lion's share of the take. It's a lot of trouble to set up one of those games and is damned hard on the nerves hoping you got all the bases covered. But the profit from that kind is usually up-front cool cash without consecutive serial numbers.

"Of course there was no such thing as a safe bet where your grandma was concerned. She could read me like a school primer right from the start."

He really wanted to be invited into Loralei's room, but not at a price he couldn't agree to. So he figured whatever question she asked, his best option would be the truth anyway. He nodded a quick yes.

"You must tell me who you seek in Topika Springs."

"Uh, I'm looking to see some old friends," he replied carefully. "That is, I used to live around here."

"No," she reached out and cupped her palm to the back of his left hand, "I mean the woman you have come back to see."

Spacecase swallowed slowly and said, "Well, there was this girl, Molly. But we were both just kids, and her old man don't like me, and I really don't expect she'll be interested to see me anyhow." He stopped. She was smiling.

Jim Erkiletian

Then she slowly inclined her head toward the room, and opened the door for him.

Inside the small bedroom, she closed the door behind him and stood for a minute with her hands on the latch. "Tell me then," she asked, with a slight Mexican accent tipped with Apache, "Say you find this lady and she is attractive and alone and, say maybe her old man's away on a trip, or something. What you intend to do about that, ay?"

Spacecase figured this seduction was probably going to be tougher than he'd anticipated. He decided maybe he should try a little boy act, to see if he could soften her up. Little boys can get away with more. "Aw, I shouldn't have told you about her. She's not even my girlfriend." He curled up the brim of his hat shyly, and pretended to shine the toe of his boot on the back of his trouser leg.

She smiled again, obviously enjoying his little play-acting bit. Then she matter-of-factly strode behind a Chinese screen, tossed some petticoats and a harness up on top of it, and started unbuttoning her dress. "Have a seat," she called from behind the screen. "And pour us each a drink."

There were two chairs, and a couple of bottles and glasses on a cupboard beside the door. "What's your pleasure?" he asked.

"One's orange juice and the other's homemade rice liquor I got in the Frisco Chinatown. Go light on the booze, or it'll make you see snakes. About a thimble full in mine."

He made up two glasses, was stirring them as she came out from behind the screen wearing a very soft, white doeskin robe, tied at the waist. She was combing her frizzly black hair with what looked like a little curry brush.

"Is your name really Buzzard O'Toole?"

"Yep."

She took a sip, nodded approval to tell him he had made it right.

"Who is this girl? Maybe I know her. I been around here a while."

"Uh, I'd a whole lot rather talk about you, and where you're from and like that, if you don't mind."

She stood up and folded her arms. "Now listen here, buster, you let me do the thinking and I'll come up with a deal that'll work for both of us. How do you expect me to help you find this chichita if you don't tell me her name?"

"I don't expect you to help me find her. In fact, I don't know if I even want to go looking for her, being here with you and…"

She touched his hand, very lightly, and looking him in the eyes, repeated, "Her name is…" and waited.

He hesitated. "Wrangle. Molly Wrangle."

"Judge Wrangle's girl?"

"Uh, yeah, I guess. I mean I heard her old man had got to be a judge."

When old man Wrangle had got the law on his side, some of Spacecase's old buddies had moved out of the area entirely. He didn't know it at the time, but one of his old pals had ended up swinging from a rope out on

Alcatraz Island, not six months earlier, after crossing Judge Wrangle. A mean cuss with a hot temper, he hadn't made the scramble that tears the skin off your fingers, from cattle puncher to judge, without taking out some heavy dudes en route. Fast, accurate, down the centre of the line with hot lead slugs powerful he'd made his life quite comfortable for himself and his children. The only people he hated worse than non-whites were half-breeds.

"Well, I can see some possibilities," Loralei muttered, finishing her drink and pouring another, with only half a thimbleful of booze this time. "I think your girlfriend's in town, all right. Unless her papa sent her off to some European boarding school or something." She walked across the room, around the bed that took up about a third of the apartment, and looked out the small window.

He watched her, started to say, "She's not my girl…"

"I tell you what," Loralei resumed, interrupting as if she hadn't heard him, turning back to face him. "I'll go down to town tomorrow and see if I can get a line on this Molly Wrangle. You'll stay here and wait for me."

A frown crossed Spacecase's face. Things were getting out of hand, here. He finished the glass of orange juice, said, "Hey, I don't much want you looking up an old friend of mine. I mean, she doesn't even know you."

"Get smart, O'Toole," she said softly. "You can't just waltz into this town and cozy up to Judge

Wrangle's only daughter and expect to keep your manhood intact. That Irish drygulcher plays rough."

He could think of no reply that would not either contradict her presumption of his possession of a manhood, or call it into question. "Well, then, what are you planning to do?"

"I can get in touch with her, on some pretext or other, and tell her you'd like to see her. If she says no dice, you're ahead of the game, because you haven't wasted a bunch of your time and maybe got yourself shot to pieces for nothing."

Spacecase was flabbergasted. "Uh, why would you want to do that for me?" he asked.

She tossed back her juice-and-saki, stood and stretched, went straight to the bed and pulled the covers back. "I don't know. Yet. Might be something in it for me, some way or other. Girl on her own, like me, might find it useful to have a judge on the payroll, so to speak." She climbed under the comforter and the quilts, snuggled way down, and peeked coyly out from under. "Besides, you blow nice back-up mouth organ. You coming to bed? It's cold in here."

He stood quickly, almost stumbled, then carefully stepped across the room, sat on the edge of the bed, and started pulling off his boots.

She reached from behind, with both arms around his waist, and very slowly unfastened his belt buckle. He began to develop the normal male reaction to this sort of treatment. She unbuttoned his trousers and suddenly there was a straight razor in her left hand, half-an-inch from the head of his erect penis.

"One thing we should understand, amigo," he heard her steady voice saying through a sort of misty haze. "We don't know each other very well yet. And I don't want to get involved with you until I know what's the score with this Molly and with you. So we gonna just be friends, and you can sleep here but you touch me and I cut you up. Understand?"

Spacecase said "Yes, Mam!" with every ounce of sincerity and humbleness that he could muster. She turned back to face the wall, and he couldn't tell what she had done with the razor.

He sat for a minute on the bed, thinking over this new development. Then he removed his coat and shirt and tossed them over the bedstead.

"Uh, pardon me, Miss Loralei. Do you ever have dreams?"

She laughed, a loud chuckling laugh like he'd heard from drunk pirates and old mule skinners. "Now and again," she said to the wall. "I usually manage to wake up before doing anything bad."

Spacecase decided to leave his underpants on. But he took off his undershirt and socks and snuggled down into the bed beside her. He claims they both slept peacefully. Who am I to suggest otherwise?

In the morning he woke first, and waited very quietly for her to stir. But she was sleeping, sound as a gold dollar, and he had to take a leak so he thought himself into a kind of trance, and slipped out of bed without waking her.

The toilet was in a separate room at the end of the hall, so he took her key from the nightstand and stepped out the door. When he got back she was up and getting dressed behind the screen.

"How the heck," she called, "did you manage to get out of bed without waking me up, whiteman?"

He laughed. "I figure that makes us even."

"Even for what?"

"That danged razor you pulled on me last night. You didn't need t' do that, you know."

She came from behind the screen wearing riding britches and a loose plaid woolen shirt. Her hair was neatly tied and bundled into a head scarf. "I'll need some money to get into town. If you don't have any, I can hock your boots at the bar and bring you back some moccasins or something."

Spacecase decided to trust Loralei a little more, then, and let her have a look at his bankroll. His $600 was a veritable fortune in those days. People had retired for life with less, had their throats slit for much, much less. He'd been planning, when he got to town, on blowing a hundred on a horse. And going for a ride in an automobile.

He gave her $20, told her to be careful, and suggested that maybe he should go along. But she insisted that she would be better off playing this gig solo, and not to worry because she knew what she was doing. And she kissed him gently on the forehead before she left.

Spacecase hung around the bar all day, reading a paper, getting a haircut and shave from Marvin, the handyman and local barfly. He swapped some stories with Ollie, the bartender, and played some solitaire at

Jim Erkiletian

50 cents a hand. Bartenders often picked up a few bucks on the side, selling you the deck for four bits, and paying you back five cents a card for a one-time run through of the deck. The odds were always with them, so you had to cheat in order to win. If the bartender caught you cheating, he was honour-bound by the code of his profession to break at least one of your arms.

Spacecase had lost thirty cents or so, to establish himself as a potential mark and good-natured loser, and made a friend of Ollie, when Bert, the piano man, came in to relax and loosen up before the gig. Bert had some of that purple marijuana weed that grows out in the desert. You may know it, the stuff that makes you feel like you're on an otter slide that just keeps going on forever until it finally splashes you into a big blue pool of warm ocean with a bevy of mermaids to laugh at you and beat you at playing water tag. It was, of course, quite legal in those days.

Spacecase and Bert went up to Loralei's room and smoked a little, then played some tunes on the harmonicas. Spacecase had three of them, in three different keys, and Bert had blown a little harp in his day, so they traded tunes for a while.

They worked out some songs to do that evening in the bar, after Bert established Spacecase was solvent enough he wouldn't be expecting a cut of the take. "I'm only playing for tips, anyway," Bert said. "And I'm already giving Loralei and Harlin the banjo-man a cut. I take the bigger cut, because I pay for my own room half-a-mile up the trail."

Bert was living in one of the old miner's shacks, which were rented out to drifters and hired-hands working on some of the farms in the valley. Most were empty. Bert's, coincidentally, was next door to the one Bierce had fixed up for a retreat.

In the six years he'd been away, nearly everyone Spacecase had known as a boy had moved on or been hanged. Topika Springs was essentially a ghost town, just holding on to past glory with the occasional tourist and a few people working as hired hands for the half-dozen families who had made some money in the gold heyday and decided to stay on instead of going someplace else. Gold towns don't lose the glitter overnight. They just sort of fade into ghost towns that shimmer in the misty night, like false dreams recalled from senility in an old folk's home.

When the sun started setting, neither Bert nor Spacecase was feeling any pain. Nevertheless, they decided to worry a little, and speculated on whether or not to rent a couple of horses and ride into town to make sure Loralei was O.K.

They went down to the bar and asked Ollie if he wanted to loan out a couple of horses so they could go looking for Loralei. Ollie said he'd maybe sell one of his horses, for two hundred dollars.

Spacecase asked what it would cost to keep his bankroll in the hotel safe. Ollie replied that that was a service provided by the hotel. So Spacecase handed over $200 of his roll, and said he'd like to try out the horse for a few hours.

Ollie told him to take the dappled gray stud in the far stall out back. "His name's Warrior. Good horse, but too smart for most riders."

Bert decided to stay, in case Spacecase missed Loralei somewhere along the trail or in town.

The sunset was spectacular, out over the ocean, as he rode down the winding trail through the cedar, spruce and Douglas fir forest. The pony was more familiar with the trail than Spacecase, fortunately. Spacecase was careful not to hurry the horse, and they were getting along fairly well by the time they'd covered about half the distance into the town.

He was coming down off a rock bluff when Warrior laid back his ears, then cocked them forward. Spacecase reined to a stop and listened. Shortly, he heard a horse on the trail below. Listening more carefully, he was able to make out the clip-clop of two horses, but it was too dark to see them yet.

4. Up the Creek Without…

Unnatural: n/adj.   What others want to do, but shouldn't.

Spacecase waited until Loralei's horse nickered, letting her know there was someone else on the trail. Both the riders stopped dead, waiting.

"Halloo," he called. "Where ye bound?"

Neither of the riders answered, and Spacecase couldn't tell in the darkening rain forest who they were. He surmised that they might be women, because women would be more cautious about giving away their gender to a stranger on a dark trail.

Most men, on the other hand, would have answered right away. Unless they were up to some skullduggery, like trying to hide a bunch of stolen gold. Or a dead body. Or maybe were looking to relieve you of your money belt. He would be able to tell by their answer, which sort he was dealing with.

Or lack of answer.

Probably.

After what seemed to him a considerable long time, he recognized Loralei's laugh, and there was a laugh as well from the second rider. Then there were whispers, and the horses began to plod forward, picking their way among the rocks and tree roots.

When they drew up even with him, Spacecase recognized Loralei, but he couldn't tell who her companion was. He thought it was a man, dressed in a fringed moose hide jacket and leather riding chaps, with a wide-brimmed hat covering her face. Of course it was Molly, all grown up and curious about seeing him again.

"Something women like almost as much as loving with a man," Spacecase figured, "is setting up other people for loving each other. Playing Cupid. It's dang near a profession with some of them, more sex on their mind than in the sack with their own husbands or lovers."

Spacecase first saw Molly in 1907, when she was fourteen, and new to California. She and her ten-year-old brother had ridden into Topika Springs with their father and about forty head of cattle they'd punched all the way from Colorado. They'd started with over two hundred head, but had lost a third to bad river crossings, a bear, barbed wire, rustlers and paying to cross Indian lands.

They'd sold half the herd at the rail head in Salt Lake City for traveling money, but the rest was clear profit.

Old man Wrangle had set up a trading station on the old Oregon Trail, swapping one fat cow for seven-to-ten skinny ones, to folks traveling west. Lots of people had cattle that were wasted and skinny by the time they had walked over the Rockies. Most of the grass near the trail had been eaten by the thousands of sheep and cattle that had already plodded that dusty path, going both directions.

Travelers on the trail often needed milk, especially if they had kids to look after. They were willing to trade down, if not very happy about it. Wrangle didn't win any popularity contests, but he did manage to build himself a good herd. By the time he got to California, he was already sitting on a fat money belt. And his own kids had always had plenty of milk to drink during those years when they were growing strong teeth and bones.

Molly was the most interesting tomboy Spacecase had ever seen. She sat her pony, a little sorrel mare, like it was the only place she'd ever been. The pony obviously loved her right back, too.

He was lounging around in front of the pool parlor on Main Street with some of his buddies, just about having decided to take a hike over to the pond and see if they could catch some fish. He'd only been in town for a few months, but the other young punks that hung around the street here were smart enough to recognize a good con artist when they met one. They'd taken him in like a mother wolf will take care of a human baby. (That's another story, about the wolfboy Fairly who's folks had been burned out of their tepee by a bunch of scalp hunters working for the mining companies. Less than ten months old Fairley had managed to crawl into the nearest wolf den. It's a good story. But sad.)

Topika Springs was a dying town by that time, but with a fair amount of left over bustle from the rush. Smart locals were putting their money into fruit orchards, cattle and sheep, but there were still quite a few businesses operating on the dregs of the gold trade. Lots of people had managed to stash away little bits under their mattresses, and there was enough coming out to support a thriving population of get-rich-quick idealists and wish worshipers.

Spacecase, being fairly husky, was able to pick up a few days of work now and then on the loading docks, and on the farms at haying time or fruit-picking time.

His new mother was young and pretty enough to be able to keep a pretty good larder, although he didn't care to spend much time with her. She wasn't his real mother, after all. He didn't see much of her, although he was still sleeping at her house most nights.

Most days he preferred hanging out by the pool hall, playing the odd game of pitching pennies or otherwise exercising the rights of young men not to work if they didn't have to. That's where he was the day Wrangle and his kids turned their herd onto the street, heading for the stockyard down by the livery stable.

Spacecase was smitten.

She looked him straight in the eyes as she rode by, her face expressionless. Her moose hide coat covered her, but she arched her back slightly, and the bulge of her small breasts against the front of her shirt left no doubt she was female. One of the other guys whistled, but she didn't respond.

Then she was driving the cattle again, oblivious to everything but the plodding stock. Later, in the Fall, she was sent to school with the other kids, and Spacecase decided to happen to be wandering by that way when school let out, to see if he could get to talk with her.

This time she was dressed out in a frilly little dress that accentuated her trim waist, but covered her from the high neck almost to the toes.

He offered her some peaches he had picked earlier while taking a short cut through Harlin Crumpet's orchard. Old lady Crumpet had seen him, and yelled at him from her porch to "get yer hands off my peaches, you ragamuffin, afore I skin yore ass!" He was feeling like sharing them.

He told her where he'd got them, and warned her against getting any for herself. The picture he painted of the Crumpets would have sent a grizzly bear to flight with its tail between its legs. Besides hoping to impress her with his own fearlessness, he was intent on making those peaches seem more valuable than they were. Good bargaining tactics, he figured.

She graciously accepted his gift, and suggested that he might be allowed to walk a ways with her, and her little brother. But she cautioned him about her father right from the start.

"He doesn't like boys talking to me," she said. Spacecase was to come to fully appreciate the term understatement' from that remark.

Over the next few weeks he got to know Molly a little, and took to waiting for her to get out of school on a regular basis. The other guys teased him, but he didn't pay much attention this time. She was different from other girls. The bull whip she wore coiled under her long skirt indicated when she said no, she meant no. On the other hand, the possibility she might say yes was made that much more intriguing.

He was getting to like her.

Worse luck. By the end of a couple of weeks of him meeting her after school every other day or so, she was getting to like him back.

There was an old barn on the way from the school to Molly's house, that Tim McWhorter used to store winter hay for his horses and sheep. Spacecase and Molly decided to stop in there one day, if they could talk little brother Mickey into doing something else besides dogging their footsteps.

Spacecase had been doing a little work on the loading dock of the warehouse, behind the general store. He was pretty well heeled, for a fifteen-year-old. He managed to buy the kid off with a nickel, to go down to the candy store and bring them back some sweets.

Spacecase and Molly got to spend a few minutes alone together, there in the barn, and were getting a bit closer each day. Then little brother found out from one of his classmates that the going rate for not hounding big sister and her suitors was a dime, rather than a nickel. He figured he'd been cheated.

Mickey informed Spacecase that if he didn't get a dime from now on, he was going to squeal, and that he wanted a dime for all those times before. He'd figured it out, and computed that he was owed fifty cents, all together.

Spacecase listened through the argument. Molly said she thought maybe little brother Mickey could use some flying lessons off the top of the barn roof. But Spacecase decided it would be easier to just pay him off. He told Molly that he was really coming to enjoy that little space of time they had together, and that he didn't want to risk losing it.

Molly liked him a little more for being so generous. But that fifty cents was too much for Mickey to handle. As soon as he got it, he ran down to the store, sneaking through the back lane and looking up and down the street until none of the other kids were anywhere near. Then he bought as many licorice drops, jawbreakers, chocolate candies, dried apricots and dried plums as he could get for fifty cents, and proceeded to gobble them down. He had no way of telling when a bunch of ragged kids might come down the street and demand the shares that being friends entitled them to have. So he didn't waste any time.

Before he got halfway back to the barn, he had the worst stomach ache he'd had since the time he ate a bunch of green apples. It was so painful he thought he was dying. So he didn't even go by the barn, took a short cut through the old creek bottom, went straight on home and told his pa everything, so as to confess his sins so he wouldn't end up in hell.

The church wins again in its ongoing struggle to preserve young lovers from learning how each other's made. Literally.

Old man Wrangle grabbed his shotgun and a couple of special shells he'd made up for just such an occasion, jumped bareback onto his fastest horse, and headed up to the old barn at a full gallop.

Spacecase and Molly had become accustomed to gauging their time together by how long it took Mickey to get to the store, eat a bunch of candy, and get back to the barn. They were cuddling in the hay, in the process of discovering how nice it feels to have her pretty little breasts snuggled against his bare chest, when they heard the horse coming. They held a brief conversation, partly about love, partly about sex, and partly about how he could get away. Very brief.

There was a rope hanging from the end of the barn opposite to where the horse was coming from. Spacecase swung down it with his shirt still only half on, to get a start for the newly-ploughed field across the pasture. He knew the horse would not be able to travel as fast on the soft earth just beyond the rail fence. The hedgerow also offered some little cover.

Old man Wrangle hollered "Molly!" and pulled his horse to a stop on the other side of the barn, just a Spacecase's feet hit the ground. She didn't answer.

Up to that point Spacecase was sort of considering the noble ideal of actually confronting Molly's father and standing up to him, man-to-man, so to speak. Molly had been adamant that avoiding the old bear was the more sensible course, but what did girls know. At any rate his brain was thinking if he stopped and waited at that end of the barn, maybe he'd get off with a warning. And Molly could have escaped out the other side of the barn. Maybe.

When he heard the old man yell, however, his body took over command from his confused and love-addled brain. The obvious underlying wrath in the yell opened an adrenaline switch that hit his spine like a triphammer. He took off running for the hedge, mentally thanking his mother's people for the beautifully comfortable moose hide moccasins he was so lucky to be wearing.

Wrangle heard the footfalls, and charged around the edge of the barn, cocking the hammer on the buffalo gun. Spacecase heard the report of the gun, sounding like thunder in his ears, just a split second after he felt the four little pieces of rock salt bust through his jeans, two in each cheek. He was almost over the fence, and the blast sent him sailing over the top rail and sprawling into the field beyond. The pain kept him going, far faster and far longer than he could have moved otherwise.

Wrangle turned back at the edge of the ploughed field as Spacecase rolled down a bank into the thicket beyond. He kept going for a few days, figuring he would circle around and head back eventually. But once he was out on the trail there was the tendency to keep pushing it to the limit, to see how far he could get. He couldn't sit down for any length of time, so might as well do some traveling. He hadn't seen his mother for a couple of years, by that time, so he headed up north along the coast. Hopping freights and hitching rides on wagons and boats, he made it up to Hyder in the Alaska panhandle within a month, and stayed with his mother's people for a few days. That's where he first met Chi'klavea, who made him some medicine to ease the pain in his butt.

Then he took the old gold trail to Dawson City in the Yukon.

When winter started to move in on him in the North, he headed back South. He was figuring on going back to Topika Springs, because he still considered Molly to be his girlfriend, but he caught up to a band of four young Poncas braves who were exploring the Western country. They accepted him as a sort of fellow refugee and wild card.

They were heading down into the Southwest desert country, ostensibly looking for adventure, understanding, and maybe some of that Mexican gold and silver they had heard about. He decided to travel with them.

"I was always a good runner, kid," he often reminded me. "It's one thing they can't take away from you, without catching you first at any rate. People who live close to the land know how important it is to have a good one-manpower means of transport. Plus it has the added bonus of reminding you to travel light."

5. The Sun's favourite children…

Economics: v.t. The study of how men reduce their options in order to gain control over their fellow men's resources.

The Poncas had been robbed of their land in the Dakotas by a crooked Indian agent some forty years earlier, and had been forcibly moved from good farms onto desert land with bad water in Oklahoma. They were literally dirt-poor, didn't even have horses any more. These boys had grown up amid horrible poverty, but they had become self-reliant and competent adults on land that could only support humans who knew how to scavenge from the scavengers. They were skinny and tough, like turkey necks, but all over.

They had heard that somewhere in the deep southwest were people who had never used horses, and who still resisted taming wild horses even in that day. They were curious. They made their way south along the coast, working on small farms and occasionally on the docks in the logging and fishing towns. Once in a while they were able to hitch rides on steamships that carried everything and everyone, including travelers and adventurers (we'd call them tourists today) up and down the California coast.

At San Francisco, Spacecase decided to stay with his new companions rather than make the detour to Topika Springs. It was a tough decision, but he knows it was the right one at the time.

Jim Erkiletian

Spacecase first noticed, on those steamboats, that some of the men and women appeared to be more interesting than others. They dressed in high style, yet comported themselves with a reserve that indicated competence and inner strength. They always seemed to have money, and, as he learned from doing shoe shines and running errands, they tipped well. He discovered they made their money by taking it from other passengers.

He also discovered they were willing to tip handsomely a shoeshine boy who was willing to mention how much money he had seen in the pocketbooks of other passengers. Many gentlemen who took great pains to conceal the amount of their holdings from their fellow passengers, had no such qualms about bragging of their success to a ragged kid in business for himself. Such information could be valuable in many ways.

These other passengers, in contrast, almost never tipped at all. Although they seemed to be wealthy, they didn't seem to know how to go about having fun. In fact, they didn't seem to want to learn.

"Money's there to make our lives easier, not harder. Some of those folks did nothing but hoard their cash, and no matter how much they had, they were always trying to make more."

"Its not much fun being poor," I observed.

"More fun being poor and free than being rich and trapped by your money," he replied.

Spacecase remembered those days as particularly good, except for the pain in his butt that made it hard for him to sit for any length of time. Even that had its good side. It kept him from getting lazy.

There were five of them, looking out for each other, and the fishing was usually good even when the money was not. By the time they got to Mexico, later that winter, they had managed to swap an abandoned wagon they were able to fix up for a couple of fairly good dugout canoes. An Oregon-based Salish family, who had decided to invest in horses and travel on land, swapped them the canoes just south of San Luis, California.

At Tiajuana, on the Mexican-U.S. border, they sold the canoes and asked around until someone told them how to get out into the back country, and what they'd need to go there. Everyone they met who had been even close to that country said WATER, so they bought good canteens with their shoeshine money. They picked up some odd bits of gear, two axes, a blanket apiece some tough canvas clothes, and set off into the Mexican desert on foot.

Any person from the coast would have told them they were crazy to head out into that parched land, especially at that time of year. But they were young and confident, and innocent enough to figure they could get by.

The nights were cool, but not real cold yet, and they knew some of the tricks of finding water in a parched landscape. The Poncas had some experience of such lands, and were able to sniff out water, and tell where it was likely to be found by the lay of the land. They

Jim Erkiletian

were good at following little-used trails through brush-and-thorn country.

They had enough jerky and water for five day stretches, and were able to find a real good spring protected by overhanging rock on their sixth day out from the last village. They weren't adverse to eating lizards and snakes, if they had too.

They had been told the Taratumara don't like strangers, had a habit of disappearing anyone who wandered into their country. It was also said they were tough on a scale that none of these young men had ever had the opportunity to measure.

The tenth day into that parched and arid land, they camped on top of a broad mesa that gave them a view for a hundred miles in three directions. The only thing moving in that vast distance, when they woke in the morning, were half-a-dozen dust devils, and a solitary figure. Way off in the valley they could barely make out the shimmering image of a man, or possibly a woman, running in the morning sun. A tiny droplet of water away in a great bowl of wind and rock.

"That's one of the honchos we're looking for," Young Bear, the oldest, said quietly as they watched the figure, like a tiny speck of brown sand moving across a red and yellow sheet of crumpled newsprint.

"How do we manage to catch up with someone like that?" Spacecase asked.

The other braves didn't say anything for a few minutes. Then Young Bear said quietly, "Don't worry. If we can see him, you can bet that he, or his people, have already seen us." He turned to the small cooking

Windigr

fire they had built to make tea for breakfast, kicked sand over the glowing coals, and picked up his knapsack. "Don't make any hasty moves. We're being watched right now, and you can bet your last bundle of sweetgrass on it."

Sure thing, Spacecase figured, from the way he'd said it.

They started on a downhill trek that would take them right into that man's country, on a trajectory that would roughly intercept his course in about two days. Assuming he would not change direction. And would be willing to accept them.

This last bit was crucial. When they got close to him, they would be completely at his mercy. They had drunk the first half of their water since the last water source, and had been on the verge of turning back.

That day they went from shady place to shady place, down rough hardrock cliffs with overhangs that turned into straight drops of three, four, five hundred feet and more. It was deceptive country, designed to throw a human mind into rolling shapes of silent windblown memories. Millennium of wind-and-rock spirits and hard-bitten wild dryads screamed in the distance.

The winds along some of the cliff faces, hurtling across hundreds of miles of open space, then forced into long, increasingly narrow box canyons, shift to updraughts that can toss a man in the air as gently as a mad bull. If you were lucky, you'd come back down on to the rockface. The chances were about fifty-fifty."

That evening, as they huddled around their campfire, they discussed the alternatives. They could go on. But the possibilities were that a) they might meet somebody who would try to kill them or b) they might meet someone who wouldn't help them survive. They discussed the possibility of turning back, to try again later. General consensus was they had come this far…

They decided to post a watch in two-hour stretches, with the stars deciding who would follow who. They asked Young Bear to forego the standing watch so he would be more sharp and clear-headed the following day. It was an honour to Young Bear to be chosen by the band for this, and meant they in turn depended on him to make first contact with the men they were seeking. Much depended on Young Bear now. If the stranger proved hostile, Young Bear would be the first to die. He must be attentive, to learn that man's manners, and he would have a very short space of time in which to do so.

That the Taratumara would decide the etiquette of first contact was axiomatic. It was their country. Of course they might wish to open the dialogue with someone other than the chosen leader of the group. Or kill him first to test the others.

Spacecase asked for, and got, the next-to-last watch. He figured he needed a straight stretch of sleep, because he wanted to be close to the action when they met the runner on the following day. The others had come to recognize that he might be a special asset in some way, with his combination whiteman/native background.

He rolled into his blanket and slept.

The warrior chosen to precede Spacecase on watch, Yellow Buffalo, wakened him, in the dusky misted morning. Clouds had obscured the stars, but Spacecase could tell the time was about right, by the glow of the moon, shining through the clouds. She was nearly across the sky from where she had been, and still bright enough to cast shadows. He moved over by the fire and built it up a little as Yellow Buffalo went to take a leak.

As Yellow Buffalo was buttoning his fly, he felt a chill, like ice, against his back. It was the flat side of a very sharp obsidian blade. He slowly raised his hands and went where the spear against his back told him to go, forward across a sandy dune and along a small arroyo, where he was confronted by four more warriors.

"We come in peace," he said in sign language, repeating in a quiet voice in Navaho and Apache.

The nearest of the four warriors motioned with his own spear, and the blade was removed from the small of Yellow Buffalo's back. Yellow Buffalo relaxed visibly, but remained expressionless, carefully avoiding the eyes of the older men standing before him.

The Taratumara warrior kneeled and drew a circle in the dusty sand. He drew legs on the front and back, and a head, to indicate the Great Bear. Some folks say the Great Turtle. (Others call it North America, after some European geographer who figured out something native children have known for millennia, that our Earth is round.)

These warriors obviously wanted to know just where their visitors were from. So Yellow Buffalo pointed to the spot on the map, down about halfway through the stomach. The men all nodded thoughtfully. They had heard of that country, but had had no visitors from Oklahoma for several generations. They talked about it for a while in their own language.

Yellow Buffalo couldn't understand exactly what they were saying, except for a word here and there. He could tell, without a doubt, they were arguing over whether it had been four or five grandpa's back that Oklahomans had been seen here. They finally decided on five, and held up five fingers for him.

Yellow Buffalo nodded that he understood.

Spacecase, meanwhile, had noticed Yellow Buffalo's extended absence. He very quietly woke the others and whispered to them that either Yellow Buffalo was pissing a river, or he's been captured. When Young Bear woke, and was informed Yellow Buffalo was missing, he suggested they all stay together, but spread out in a circle so that each would be able to keep track of the two men on either side.

Meanwhile, the warrior questioning Yellow Buffalo stopped, listened intently. There was the sound of a cricket, or something, to the south. In fact it sounded exactly like a cricket, except for a slight rise in inflection at the end.

The warrior signed to Yellow Buffalo that he was to speak loudly, and that he was to tell his brothers to keep still. Yellow Buffalo called to the others that they were to hold position and wait, that he was communicating with a man from this country.

This uneasy situation lasted for another hour, during which neither side made any movement from their positions. The Taratumara discussed the situation carefully, and Yellow Buffalo listened carefully. Finally, a warrior brought some water for Yellow Buffalo. They had decided these young men were here to learn and open communication, rather than to rip them off or fight. They were invited to accompany the band further into the desert.

Spacecase spent over half a year with the Taratumara, learned some of their language, and developed his skills as a runner.

"For those people, running is a high art, especially meaningful if they can have the noonday sun burning down on their glistening bodies," he said. "If they ever got interested in competition, they'd blow the Olympic races into a whole new game."

"So why don't we get some of them and set up races?" I asked. "Seems like you could take bets, and we could take in a bundle." By that time I'd learned that living on the road requires a resourcefulness that recognizes opportunity when it springs up.

He looked at me and smiled. "There's some things you don't do for any amount of money, Yeuzor." He was carving a peak-stick, one of those little paddles northerners use in winter to knock down the peak that grows in the outhouse. In cold country, if your outhouse is dug too shallow, the little mountain of turds can come right up even with the seat, along toward spring. Besides a catalog and a tin of wood ashes to pour in to kill the smell and neutralize the acids, the peak stick is one of the most important accouterments of a Northern outhouse.

He stopped and eyed the design of a whale he was cutting into the blade of the tool. "Take this peak stick, for instance. If someone wants to buy it, some tourist or Eastern dude say, I could tell them its a little baby canoe paddle. I don't see no harm in that kind of a white lie, to get a better price. And what the hell, it might just be a little paddle, eh?"

I nodded slowly.

"But when it comes to changing a man's perception of his own art, or making him feel different about what is important or worthwhile, we have to step carefully. Or not at all."

"You mean they wouldn't understand the idea of running to make money?" I asked.

"Sure they understand," he said. "But they don't see any sense to the idea that anyone should run faster than anyone else. Everybody runs at their own speed. And everybody wins."

They seldom use a bow or spear for hunting. Instead they go in groups of five or six into the desert, looking for the small herds of antelope that manage to eke out a living there. Then they run, choosing the strongest animal to cut out from the rest of the herd. This one they pursue, sometimes for days, across the blazing sand, naked but for the small pouch of cactus buds they wear around the waist.

They eventually exhaust the animal. When it collapses in the sand, they stand around it for a time, in reverence for the spirit of the run, and the land, and the sun that brings life. Then they return to their camp.

The antelope walks back with them, for his own reasons. Partly because the antelope is lost from his own people, and partly because he recognizes their superiority in the art of running, an art of which the antelope is among the most cognizant.

"You see, everybody wins, even the antelope who will live out the rest of his days among the greatest runners in the world. Antelope heaven, so to speak. And when they eat him later, the antelope will become a part of Taratumara consciousness, forever running in the desert sun."

Such people are not easily conquered. Their legends told of Aztec incursions into their lands. They had met Spaniards as well. Neither invaders had discovered more than a dry, sandy death. The memories of great empires, ancient and modern, are no more than jokes and folk tales in the lore of those people.

They knew of the coming of the white people to their north and south, and had discovered how the yellow metal that grows in certain parts of their country could make those men crazy. They had taken steps to protect their lands and peoples from that insanity. Yet they had come to realize the edge it gave them in trade.

Their trade stories, which Spacecase and Young Bear were able to validate for them, indicated that if they failed to protect their land from those who seek the yellow metal, they would lose all. In some places, even strong and powerful natives had become infected with this sickness, known in the whiteman's tongue as greed, the wishing to own more than other people. It had caused them to destroy their hunting grounds and farmlands in pursuit of this illusory and false wealth. It made their children less wealthy than their grandfathers, and in some cases, poorer even than their fathers had been.

The Taratumara keep their sources of gold hidden to all but each other. In cases where it is necessary to trade, they bring their gold to the settlements or the trading post, and swap for what they need. But there has been no further selling of their lands, except for these bits of yellow rock.

They've only seldom had to protect their lands by force. The sun and desert took care of most prospectors. And if a man were to enter that country and be so unlucky as to actually find a good showing, he was easily prevented from leaving. The Taratumara take great care to insure that the land that nurtures them is in turn nurtured by them. There would be no large machines tearing great gouges from their country.

They had heard the words of Chief Sealth, the warnings that told of a people who would take the wealth of the land as quickly as possible, and convert it into something useless. And of the many who had been paid for their lands, the source of their strength and their lives, with paper and empty promises.

"The Taratumara," according to Spacecase, "will have their lands and their gold forever. Unlike the white men who will eventually find that gold is only a pretty, yellow metal worth far less than a cup of clean, sparkling water or a piece of green earth."

Funny talk for a gambler.

"They have gold to spend, anyway. That's more than some folks," I said.

"Sure they do," he replied. "And they only take it out a little at a time. They don't dig it out all at once like they did in the Yukon, leaving big dredged-out creekbeds that won't support healthy forests again for a thousand years."

Spacecase indicated many times that the women in that country were beautiful. As pretty as a Taratumara maiden was one of his regular remarks. He may have had a sweetheart there, or some kind of relationship with a woman. But like the mythical gold mine that is supposed to exist in that country, she is one of his secrets. Even from me.

6. Perfume and Red Roses...

Perverted: n/adj. What others want to do that is beyond the bounds of human decency.

About half a year after he trekked into that country, Spacecase let his wandering spirit take over again, headed on across northern Mexico, up to Brownsville, Texas. Two of the Poncas braves kept him company. They were all three able to sign onto a cattle boat hauling beef across the Gulf of Mexico, supplying New Orleans.

At New Orleans they split up, the Poncas heading for Ardmore, Oklahoma, and Spacecase signing on to a riverboat for a run up the Mississippi.

Young Bear and Yellow Buffalo had chosen to remain with the Taratumara, settling into that way of life like ants in a sugar jar. "Their children are probably running through the desert right now, munching cactus buds and loving the feel of their feet on the sand, the wind in their long hair, the blazing sun on their faces and backs and arms and legs."

He says it like of all the places he's been, that was the best. That's why he doesn't talk about it much, I suspect. It may be his final hideout. The last resort of an outlaw, hounded and hunted down by the law and civilization.

By the time he made the eastern coast, Spacecase was making good money dealing blackjack and running an occasional poker game, especially up around

Chicago. He rode back into Canada on the Great Lakes, and ended up down in New York, before making that jaunt to Europe that got him hooked up with the circus.

"The world is round, the seasons are round, the sky is round, and men are round, grandson." He'd usually be smoking a corncob pipe when he said that. "They ain't meant to be squashed into little square cells or boxes."

"Was Molly as round as you remembered her?" I asked him.

He hesitated. And took the opportunity to inhale some more of that herb he was burning in the pipe. "Rounder," he finally said.

When Loralei got into Topika Springs, she asked the first person she met where the judge's house was located. It was a few miles out of the town, but easy enough to find. When she got there, she left her pony at the hitching post, a cement black kid in a jockey suit holding a brass ring.

She walked around to the back where a live black woman was hanging out clothes, and asked her if Molly was around.

"I think that spoiled little brat is sleeping off too much hootch and too much party from last night," the woman said through a mouthful of clothespins.

"I have some male for her, that was delivered to me by mistake," Loralei said, sort of truthfully. "May I take it too her?"

"I can give it too her," the woman replied.

Loralei smiled and said, "I'd like to deliver it in person, if I could. Maybe you could take me to her."

The woman looked her over, then nodded her head toward the rear door. "Upstairs. The second bedroom on the right."

Loralei walked in through the kitchen and found the staircase, tiptoed carefully up.

Finding the door to Molly's room slightly ajar, Loralei tipped it open with the end of her parasol. Molly wasn't in her bed. She was sitting at a little writing table, writing a poem. Loralei could see tears flowing down her left cheek in the mirror on the wall beside her.

"Hello," she said quietly.

Molly looked around, startled. "Who are you?"

"Not your fairy godmother. Nor the bearer of bad tidings, either. Are you in the mood for a surprise, friend?"

"Not if it concerns horses, men or whisky," Molly answered with a straight face, which changed to a quick, wicked smile.

She was indeed in the mood for something new. Surprise usually means something good for rich, intelligent young women who also happen to be marooned in a country full of healthy young men trying to do things for you and threatening to fight duels with each other and other stupid nonsense.

This duel business was getting to be a bother. She was spending so much time talking some of those hotheads out of shooting each other in the process of trying to win her hand, she could hardly find time to write. She didn't know for sure what she wanted in a man. But she did know she didn't want any jerk playing around with her body who was stupid enough to get himself killed protecting her honour. Whatever that was.

Consequently, she had learned to put on a real good drunk act, complete with phony hangovers. That way they would still ask her out and take her to the various shindigs, but she could get rid of them easily, later in the evening. Most of them had learned to leave her alone until after noon of the day following any partying.

There was always daddy's temper in case any of them got overly familiar.

Molly jumped up from the chair and started changing into her riding clothes when she heard Spacecase was back. Of course she wanted to see him. He was the first male she had ever kissed with. That was damned special, and she had been thinking about him, wondering what had happened to him, off and on for six years.

"Have you told anyone else?"

"No," Loralei said. "I told the lady in the yard I had some male for you that got sent to me by mistake."

The two women doubled over in a fit of giggling for a full five minutes, hugging each other to keep from falling on the floor. Then Loralei wandered around the room inspecting the pictures on the wall as Molly finished primping. Most of the pictures were thoroughbreds on bluegrass farms in Kentucky, and there was a Lakota headdress on the wall above the bed.

Molly quickly composed a note for daddy with a goose-quill pen. It indicated she was going to be spending the evening with a dear woman friend who had sent her an invitation to a birthday party.

Loralei watched over her shoulder, then wrote out a phony invitation note on a little card and put it onto the writing table. She signed it Mrs. Rhudolphe Bourbon-Tudor, the first good aristocratic-sounding name to pop into her head.

Molly took a look at it, said, "How'ja do, Mrs. Rudolph," and curtsied. "What the heck am I supposed to call you?"

"Loralei's what they call me around the lodge," she replied. Then she picked up the scrap of paper with the poem on it and read it through slowly. It was in rhyme, fashioned into a trio of verses that lilted into the wind like a three-masted schooner. And it had a couple of hidden meanings underlying the real words.

She laughed. "Mind if I take this along?"

"You like it?" Molly asked.

"Yeah," Loralei answered. "I want to sing it."

The two women headed out to the stables, saddled up Molly's appaloosa, Whirlwind, and walked her around to the front where Loralei's horse was waiting. On the way back they stopped into the haberdashery and picked up a few things that they didn't really need, to establish a camaraderie of shopping together. They took care to avoid the centre of town, the courthouse where Molly's father would be, and the Wells Fargo office where Molly's brother Mickey was working.

Molly actually got on pretty well with her brother, considering they were both relatively spoiled rotten by their dad. They had learned to give each other room to move, and not try and run each other's lives. Still, she didn't really trust him since that time six years before.

When the two women met Spacecase on the trail, they had been discussing how to deal with him. Loralei had figured out that he was the type who would have lots of money one day, be stone cold broke the next, and not really cognizant of his own rollercoaster lifestyle. Molly was half-interested in throwing her arms around him and welcoming him back, the other half in whopping him with a riding quirt for never having even sent her a letter.

In the end, they just shook hands and discussed their lives as they rode back to the Eldorado. Loralei rode a little ahead so as to give Molly and Spacecase a little privacy.

"So, Buzzard O'Toole," she asked straightaway, "why didn't you think it necessary to even send me a post card, huh?"

"Shucks, Molly," he replied, "it's hard to write standing up. And then I was down in country where the only mail travels by moccasin telegraph."

Molly's father had inadvertently barred that communication device from his house. He hated natives with the passion of a true racist bigot who would have shot any man who called him an Indian-lover. As a matter of fact, he would have shot any man who called him a racist bigot, too.

"I thought he'd killed you, at first," Molly said. "Then when you didn't even write, I wished he had."

When he'd ridden back around the barn, six years before, to find Molly crying, old man Wrangle had softened up some and told her he was just shooting rock salt. Then he sent her back up to the house and told her if he ever caught her with that half-breed again, he'd use real buckshot, or worse. She believed him.

They made it to the hotel a couple of hours before the main show was scheduled to begin. Spacecase and Molly sat around and talked in the bar while Loralei took a bath down in the basement laundry room.

As the show progressed that evening, Molly excused herself to also take advantage of the hotel bath. Then both women encouraged Spacecase to avail himself of that same service. Eventually the three of them were all cleaned up with, interestingly enough, only one place to go.

After the show, they invited Ollie and Bert and the banjo player, old man Crumpet (the same Crumpet Spacecase had stolen the peaches from, coincidentally), up to Loralei's room for a drink to unwind.

Ollie said he had to cash out and sweep up, and his wife wanted him home. The others went up to Loralei's room, proceeded to finish off what was left of her rice wine and orange juice, and indulged in some more of Bert's killer weed.

By sunup they were all lying on the floor giggling and talking and exchanging lies and adventures as if they'd known each other for years.

Spacecase thought about getting another room to spend some time alone with Molly, but that didn't seem right, to leave Loralei all alone. With two other guys… On the other hand, Molly seemed real happy to just be friends, the way she was acting. He didn't much want to leave her alone, either. With two other guys…So he was in some kind of a quandary when the five of them eventually passed out on the bed, fully clothed, like a bunch of cougar kittens in a haystack.

At some point during the evening, Spacecase remembers Loralei taking out the poem Molly had written that morning. It went something like…

> *Floating on a harvest moon*
> *Shining through the windy night*
> *Our silent windows echo madness*
> *Lost in shadowmaker's flight*
>
> *Our forests tell us*
> *With their mysteries*
> *All we ever need to know*
> *We take for granted all we're given*
> *Til it's gone for ever more.*
>
> *The world turns*
> *In spiral spinning*
> *Winning through the August sky*
> *Taking us poor simple creatures*
> *Journeying to learn to fly…*

Loralei started to read it out, but Spacecase said, "Wait a minute. You read it and I'll do some background music." So he blew some low and soulful blue notes he'd picked up from some cajun musicians in Louisiana. Both Bert and Harlin said it was the cat's ass, what the hell ever that meant.

They went through that poem about fifteen times in about fourteen different ways. By the fourteenth time through, Harlin was plunking on banjo, and both women and Bert were harmonizing on the tune. They sounded great, to each other at least.

Some time during that evening one of them came up with the notion that it would be great fun to head out to New Mexico. There was supposed to be a gathering of some elder artists and spiritual people taking place out there in the next summer. There was a rumor some artists from Europe were thinking about settling into that country. Famous artists and writers.

Loralei had grown up just southwest of Taos, down in Arizona. She was Geronimo's niece, actually, and had something of an extended family over into the Taratumara land that Spacecase had visited with his Poncas brothers.

Molly said the people she'd grown up with had fought the Apaches, at one time, way back in their past. She said they hated having to fight Apaches worse than anybody, judging from the stories.

Bert had come up from Tiajuana, Mexico where he'd lived for a couple of years since he'd nearly got himself lynched in Mississippi for loving a white woman too much. "She was just so damned curious to see if I was built any different than white folks, uh, male white folks, you know what I mean,…that I just had to take pity on her and let her find out for herself. Unfortunately she had to relay such stupendous news to the ladies at the hair shop and it was all over town in about five minutes, give or take."

"And just what did this news consist of?" Molly had the audacity to ask.

"Why, that us black men aren't built any different that any other men, of course," he answered with a straight face. "What were you thinking?"

"Precisely that," she replied with an even straighter face. "So it must have been the black folks who ran you out of town."

"Right," he said. "The black men."

Then they all broke down into a fit of giggles that infected all their grass-addled brains, until the whole room felt like it had been sprayed with some kind of ticklish power that sets the funny bone to vibrating.

Spacecase, before he passed out, realized he was mentally tallying up the gear they would need to make that trip out to New Mexico. It fit in real nicely with his plans, because it was just across Texas to the mountains of northern Mexico where he would expect to find Bierce riding hell-bent-for-revolution with Villa and his bandit revolutionaries.

He was on the right track. But he had reckoned without Molly's father's continuing wrath. Judge Wrangle wanted his only daughter to marry some rich aristocrat. Barring that, he would a whole lot rather she married a Comanche or Arapaho, as long as he was a chief. But a halfbreed like Spacecase? About as bloody likely as a Protestant Pope, or a bear sauntering into the outhouse and sitting up on the seat to drop a poop.

And a halfbreed who wasn't even remotely interested in matrimony? About the same likelihood. If he didn't have a stroke at the thought of such a match, Judge Wrangle would be fit to be tied. With chains and big iron padlocks. A wet banty rooster on the warpath might look pretty tame compared to Judge Wrangle on a good day, let alone a bad one. He'd be coming looking for his daughter real soon, and he wouldn't be loaded with rock salt this time.

He'd be bringing a gang of very fast reckless young hooligans to back him up. Or maybe front him up, would be a better choice of words. He'd be sure to keep his posse close enough that he could duck behind any one of them if the other guy was still standing after the first exchange.

He was a judge, after all. There would be little chance of escape. Like most Americans, Wrangle had learned from the natives the advantages of being able to move, across vast distances if necessary, at a moment's notice.

Wrangle would have been even more outraged at his daughter's choice of friends if he had known Spacecase was indeed part Irish and, heaven forbid, English. His name, O'Toole, was inherited from those Irish immigrants who had sold out the worst, in the reckoning of many Irish Catholics and Protestants alike.

Spacecase was the black sheep of the family, but his lineage was well-known to the British aristocracy of the day. His Oxford-educated grandfather, scholar and pioneer scientist Erasable O'Toole, had penned O'Toole's Postulate to Murphy's Law.

Murphy's Law, for those unfamiliar with the Western scientific tradition, states: FOR ANY GIVEN VARIABLE THAT CAN ADVERSELY EFFECT AN EXPERIMENT, THE PROBABILITY IT WILL OCCUR VARIES INVERSELY WITH THE EXPERIMENTER'S ABILITY TO PREDICT AND ACCOUNT FOR IT.

In layman's terms: If anything can go wrong, it will. O'Toole's Postulate states, roughly, Murphy was an optimist.

Spacecase's father had served in various British campaigns, in India, Russia, Africa, as valet and aide-de-camp to Colonel Flashman of the Royal Dragoons. Unlike his Colonel, he was never decorated for acts of heroism and bravery, two qualities he considered highly over-rated. Which was the main reason Colonel Flashman kept him around, to help him get out of any unpleasant scrapes. Flashman was something of a coward, himself, as he admitted in an autobiography in his later life.

It was likely the career of his father that made the youthful Spacecase aware of the futility of fighting other men's battles, and the utter futility of fighting for an empire or government. Hence, while one may have assumed Spacecase's Irish blood would have counted for something in his attempt to woo Molly, it was simply not so. As modern sociologists know only too well, the most bigoted racists tend to be especially prejudiced toward their own kinfolk.

Wrangle hated the Irish more than he hated all other ethnic groups put together. It had something to do with knowing that all kinds of folks he'd never met would show up to share his wealth, if he was to admit some connection to the clans of his forefathers. But it went deeper than mere economics. Wrangle knew, way down in his soul, how mean and sadistic his temper could become when it's set off, and how little it takes to ignite his short fuse. He naturally blamed it on his Irish blood, instead of the yew stick his own father had used on his butt every time he'd done something new or daring as a kid.

When Spacecase woke up in the morning, sandwiched in between Molly and Loralei crosswise on the bed, he thought he was in heaven. Bert was over on the other side of Molly, and Harlin was dozing the other side of Loralei.

Spacecase stretched and everybody sort of started moving around. Then Harlin jumped right out of bed and said to nobody in particular, "Holy shit. My woman's gonna take after me with the double-bit axe, again. I better git on home."

Molly said "I thought you were going to take off for New Mexico with the rest of us?"

Crumpet sat back down on the edge of the bed and thought about that. "You really aiming to go?" he asked.

Windigr

Loralei stretched and sat up beside him, started massaging his shoulders. "We better get a move on if we intend to make Taos by winter," she said quietly.

"Well," Crumpet replied thoughtfully, "it would be some safer than facing that axe, for me anyhows. But seems to me Molly's papa's nose will be so far out of joint it might get stuck in his nostrils."

"Maybe we could send him off in the wrong direction," Molly suggested.

They discussed it for the rest of the morning and decided that they could leave a heavy false trail, and make off with the Wrangle buckboard and plenty of supplies if they did it right. By the time he doubled back from following the false trail, they could be over the mountains and gone. It all seemed so simple. Like for catching birds, all you have to do is put salt on their tails, and they get stunned. Can't move.

"Another lesson, grandson, in being wary of simple plans. They can go wrong in the most complicated ways."

"What kind of heater were you packing in them days?" I asked him.

He took his time in answering, as usual. "You know," he finally said after fooling around with the campfire and adjusting the stick bread over the coals so it would bake just right, "it ain't the heater you're packing that makes the difference. We won't get your grandma's medicine bundle back from those thugs, even if we had a whole battalion carrying tommy guns. It's something else."

I waited politely for him to explain.

"When old man Colt came out with the .45 caliber revolver, he called it the Peacemaker for the most idealistic reasons. He figured democracy isn't real unless everyone is equal, and there ain't nothing more equalizing than everyone toting his own big cannon."

He looked at me carefully, chewing on the end of his pipe after again adjusting the stick bread. "Billy Bonny once told me he thought democracy must mean more than everybody being able to kill everybody else. He was carving the twenty-fifth notch into the handle of his .44 at the time, and musing that if that was all there was to it, he should be allowed to vote twenty-five extra times, now."

I had read a little about Billy the Kid. "I thought he only killed twenty-two men," I said.

"That was before him and Pat Garrett cooked up that scheme to collect the reward money by declaring Billy officially dead. They never got the money, but most of the Pinkertons stopped looking for him after that."

"So what about grandma's medicine bundle?" I asked him then.

"We're getting closer," he said.

7. Deals off the Bottom…

Justice: n/ A system of reward and punishment that flourishes when there are increasingly large numbers of law breakers. Closely allied to the political system that makes laws.

It was old lady Crumpet who brought the posse around to seeing their mistake. When Harlin came straggling in about noon, she indeed took the axe and chased him around the house a couple of times. Finally he hid inside the outhouse to wait her out.

It was raining a slow steady drizzle. She cussed him a bit. Then she went back in the house and watched out the window. She could see the outhouse door, all right, but she didn't count on him borrowing out under the back side, through the hole. He didn't smell too nice after, but it gave him the time he needed to sneak around to the corral and saddle his old mare, Dixie.

They made it through the gate and out onto the road before the old lady could get around to that side of the house with her shotgun loaded. She watched him disappearing around the bend in the trail, then she walked over to McWorter's pasture and borrowed one of his horses. Harlin hadn't forgotten what a good tracker his wife was. He just didn't figure she would be coming after him with the rain coming down, and because the grapes needed to be rescued from the starlings and crows so often that time of year.

Molly and Loralei, meanwhile, had ridden into town and loaded up the buckboard with blankets, food, a couple of trunks of clothes, and whatever they figured they could swap for what they needed. They lashed some big water barrels to the sides, and picked out the two best Winchester lever-action rifles from the judge's collection.

They told Minerva, the black woman who did the washing, they were heading up the coast for a few days. And they left the judge a message to that effect, adding they were taking the horses to give them some exercise.

Wrangle probably wouldn't have become suspicious for a couple of days, if Mrs. Crumpet hadn't spied out the band at the lodge, getting ready for the trail. She knew better than to tackle the whole bunch of them alone, poor defenseless old lady with a shotgun. But from her perch in the crotch of an apple tree out on the edge of the trail, she recognized Molly.

Luckily for Spacecase, she didn't recognize the tall dandy on the dappled pony as the same brat who'd stolen her peaches four years earlier. Or, more fortunately, the Halloween mooner from before that.

When Spacecase had first come to California, the other boys had been interested in what sort of rite of passage they could pressure him into. He wasn't the type to take any old dare, especially anything too dangerous. He didn't like fighting, just turned away when challenged. The boys suggested he might be chicken, flapping their arms and cluck-clucking at him, but he just said he didn't see any sense in trying to damage each other. He suggested there were lots more fun things than beating on each other, some of which were a whole lot more profitable, as well.

The boys grudgingly admitted he had a point, but they weren't too sure what it was. They refrained from punching him in the nose long enough for him to explain, making it clear they retained an open option, should he fail.

He understood he had to do something crazy enough and daring enough to prove to the other boys he was worthy to be part of the gang. Otherwise they simply wouldn't trust him, and worse, he'd be relegated to bottom of the pecking order for the duration of his stay in Topika Springs. Not pleasant prospects.

He asked them what they had around there good to eat or drink, but dangerously hard to get ahold of.

They informed him old lady Crumpet was particularly dangerous with a shotgun, and had some of the best peaches in her orchard. One of the more daring things he could do was steal some, but peaches were out of season, so maybe he'd just better put up his dukes and take a thumping like a man.

Spacecase knew there had to be something more interesting than just the stealing to make these guys respect him.

"What would she do if I showed her my bare butt?" he asked the young hoodlums lounging around the boardwalk.

They all agreed she would certainly put a load of buckshot in it, if she could. They also agreed that it would be more than ample as an initiation rite if he could pull off such a stunt and survive.

Jim Erkiletian

Thus, on Halloween night, when bunches of kids were roaming the countryside on their house-to-house goodies drive, Spacecase and his crew made their way over to the Crumpets, stationing themselves in the bushes just beyond the gate.

They watched for a while, as a couple of groups of kids ran giggling up to the door yelling "Trick or Treat! Trick or Treat?" They observed carefully how Mrs. Crumpet opened the door, jumped back pretending to be scared and surprised all at once, then handed out candies.

Spacecase had bought a cardboard mask, an ugly demon face with a big pointy crooked nose, colored purple and green. He cut a piece of the mouth out so he could see through the hole better, and put it on upside down.

They waited until no kids could be heard approaching the house from any direction. When it got real quiet, Spacecase ambled up onto the porch, yelled "Trick or Treat" in a high, squeaky voice, turned with his back to the door and bent over so he could see through the mask between his legs. Then he unbuckled his belt and pulled his pants down just below his bare ass.

Mrs. Crumpet opened the door, holding the kerosene lamp just to the side and above her head so she could see. She focused first on the mask, staring evilly from between the legs. Then she noticed the bare bum aimed directly at her nose. The little white doily hat she wore flew right straight up in the air from the contraction of her scalp muscles.

All set to act frightened, she was doubly surprised to find she didn't have to pretend. She very quickly channeled her fright into anger. Caught between conflicting signals, Mrs. Crumpet bounded for her shotgun, but lost the element of surprise somewhere amidst the resulting confusion. Spacecase and his crew were well down the trail into the night when they heard the shotgun blast, fired aimlessly into the dark.

Fortunately Mrs. Crumpet was unaware that Spacecase had played the lead role in this particular episode, else she may have charged in right then and blown him away. Instead she scampered down from the apple tree and rode straight into town and over to the courthouse where she informed Judge Wrangle his daughter was being kidnapped.

The Crumpet's hadn't been getting along well since the time Mrs. Crumpet had quilted the Garden of Eden picture. It was a full-colour blanket depicting Adam and Eve, the Snake and the Tree of Knowledge of good and evil. Adam was bowing his head, supposed to be remorseful-looking, with an apple half-eaten in his hand. Eve and the Snake were looking on. Adam and Eve were decked out in big green fig leaves, although careful reading of the Bible would indicate the fig leaves came somewhat later. Mrs. Crumpet was an artist with a needle, and well aware of the artist's license in such matters.

One evening, shortly after she had finished it, Mrs. Crumpet decided to show her latest creation to the group of ladies she had tea with once a week. She unrolled it on the table to the admiring gaze of the ladies, to find to her horror that someone had added a caption to the piece. Along the white border, below six months of meticulous hand-stitching, in indelible India ink, was penned: "ADAM DISCOVERS HIS PECKER for the FIRST TIME…"

The ladies had, of course, pretended to ignore the caption and admire the fine needle work instead. Mrs. Davidson-Smythe, the most admired and socially graceful of the group, was unable to suppress a loud guffaw which she quickly turned into a diplomatic sneeze. Mrs. Crumpet folded over the captioned portion at the bottom as soon as she read it, and made a mental decision to kill Harlin in as slow and painful a way as possible.

Naturally, those members of the group who had not had time to read it quizzed those who had at later times. Mrs. Crumpet knew she had become the object of considerable gossip, and had been spoiling to get back at Harlin for weeks. Getting him arrested for kidnapping would be just the ticket. Maybe Judge Wrangle would let her put some buckshot into his hide, or even take a hand in the execution.

Judge Wrangle didn't believe her at first. He had talked with Minerva, less than an hour before. He hadn't been able to place Loralei, but it seemed unlikely that his daughter was being taken against her will. He knew her that well.

Nevertheless, he decided to look into it. He rounded up half-a-dozen of the local toughs from the saloon, told them he'd skin the first one who harmed his daughter, then deputized them so they would know it was all right to shoot anybody else involved. They made it to the Eldorado less than three hours after Spacecase and the others had left.

Ollie told the posse that he didn't know where the group had gone, but that he'd heard they were headed up the coast. It didn't take Wrangle and Mrs. Crumpet long, however, to discover that the north trail hadn't been used for days, and that four horses and riders and a buckboard had taken the eastern route quite recently.

They figured the group was only about three or four hours ahead of them. Since there was only an hour of daylight left, they decided to bed down at the Eldorado and ride out early in the morning. They might be able to catch "them kidnappers" while they were having breakfast. They could make the women cook up a good meal for the posse, before hauling them all back to town for the trial, and hopefully, a few hangings.

Spacecase and the others traveled late into the night, so were somewhat further ahead of the posse than Wrangle and Crumpet thought. Hence it was a hungry and tense bunch who, the following afternoon, spied the buckboard and riders across Long Valley, the one that flows down from the north into Roughneck Canyon.

Harlin Crumpet, bringing up the rear, spotted the posse first. Checking through Molly's spyglass, he made out his wife's battered fedora with the little crossed swords that he knew so well. "Bingo," he said quietly. "She still loves me after all these years. But she's gonna kill me for sure this time, so I better just keep on riding."

Bert said, "Don't worry Harlin. We won't let her get you."

"What will they do?" Loralei asked Molly.

Molly considered for a moment. "Probably surround us and shoot at us, then maybe put us through some mock trial so they can legally string us up. Except us women, of course."

"Not way out here, they won't," Harlin said. "Unless we give up with our hands in the air, they'll be looking for any excuse to gun us down."

They decided against trying to outrun the posse. It would be harder to cover each other in a running fight. So they headed up into a small box canyon, turned the buckboard on its side and stacked brush and poles to make a quick corral for the horses. Then they took up positions in the rocks as high up as they could scramble. They had an overhang at their backs, and a depression to give them cover. It wasn't the best position, but they could cover the horses and the buckboard, at least.

When Wrangle saw the buckboard, a couple of hours later, he didn't waste any time on negotiation. He sent three of his men around to try and get above and behind the kidnappers. Then he fired a few shots in the air hoping to draw some fire so he could find out their positions.

Spacecase and the rest kept their heads and didn't shoot back. But one of Wrangle's gunmen happened to stumble into their midst. He'd been warned not to hurt Molly so many times that he didn't dare shoot first, so Harlin and Spacecase got the drop on him. But he gave out a yell that let the others know where he was. Then he took off running back down the hill.

None of them had the heart to put a bullet in his back, even though it lost them a chance to cut the odds down.

Molly didn't want anybody to get hurt, so she told the others that she was going out to talk. Judge Wrangle might even let her go, as long as he knew she wasn't being taken against her will. Even if he took her back, maybe he would let the others go, and she could catch up to them later. Maybe.

The others said they were more inclined to fight. Spacecase felt she was their ace in the hole. Without her, those deputies would just try to kill the whole bunch. But they were out-numbered and would be surrounded soon. Then it would be just a matter of the posse picking them off one at a time. They had to do something, so Molly yelled that she was "Coming out!" and strolled down onto the no-man's-land until she was beside the buckboard.

Judge Wrangle and Mrs. Crumpet rode out to meet her.

Spacecase had the judge in his sights then, and kind of wanted to pay him back for the rock salt. But he didn't want to kill the old guy because he figured that might make it kind of difficult for Molly to relate nicely to him. He had Molly's Winchester balanced on a branch, but not cocked. His Webley .38 caliber revolver was still in his holster.

Then Molly turned and started to run as Judge Wrangle slipped his lariat from the saddle horn. He tossed a loop over her head with the skill of an old cattle driver, tightening around her shoulders.

She pulled a Bowie knife out of her boot and tried to cut the rope, but the old man was on top of her, whipping the end of a stringer around her ankles, as his cow pony backed up to keep the rope taunt.

Spacecase couldn't get a good shot without maybe hitting Molly, and the guys from below and to the side opened up with a covering fire that kept all of them down for seconds that seemed like hours.

To Judge Wrangle's thinking, as soon as Molly was safe, it was open season on the rest of the crew. Might as well save the taxpayers some money and just finish them off. Besides, he owed Mrs. Crumpet a favor for being so helpful and all. So he hauled Molly back behind some rocks and told his men to "kill those dang kidnappers" over the sound of Molly's yelling and swearing, and trying to kick his horse out from under him.

It took all four men and Mrs. Crumpet working together to finally get Molly bound and gagged and tied onto one of their horses. The judge had had enough, so he smacked her on the side of the head with the flat of his hand a couple of times, and repeated his instructions. He told the posse they could have any leftover horses and the buckboard for their trouble, then headed on down the canyon with Molly in tow.

The posse, especially Mrs. Crumpet, went at it with a relish.

Spacecase and the others had their hands full with two toughs sneaking around behind them and heavy fire coming from below. They had the better position, and good rifles and plenty of ammunition. But they were out-gunned seven against four, and had no retreat. So it would be just a matter of time before they were picked off, if they stayed in the trap.

"It was a Long Shot, the very worst kind of bet, grandson," he said. This Long Shot was one that didn't really pay off at all, except that maybe they would be able to figure out some way to save their skins. All the luck was riding with the other side. It would be hours before it got dark enough to sneak out. If they could sneak out. Plus there didn't seem any time for putting together a plan, with bullets flying all over from two directions.

Spacecase scrambled over beside Harlin, asked him "What do you think?"

"Maybe I could go out and talk to Matilda…"

"Naw," Spacecase replied. "We already tried that. Besides, she's trying to shoot your ass." Indeed, Mrs. Crumpet's shotgun blasts were sending little bundles of lead shot uncomfortably close, even though she was quite a distance away.

"She's deadly with a quail gun," Harlin remarked casually as he reloaded his Colt .44 cap and ball.

"Maybe we can fool them somehow into thinking we're some place else," Bert suggested.

"I don't know," Loralei said. "But I figure we got about ten minutes before they get above us. Then we're sitting ducks." She paused to fire a quick shot toward the rocks that hid the two flanking gunmen, then said.

Jim Erkiletian

"One thing sure, we can't get out of this with fancy gunplay alone."

Now Spacecase had learned one valuable lesson from that eagle. And a big timber wolf had taught him a similar bit of backwoods lore. It was that year he'd gone into the north after leaving California with the rock salt in his butt. Early spring of 1909. He was hunting moose or caribou in the Yukon bush by himself.

He'd been about two days out of Whitehorse, on a long ridge trail up the side of a valley. From the top he could see the whole valley floor, small green pastures bounded by gullies and hedges of saplings and brush. There was sign of wolf, bear, lynx and even wolverine along the ridge trail. Lots of predators used it, as lots of herbivores used the valley bottoms for grazing.

He walked the trail until he was right at the top of the valley, then sat down to wait a spell when he found a soft spot of caribou moss. "It was a real quiet day, with hardly a sign of wind," he said. "I had a little rollings with me, kinikinik, and decided to have a smoke while I watched the valley for moose.

"Just as I was most relaxed, with my rifle across my legs, sitting cross-legged and musing on the peacefulness of it all, there was this crash off to my left and just below me. It startled me so much, coming all at once and cutting through the silence like that, that I dang near did a back somersault. My feet shot right straight up in the air, and my rifle bounced up under my chin. I thought a tree had fell over and just missed me or something.

"Looking around I saw a grey shape with a tail disappearing into the woods about fifty yards across the top of the valley. Big timber wolf, just tearing along. He had been hunting, like me, waiting up there at the top of the valley for grazing animals to come around. And he must have seen me coming, unless he was sleeping or something. Anyway, by the time he saw me, I must have been right visible, and packing a rifle. So he decided to stay put, waiting to see what I was going to do. Hoping I would just keep going.

"Where he was sitting, I must have walked right past him, maybe two feet from his spot. He could have jumped out and grabbed my foot and tipped me right over, if he'd had a notion. He hadn't moved a muscle, even when my foot had almost grazed his tail.

"When I sat down for the smoke, he realized he'd have to do something. It was only a matter of time before I spotted him from that position above him. And the closest bunch of trees was nearly half-a-football field away, across a sidehill. If I spotted him before he started running, I would have a clear shot for all that way. Wolf had some hard decisions to make, and some real hard choices.

"He made it to the trees with time to spare. And even if I could have got a shot off, it would have been dumb luck to get anywhere near him. Surprise is the one thing that wolf had going for him. And I wasn't able to aim my rifle for an hour after that."

"So how did you get out of that canyon with Loralei and Bert and old man Crumpet?" I wasn't about to let

Jim Erkiletian

grandpa get off the track onto another one of his stories. He'd done that to me too many times before.

"Oh, that," he replied. "I forget."

Then he didn't say anything for a few minutes. Just sat there musing or something.

"So what about the wolf?" I asked.

"That Yukon wolf got us out of that trap just as sure as I'm here with you. This is how we did it. And this is how I paid." He rolled back his shirt and showed me a long scar on his chest just above his left nipple. Then he rolled up his pants leg and showed me a similar scar, but bigger and longer, on his leg just below the knee.

8. No Man's Landing...

Military: n. An organization dedicated to the art of organization.

First, they had to take care of the flankers.

Harlin had been captured early on in the American Civil War by a Confederate cavalry officer who had taken over 2500 Yankee prisoners with twelve men and a wooden bridge. He'd spent most of the war in a stockade, until he'd managed to trade his prisoner status for a move west in 1864. Of course he'd never forgotten that wooden bridge, or the value of accurate intelligence on the enemy. Providing the intelligence is not provided by the enemy.

The rebel lieutenant had marched his twelve men, their horses and single wagon, back and forth across that bridge all night long, shouting orders and rattling sabres. In the morning he rode right into the enemy camp with his entire twelve-man force and demanded the surrender of the whole bunch. Said he had them surrounded, and would open up from all sides.

Those yankees weren't stupid. They'd been counting and estimating all night. Besides, nobody would be fool enough to ride into their camp if they didn't have plenty of back-up. Naturally they surrendered.

Harlin told the others to cover him, took one of the Winchesters and his .44, and moved up into the rocks behind, so he could out-flank the flankers. When he got above them, he signaled for the others to hold fire, and waited until the gunmen decided to make a move.

Then he opened up with his .44 in one hand, the Winchester in the other, so they would think there were two of him. He even managed to wing one of them. They both scrambled back down the hillside, figuring they were out-flanked from above. It bought the group some time.

Then the posse got nasty and shot up the water barrels on the buckboard. Now they were in a bind. The odds were still seven-to-four against them, but it was a Mexican stand-off, neither side able to make a move on the other without risking blood.

"I always been careful to have a good escape route planned since then," he said. "Even if you're just bedding down for the night, you need to think out how to get out if your fire gets loose or some uninvited guest arrives."

Spacecase knew the posse was short a horse, since Molly had been tied into a saddle. And the horses they did have were tired, while his had had a time to rest. If they could get to their horses, and out of this box canyon, they could probably outrun the posse. But there didn't seem to be any way to do that without running a gauntlet of fire.

Mrs. Crumpet had taken over command of the posse, and was intent on putting the lot of them six feet underground. And she thought, by this time, that the honcho with the Winchester looked kind of like the same cuss who had stolen her peaches back six years ago. He'd become her second priority after her old man.

Harlin crawled back down into the hollow with the rest of the group and reloaded his .44. "Too bad we ain't got Chief Joseph to give us some advice right now."

Chief Joseph of the Nez Perce had fought a six-month running battle with 10,000 U.S. Cavalry over some 1500 miles of territory, back in 1877. With fewer than 150 men, women and children he'd avoided trap after trap, ambushed the ambushers over and over, and come within fifty miles of the Canadian border before being finally overwhelmed by sheer numbers. In the process he'd provided the world with the finest example of the superiority of guerrilla over conventional warfare ever encountered in military history.

"He'd probably tell us we should have stayed with our horses." Spacecase replied. "We have to get to them, somehow, and out of this box."

During a lull in the battle, Spacecase climbed up on top of a boulder and estimated the distance to the horses. There would be about a hundred yards of rocky sidehill to cross, plus another two hundred yards of hard riding to get past the posse and far enough down the canyon to get a good head start. Chances are they would die on the hill if they made a run for it.

He could see Warrior and Dixie, and the other horses, peacefully munching grass. They were saddled and ready to run. But they might as well have been a million miles away.

Jim Erkiletian

He jumped back down just as the posse noticed him and started shooting again. He recognized the boom of Mrs. Crumpet's shotgun, felt the wind of many small pellets of buckshot flying just over his head. At least the rest of those gunmen had proven to be not particularly good shots.

"Harlin, how much powder you got in your horn?"

The old man eyed it carefully. "About enough for another thirty shots," he said. "You got an idea of something better we could do with it?"

"Maybe we could make a bomb."

They thought about that for a minute.

"What kind of bomb?" Loralei asked.

"Maybe a smoke bomb. We got that tin of kerosene from the wagon."

"Great," Bert said. "So how do we deliver this tin of flaming kerosene. Those hombres are a good hundred yards down the hill and behind the rocks."

"I might be able to help with that," Harlin said. He pulled the tamping plunger from under the barrel of his .44 and twisted it off the pistol. "Strap her on to the end of that."

"Man, this is crazy," Bert said, shaking his head and pulling out a boot lace to make a strap for the kerosene tin.

He and Loralei made a tiny hole in the cap of the tin, just big enough for the end of the plunger to fit, but small enough so the twisted metal where it had broken wouldn't slip down in the can. Harlin tamped some powder into an empty .44 cartridge and loaded it into the pistol. Spacecase, meanwhile, kept the posse busy with an occasional shot over in their direction.

There wasn't much activity from the other side right then, because Mrs. Crumpet and her gang were convinced they had the upper hand. They figured they could just play a waiting game, and either the others would have to try to get by them, or have to leave their horses behind and strike out on foot. They knew there probably wasn't any water up on that hillside, so they figured they didn't have long to wait.

The kerosene leaked a little around the hole where the plunger went in, but they tied the boot lace around it tight and tucked it in at the edges so it wouldn't slip down into the can when the plunger was fired. Then they carefully lowered the plunger down the barrel of the gun as far as it would go. It wasn't quite long enough to seat against the powder in the cartridge, but almost.

Bert asked Harlin, "How many times you done something like this before?"

"Waal," the old man drawled, "I reckon this here's the first. We got no way of telling how far the damn thing will go when we pull the trigger. So the rest of you better sort of stand back a ways."

None of them could see any reason why it wouldn't work. It was a sort of jury-rigged mortar.

The posse was gathered behind the largest rock in the valley below, so were temporarily bunched up. "No time like the present to find out if this thing is going to work," Harlin suggested.

Spacecase put his hat on a stick and poked it over the top of his covering rocks, drawing considerable fire for a few seconds. Then, as Loralei and Bert returned the fire, Harlin carefully aimed the kerosene can on the plunger a little above the biggest rock covering the posse. He knew a little about trajectories, and was well aware of how to aim the pistol over fairly long distances. It had a twelve inch barrel, and would throw a four ounce ball of lead over a mile with some accuracy. But he'd never fired a tin of kerosene before.

Spacecase lit the boot lace fuse just before Harlin pulled the trigger. Then he dived for cover as the hammer came down on the cartridge, sending big flashes of fire out the sides of the pistol.

Harlin had overloaded it as much as he thought he could get away with. The little kerosene tin weighed quite a bit more than a chunk of .44 caliber lead. The recoil knocked his arms right back over his head and showered sparks all over his leather jacket.

The tin flew through the air like a rocket, arcing down on top of the rock and bursting open along a seam, scattering gunpowder-laced burning kerosene over a wide area. Little sparkles of burning gunpowder followed the can through the air. Some lit in the tinder-dry pile of tumbleweeds and sage against the side of the rock, bursting it into flame as well.

The gunmen below broke and ran, firing their pistols wildly over their shoulders. Spacecase and the rest broke and ran too, crossing the sidehill in record time with the cloud of smoke covering their retreat.

Mrs. Crumpet was the first to recover. She bounded through the smoke with her shotgun, looking every which way, to discover her targets were already mounting up and going to be riding right through any minute.

"Git yer butts movin!" she yelled to the rest of the posse. "They're getting away!" She fired both barrels in the general direction of the buckboard, but as she was a little off balance, and half-blinded by the smoke, the shot went wide, and the recoil knocked her on her can.

`The rest of the posse was scattered out in all directions, but they were beginning to get their wits back when Spacecase jumped Warrior over the buckboard traces heading straight for Mrs. Crumpet. She was yelling and trying to reload her shotgun and scrambling sideways like a crab all at the same time.

Another figure appeared through the smoke, with a rifle in his hand, so Spacecase fired his .38 toward the man's chest, grazing his left shoulder. The gunman turned and scurried back into the smoke.

Harlin rode in beside him, swung down from Dixie and managed to twist the shotgun out of Mrs. Crumpet's grasp before she could get it snapped closed. "I'm sorry, Matilda," he said, "but I think we need a little holiday from each other. We been getting right snarly since I revised your quilt."

She looked at him for a second, almost remorseful, then she looked over his shoulder and saw Spacecase. Her eyes turned red angry, and she yelled, "Harlin Crumpet, you not only run off, but you done took up with that trash who stole my peaches! Well, don't expect me to be here waiting when you get back!" She punctuated her speech with a swift kick toward his balls.

He managed to dodge and swing back onto Dixie before she could follow through with the haymaker she had aimed for his head, as Spacecase yelled "Come on, Harlin. They're starting to rally!"

Bert and Loralei were firing the Winchesters and riding along the edge of the cloud of smoke, heading for the lower canyon. Spacecase was a little behind them. He could see through the smoke the rest of the posse circling around, going to ambush the others near the mouth of the canyon.

"It was one of those moments they call epiphany, grandson," he said. "I could have ridden on out of there with the others, and maybe two of us would have made it. But two would not have made it. One alternative was for me to be the one not to make it. Now, I ain't no hero. But you tend to forget what a coward you are when things are moving so fast. So I whipped up Warrior and drove right into those gunmen. Harlin saw what I was doing, and decided to back me, even though he could see it was a foolish move."

They managed to make all the gunmen retreat for cover. But Spacecase wound up with a couple of bullet holes in his body. One was a clean grazing hole on his chest. The other broke his leg with a compound fracture.

"Still," he said, "I'm damn glad they didn't hit Warrior."

By the time they were far enough down the canyon that the posse couldn't see them anymore, Spacecase was barely hanging on to his saddle horn. They stopped long enough for Loralei to clean the wounds as best she could and bandage them with pieces of a torn shirt, as Harlin and Bert rode back to check their back trail.

They decided to keep riding. They certainly couldn't go back, and the California line was very near. They were all thinking Mexico might have to be their next home.

They traveled for the next two days with Spacecase just hanging on to life and his saddle horn as best he could. He'd lost a lot of blood, and the compound fracture to his leg hurt worse every day. But they kept on moving, even through most of the nights.

On the third day Bert and Harlin cut poles and tied them to Warrior's saddle to make a travois for Spacecase. He was delirious when he was awake, and passed out most of the time from the pain, but hanging on to that flicker of life with the tenacity of a bulldog. Loralei rode out into the desert a few times, returning with plants she made into soup, and poultices she put on his wounds every night.

Harlin and Bert rode back a few times, just to see if they were being followed. Apparently the posse had given up. It was almost two weeks later they made contact with Loralei's people in the desert.

Spacecase doesn't remember too much of how the Apache people managed to patch him back together. There were two women doing the surgery. One of them was a real sweetheart, nurturing and kind. She even cried with him, at his pain, and did everything possible to make him comfortable. He remembers her feeding him hot soup from a wooden spoon, and massaging his good leg and his back.

The other one was a competent surgeon, pitiless and smiling, with no time to waste on his pain. She cut the gangrene away with quick efficient strokes of a flint knife. Then she bored two small holes through the bone ends, set the break, and pinned it with two small pieces of deer bone carved to fit the holes. The native people may not have known much about cholera or diphtheria or smallpox, but the people who tamed the mustang knew a great deal about treating broken bones. And how to avoid infections.

Spacecase was passed out from the pain during most of this operation. They did give him something that took his mind off the throbbing leg and shoulder, but it only worked for a little while. The time he was awake he was hurting.

It took him all winter and most of spring to get his leg and arm back. They fed him the most nutritious of their food, deer liver and soups made from plants he'd never heard of. Several times lactating women were brought to him, and he discovered the healing properties of mother's milk for the second time in his life, presumably.

Harlin and Bert, meanwhile, decided there wasn't anything they could do here, and that they might as well keep on moving. They headed on out to Taos, promised to wait there until spring, if they could.

Spacecase was obviously going to need some time to recuperate.

Loralei decided to stay with him.

He paused to tamp his pipe on a rock. "She and I made your Uncle Joseph during that Spring."

"When did you make mom?" I asked.

"She was the last one we did." He put the pipe back in his mouth, carefully pushed in a wad of kinikinik, and lit it. "She was also the one who was most interested in getting away from her roots."

I made some marks in the sand with my stick. "She always seemed to be in need of something. More money or more things or something nobody and nothing could give her."

He nodded. "Like she wasn't quite complete, for some reason."

That's the main reason we were out there on the road on the trail of that old medicine bundle. He was hoping it would bring something back that had been lost, not only for mom, but for me as well.

We didn't know yet, at that time, about the accident up in Barlow Canyon. But then death never stopped Spacecase, or even slowed him down, when he got on to something.

Jim Erkiletian

9. Cactus Flowers and Sandstone Beads…

Intimacy; n. Self-love that nevertheless requires at least two participating individuals.

That was the worst winter Spacecase ever had, as far as he could remember. All the others were easy, after that. He was delirious most of the time, raving mad some of the time, and out cold some of the time.

But when springtime rolled across the desert, he got to know Loralei.

It was his good luck that two of the finest Apache surgeons were travelling in that part of the country. He's certain they saved his life, and he is aware that if he'd fallen victim to a European or white doctor, he would have been pushing up daisies by Christmas. Or rather fertilizing cactus, considering the terrain. Modern science had no understanding of the plants that prevent infections, or even the ones that fight scurvy in those days.

At the very least he would have lost that leg. The only thing white doctors knew to do in such cases was amputate and hope they could keep the gangrene from poisoning him to death. Or any of the hundreds of other diseases rampant on any doctor's hands.

"The main thing the white man's medicine has done is get a whole lot of people dependent on doctors and drugs." He was fond of saying that too. "Men were dying of scurvy in the Yukon in 1906. Why? Because of Doctors. The poor jerks that believed in them died."

Captain Cook had proved vegetables would prevent scurvy by enforcing a vegetable diet on his sailors. They almost mutinied. Some people think his own men did him in, for making them eat cabbage, then blamed his death on the savages of the South Sea islands.

Whatever killed Cook, it wasn't scurvy. Ship captains in those days reckoned a loss of a third to one-half their sailors to the disease, on a crossing of the Pacific Ocean. The fact his men survived some of the longest voyages in history, to that time, proved beyond any doubt that fresh vegetables knock the scurf.

Nevertheless, the priest in the Yukon, with some sixty dying men in his hospital, would wait all winter for the first boat to bring in onions and potatoes. He never considered that local natives never seemed to experience any vitamin deficiencies. What would they know? Savages.

Any native Yukon child knows dozens of plants inside the winter camp, or within an hour's walk, chock full of vitamins. There's caribou moss, that has everything necessary for human and caribou survival. You have to look during the summer so you know where to go in winter, but you can even get the caribou to dig it out of the snow for you, if you time it right. There are rose hips, very strong in the C vitamin, that grow practically everywhere. When the snow is too deep there are spruce needles which make a bitter but vitamin-enriched tea.

Any one of these is adequate to combat scurvy, and do a better job of it than potatoes or onions. But the Dawson City priest would wait for the boat to beg whatever amount of moldy vegetables he could get from the captain.

"That's just one way," Spacecase said, "your own racism can kill you. There are a whole lot of others."

When springtime came to the desert that year, 1915, Spacecase was hobbling around on a crutch and getting to know Loralei better and better. His worst winter was followed by one of his best springs.

"Grandma Loralei was a whole different person out there in her own country," he said. "That's where she really came alive and bloomed."

"What made her decide to leave the razor behind?" I asked.

He started to answer, and hesitated with his mouth half-open, his eyes peering directly back into his head. I waited.

Finally he looked at me, took a long strip of fir off a branch and started picking his teeth. When he finished, he drawled out a slow "Waaal now that's sort of private information, Yeuzor. I'd have to check with your grandma before letting my tongue run on that one."

What he'd flashed on was that little round house out in the desert, sunk into the desert floor, with the sweat pouring off their naked bodies from the hot, hot steam coming off the rocks above the fire. It was a very dry sauna, with water so scarce they only used a few drops sprinkled lightly from the tips of the fingers, about every half-hour.

They could hear the hiss of the instant steam, and feel the wave of boiling mist sweep over them, filling a void of indecision with a warmth that can't be done any other way. "There's no way to describe a dry sauna in the desert with dirt and grime flowing off you like a river. Every sweat gland open and flushed by hot steam."

It was four saunas before she would let him touch her. Needless to say, he was some ready by the time she came around the fire and sat beside him and began softly massaging his nearly mended leg. It didn't hurt, the way she did it. He knew her well enough, by this time, to know she was quite capable of digging those fingers in to the bone, if need be.

He winced slightly, just to see her immediately relax her grip even farther.

"It doesn't hurt," he said. "Not directly. Just makes me want to touch you back."

She stopped massaging his leg, her eyes drinking the fire. "Sounds like you're getting well quicker than I thought."

Eventually they found each was looking directly into each other's eyes, exploring something different and wonderful. It was a very short step from eyes to hands and they were both very carefully and gently flowing close together body-to-body with such an amazing warmth flowing from the centre of each others' tummys and intertwining there on the rug on that hardpacked dirt floor.

They spent longer in the sauna than usual. Other members of the tribe saw them later, holding hands. It made everybody smile. Except Loralei's father. He'd have to put on the big proper-father act, now. The stranger probably wasn't good for very many horses, either. A danged nuisance.

Spacecase and Loralei didn't notice. There was little outside stimulation for them that year, although the inside stuff was more than either one of them had bargained for. They heard about the Great War to End War through the moccasin telegraph.

The United States was getting addicted to the slogans. From "Make the World Safe for Democracy", all the way around to "Kill the Hun", the image makers were hard at work to sell the idea that heroism means giving your mind and body to a general, or even a lieutenant, to use as he sees fit.

"The yo-yos telling us to hate Germans were the same jerks who'd massacred native people all over the Great Bear. In fact, they'd murdered their own workers at Luddlow and Winnipeg and Everett. Most people weren't fooled. But, like Jim Thurber said in 'The Owl Who was God', "You can fool too many people, too much of the time."

I reckoned as how all the people, some of the time was bad enough. He agreed.

"We could see the shape of the coming peace treaty back then too," he said. "It was going to be another of those forked-tongue jobs that would wind up in another war a few years down the road."

The natives had lots of experience in what treaties mean to Europeans. Breathing spells to allow them to steal the land and build up big armies for the next war.

"White people think their ancestors stole the land from the natives, grandson. And there's a trail of broken treaties that spells it out. But there is more native land being exploited and ripped off today, as we speak, than there was back a hundred years ago. We just don't hear about it because they tell us it was a long time ago."

He was right about that. The most disgusting scenario in that little drama is the United States government poisoning Navaho and Apache lands testing their atomic weapons. And dumping their toxic wastes.

By late Spring, Spacecase was well enough to ride. Warrior had taken a liking to a little mustang mare that belonged to Loralei's uncle. He was willing to part with her as a sort of wedding present, providing an adequate bride price could be arranged. That was a problem. Spacecase still had a couple of hundred bucks left from that game back in California. But that wasn't near enough to make for a good wedding.

But Loralei made some proposals to the women, and her grandma managed to mollify grandpa. Nevertheless, he acted like he was offended at the small nature of the gifts Spacecase offered. He stamped off in a huff, complaining in Apache about young people not listening to their elders anymore.

Loralei assured Spacecase that was how a father is supposed to act, to keep face with the neighbors. She knew, as well, that her brother was on his way from Flagstaff to take care of the arrangements for his sister's wedding.

The bride price was something like money in the bank, for Loralei. She knew she could always come back here and wheedle that money out of her father, if she needed it. Better than a bank, actually, because banks steal from their own customers when they can't get anything from anyone else. As Americans discovered in the 1930s.

"Her brother must be my Uncle Bob," I said.

"Right the first time," he said. "He gets the bride price, eventually. It was him who raised up your Uncle Joseph and your ma, more than me. Lots of people do it that way, cause it's easier, and better for the kids."

"How come?" I was curious.

"Well, it splits up the work more even. And spreads out the gene flow. And it solves lots of inheritance problems. In the whiteman's world, some sweet-talking gold-digger can slide in and get some old geezer to sign the marriage papers, she gets all he has. But in the native system, a man's kids get what he has, regardless."

"Can they get divorced?" I asked.

"Sure. No problem there, for the couple anyway. But there is lots of problems for everybody else if a girl decides to go back to her own people. They're supposed to give back the bride price. It's probably spread out through the whole family by that time, so it can turn into quite a boondoggle. You can bet they do what they can to get her to go back and make up with him. If they can."

"That might be a good idea," I said. "Gets everybody with a interest in keeping them together."

He agreed. "It works the same with Bert's people, the Samburu. Every uncle and cousin and niece and grandson has some goat or something from the wedding. And it all has to go back if the marriage don't work out."

"It's even easier with my people, my mother's people," he continued. "Inland Tlingit. Most of the marriages up there, the suitor gets rejected completely. But if the girl likes the looks of the prospective husband, her father exercises his right to keep both the bride price and the daughter. Then the boy has to round up a band of warriors and sneak in at night and steal her."

"That must make for some problems," I ventured.

"Nobody gets left in the lurch at the church, anyways," he replied. "If she changes her mind, she can always go back home to her folks. Makes divorce a whole lot simpler."

"So what happened to Molly after that?"

"Molly. Now as you may have surmised, she was not the type to give up on her dreams so easily. She bided her time around her father's house for a month or so, acting repentant for her attempted escape. Then, when he made a trip to Sacramento in November, she stole ten of his best horses and set out for New Mexico again.

It was rainy season on the coast, and impossible to track her by the time Judge Wrangle got back in early December. She had told her brother she was going, and would shoot anyone who tried to stop her. Mickey spent some time convincing the old man that she was old enough to make her own decisions. He also explained that no matter how many times he hauled her back, she'd probably just escape again. Which may have influenced subsequence events, and Wrangle's decision to bring in a professional.

Some of the Pawnee braves she had grown up with had a ranch in southern Colorado, so she took the northern route into New Mexico. Some shrewd trading had expanded her herd to fourteen by the time she hooked up with Bert and Harlin some four months later at an oasis a couple of days ride outside of Taos, called Spitville Waterhole. There was enough water to support two saloons, a store, livery stable and hotel. And about three hundred people, counting prospectors and drifters.

The three of them set up shop on the outskirts of Spitville in an abandoned shack, where they built a corral out of rails and thorn bushes. Sort of a combination kraal and corral. Bert played some music now and then at one or another of the saloons. Molly sold and rented her horses, and actually made some money that year. Harlin was a good enough jack-of-all-trades that he didn't have any trouble getting work when he needed it. Or rabbits when he didn't.

Occasionally they'd ride into Taos for supplies and excitement, or over to the pueblo in the hills above the town. It wasn't long before most of the locals knew them well enough to do some trading.

Bert liked that desert country, to the surprise of Harlin and Molly. He'd been born in Africa, was originally Samburu, also known as Northern Masai.

He'd followed the Finlayson expedition of 1893 out to the coast.

"I would have just gone with them," he told Molly, "but they would've had me carrying bundles of gear. So I followed at a safe distance, then joined up with them at the coast."

"Why did you leave?" Molly asked him.

"Same reason any kid goes off traveling. To see the world. But you better believe, that thornbush country where I grew up is lots tougher than this. With lions to boot."

Molly and Bert found they had much in common, including some mutual physical attraction, during that summer. He made her a necklace with some turquoise beads he'd swapped for, and explained that was how a Samburu warrior came courting. She immediately put it around her neck.

Shortly after, she found to her delight, Bert hadn't been entirely frank with her when he'd implied he wasn't built much different than white men. He was short for a Masai, to be sure, at just over six feet. But he had participated in the circumcision rite that all Samburu warriors go through, at the appropriate age of thirteen.

"What happened was," he explained later that summer when they were all back together, "my elder took a slice through the underside of my foreskin with a flint knife. Then he poked the end of my crank down through the hole."

"Must a hurt some," Spacecase observed.

"Shit. Hurt? Like your dink has caught fire. And I was supposed to stand there and act like it didn't bother me none. Good test of how serious you are about being a Samburu, and a warrior."

"How come you to put up with such treatment?" Harlin asked.

"Well, the girls don't pay no attention to you if you ain't a warrior, for one thing," he continued. The other men nodded thoughtfully. "And you can't own any cattle or camels. But then as soon as you get the cut, man, there are all these little sweethearts in every village who all of a sudden take notice of you. They all want to be first to kiss it better, you know."

Harlin and Spacecase nodded thoughtfully again.

"It only hurts for a few hours, really," Bert continued. "But the good part can go on for quite a few years. And I got this little flower of skin on top of my knob. You'd be surprised how creative a Samburu woman can get with that thing."

"So what were you thinking about when your elder was making the cut?" Molly asked.

"Uh, I think it was how I was gonna get my first camels…" He trailed off. "No," he said, after reflecting a minute, "It was titties. Lots of titties."

10. Heads I Win, Tails You Lose...

Sin; v. A wrong action that can apparently be justified and absolved by a proper attitude toward the creator.

When Spacecase and Loralei finally got to Taos that August it was an occasion for a party. They started at the saloon at Spitville where Bert was playing and ended up back at the corral with fifteen extra cowboys, natives, Mexicans and assorted half-breed mongrels, two legged and four.

The four-legged was a big timber wolf called Brother by the youth wearing the fringed deerskin coat and toting a Kentucky rifle. He called himself Fairly, and the reason he referred to the wolf as brother was because they had grown up together. The wolf was actually four litters younger than Fairly, but they were definitely related.

Spacecase took a liking to Fairly. He came to find out the boy had lost his parents when he was a baby, still suckling, and been adopted by a wolf pack. Fairly was good at languages. He could communicate in Navaho, Apache, English and Spanish, as well as Wolf. And he had a powerful desire to learn to read.

Otherwise he was relatively uneducated in human terms. He was some sloppy at the dinner table, but when it came to enticing ladies, entertaining gentlemen, and looking after horses and cattle, there was no one better.

He appeared to be about twelve years old, which is pretty young in human terms to be out on his own. But in wolf terms he was a pack leader and elder.

"Nobody knows what the nose knows," Spacecase said often. It was his way of saying people are completely unaware of how much our sense of smell influences our perceptions and interpretations of the world around us. "Even doctors with letters after their names think we humans don't use our noses very much. That's another way of saying they just don't know how smells affects us."

Fairly used his shnozzle to read his surroundings like a book. If the wind was right, he could tell what was happening miles away. He didn't need to see or hear what was over the next hill unless it was directly downwind. Water in the desert was always right where he said it would be, day or night, Summer or Winter.

"That wolfboy could sniff out a marijuana seed under a stack of fresh-cut hay," Spacecase claimed.

Fairly had lost his first family to scalp hunters. After he got to know Spacecase and the others well enough to trust them, he told how he had lost his second family. To poison.

Most people all through that part of the country know wolves eat small rodents. Now and then they eat a cow if it's ready, that is if it's sick or old or weak in some other way. Otherwise wolves eat mice and gophers. Since mice eat grass seeds, and will turn a grassland into a desert in no time from yesterday if they aren't kept in check, the natives always considered it a sign of good luck to see coyotes and wolves walking around inside their herds of buffalo or deer. Or cattle.

"Damned hard for a human to learn," Fairly told Spacecase, "how to catch mice with your two front paws, er, hands. Took me an awful long time to get the hang of it."

The white farmers and ranchers moving into that country were scared silly of the wolves. They saw nothing more than a big, bad threat to sheep and cattle, and tried to shoot them at every opportunity. When they saw how efficient certain poisons are, they began to use them in their war against wildlife. Fairly's second family had been wiped out, four years before, by a sheep carcass injected with strychnine.

Fairly and Brother had survived because they had stayed at the den. Brother was just a pup, and Fairly had been left to babysit.

Their mother had realized there was something wrong with the meat by the time she got back, and had been able to warn them against eating it. It had taken the pack over a month to die, and they had died horribly.

The ranchers were particularly mad at wolves that year. One of Fairly's uncles, a big gray fellow, had dragged four poisoned sheep haunches from several miles apart so he could stack them in one pile and piss on them. The cowboys hated that lobo in particular. The feeling was mutual.

Little Fairly realized early on he was sort of caught in the middle. He had enough sense to realize he was going to need to live in the human world at least some of the time. So he made friends with the closest people he could find, Navaho folks who'd settled up around Chaco Canyon.

The kids took him in. Not that he needed them for survival. But they could see the advantages of having a playmate who had a wolf-brother twice the size of the biggest of them, and who could sniff out water in the desert from three times as far away as they could. Because they liked him, and looked like him some, he began to spend some time around the pueblo. Otherwise he lived in the desert and made his own way.

Those Navaho kids gave him a good education in their own language and culture. They told him about the ranchers and farmers from the East who were taking over the land. Eventually Fairly learned to wear clothes and make and shoot a bow. The summer before, he'd moved into a rock overhang just outside of Taos and begun spending some time learning how to talk to these light-skinned newcomers.

He had very little idea of where he had come from. It took Spacecase and the others many hours of discussion and guessing to figure out he must have been a refugee of the range wars between the mining bosses and the native people.

"That kid had some kind of survival urge that made him just a cut above anyone I ever met," Spacecase said. "And with that nose, plus his human eyes and ears, he could read a man, woman or horse like thick print through thin water."

"Romulus and Remus, the twins who founded Rome, were raised by wolves," I said. Just to let him know I believed him.

He looked at me sidewise, judging whether I was putting him on. Then he nodded real slow. "I believe that," he said.

It was an afternoon in the late summer of the next year, 1916, when Spacecase learned true respect for Fairly's nose. He and the boy and Brother were sitting in the shack discussing the world. Fairly liked to practice his English, and was learning to read with some dime novels. Spacecase was helping him with the big words and practicing with the cards, doing fans and shuffles and various tricks for guessing where the aces are, how to deal off the bottom, and so forth.

Molly was out in the corral, brushing down one of the horses. The others were in Spitville, Loralei selling beads and opals, Bert playing piano in the saloon, and Harlin hanging out with them to keep them covered from his quiet position at the bar or on the boardwalk.

Suddenly Brother and Fairly sat up on full alert, the latter reaching instinctively for his rifle. Spacecase looked out the window to see three riders coming, walking their horses on the dusty trail. They wore wide-brimmed hats and long oiled-denim raincoats, even though the day was hot. They didn't look good.

Spacecase buckled on his .38 and started to go out and confront them, but Fairly put a hand on his arm. "They're killers," he said quietly. "I can smell them from here."

Jim Erkiletian

Spacecase hesitated. He took his binoculars from the hook on the wall and focused in on the riders. The middle one had his hand resting on the butt of a holstered Colt. The man to the left had a rifle cradled in the crook of his right arm. The one to the right had a rifle cradled in his left arm. They were covered with weeks of trail dust. And yes, they looked like killers.

Spacecase said, "I'd better get Molly."

"Too late," Fairly replied evenly, as Brother growled low in his throat. "They've already seen her. We have to wait until they're right in range, then kill them." He cocked his rifle and rested the barrel on the window sill, just where it couldn't be spotted from outside. "You take the middle one and I'll get the ones on either side."

As far as Spacecase knew, Fairly's nose had never been wrong before. He'd learned to trust it dealing with water and animals and plants. But this was something else. A twelve year old boy telling him to kill three men because they smelled bad made him a little nervous.

"Uh, how can you tell they mean to do us in?" he asked.

Fairly looked at him as if he was a rank amateur suddenly stuck in to play the last quarter in a pro game. "I said they're killers," he replied, his voice like smooth blue flame. "That's for sure and certain. That's what they do!"

Spacecase looked through the binoculars again. They were closer now, and he could recognize them. The one in the middle had a patch over his left eye.

Patch Bishop, the bounty hunter, had a reputation. They were killers all right. Three of the most highly-paid professionals in the United States. But what were they doing here? As far as he knew, none of them was wanted. Not by the law, at any rate. Their picture would have been on the wall of the Taos post office if there was any warrant outstanding. And the local sheriff, old Tom Hatter, would have been out to get them.

"You keep Molly and me covered from here in the shack," Spacecase said. "I'm going out there to warn her."

He slid her holster with the Colt .45 onto his shoulder, slipped out the side door and walked quickly around to the corral. He was still walking with a slight limp from the wound. The three riders didn't speed up or slow down, when they saw him crossing to the corral. They just kept coming steadily on.

He tossed Molly her pistol, saying, "We got visitors. They don't look like the neighborly type."

Molly strapped on her Colt and followed him to the south edge of the corral, where Fairly could cover them both from the window of the shack.

When the riders got close enough to hear him, Spacecase stepped out in front of the corral and yelled, "That's far enough, gents. You're covered from the shack. What can I do for you?"

All three riders stopped. The centre man reached inside his coat with his gun hand and pulled out a sheet of paper, unfolded it, and turned it for Molly and

Spacecase to see. "You might be interested in this," he called back.

Spacecase stepped forward and the riders started to ride toward him. But Fairly yelled from the shack, "It just takes one to deliver that paper!"

The leader hesitated. Then he motioned for the others to stay back and rode up to Spacecase and Molly. By the time he got close enough to hand over the paper, she had her Colt pointed squarely at the centre of his chest at point-blank range, with both hands steady and two fingers resting on the trigger. Spacecase still had his Webley holstered.

As he handed the unfolded paper down to Spacecase, Bishop said, "That's a bad limp you got there, hombre." His voice was like dry ice, smoldering, but colder than frozen water.

Spacecase looked at the man for a moment. "Sprained my ankle branding some steers last week," he replied evenly. Then he looked at the paper.

It was a Wanted: Dead or Alive poster for someone with bullet scars on the left leg and right shoulder. He was said to be a tinhorn gambler, with a general description as to height and weight, and "possibly in the company of a Woman of Apache blood," a "Mr. Harlin Crumpet, Farmer," a "Darkie piano player Burtrand Carver," and "Miss Molly Wrangle of Topika Springs, Calif."

At the bottom of the sheet, in big black numbers and letters, was the offer of a $1000 REWARD.

As he contemplated this bit of information, three things occurred to Spacecase. First, Molly was in danger of having to give up her freedom and return to papa. Secondly, there was $1000 involved somehow in the net worth of his physical body. And thirdly, if Fairly could sniff out hired killers from that distance, with almost no wind, he should be able to sniff out the holder of a winning poker hand just as easily. He made a mental note to ask Fairly about that last item just as soon as he could get around to it.

Spacecase handed the poster back, said, "Sorry, you guys have the wrong place. But I never saw that one at the post office."

"That's because it ain't been released yet," the man replied. Then he looked at Molly with his single eye. "If that Miss Molly Wrangle was to return to her daddy, like a good girl, it might never be released." He folded the paper and tucked it carefully back inside his coat.

Molly stepped in front of Spacecase, her Colt still leveled directly at Bishop's chest. "If I was to be that Molly Wrangle," she said, "seems like the best thing I could do right now would be to blow you right out of this world, mister."

He looked at her with a steady one-eyed gaze. Then he patted his pocket, the one with the folded Wanted poster. "Not if she don't want this released to every sheriff in the United States." Then he slowly reached in his shirt pocket, extracting a small white card which he handed to her.

She kept her pistol aimed straight at his chest, didn't look at the card, but accepted it with her left hand.

He waited until he saw she wasn't going to waver, then said, "We'll be at the hotel for two days if you'd care to talk business." Then he wrenched his horse around and trotted back to his partners. The three of them set off in the direction of Spitville at a comfortable gallop.

Spacecase looked at the card Molly handed him. It had a drawing of the bishop chess piece, and a San Francisco post office box number in the lower left-hand corner.

They went back in the shack and sat down to talk over the new developments.

11. Howling with Hunters: The Desert's Song...

Economics: n/v. The study of rationalizations used by some men to justify the stealing of other men's resources...

"So what do you want to do, Molly?" Spacecase asked first. "You know there's no guarantee that he won't release that poster, even if you do go back."

"Hell,' she admitted, "there's no guarantee that he won't just order Bishop to blow you away, even if I do go back."

Fairly suggested they better round up the others and make some plans. Since the bounty hunters hadn't seen him, he and Brother would jog into town and inform Bert, Loralei and Harlin of the poster.

Fairly was able to follow the gunmen from a safe distance, and slip into the saloon without them seeing him. The band gathered back at the shack just before dusk.

"The whole town's buzzing, with these hired killers staying at the hotel," Bert said. "Everybody's speculating on who they're after, and anybody with any skeletons in the closet is keeping a low profile."

"Old Doc Warner's getting himself sober," Loralei said, "And the deacon is holed up in the church, praying steady. Half the town could walk under a rattlesnake without getting their hair mussed."

Jim Erkiletian

Harlin reckoned the saloons would be staying open later than usual, what with the "escalating level of general worry." He'd seen the undertaker buying up a whole lot of pine planks on credit, over at the general store.

"So how do we deal with these guys," Spacecase asked. "Even if we blow them away, assuming we could, the judge will still release those Wanted posters. And we'll all be in trouble."

No one said anything for a minute or two. Then Bert asked, "What do we know about Bishop?"

Harlin spoke first. "He and his men rode with Quantrille's boys back in the war. They did some bad stuff. But most of the people they killed died quick."

"So he's rough," Bert said. "He'll still go down like any man. We need to figure out how to deal with that poster."

Spacecase took a sip of the black coffee he'd boiled for the group. "Looks like he's got us over a barrel. What else you know about him Harlin?"

Harlin thought a bit. "He's got a good record of bringing in dead bodies. He's never made a mistake and brought in the wrong one, as far as I know." He hesitated. "He plays chess real good."

"Sounds interesting," Loralei said. "Any stories about him and women?"

Harlin turned to her. "He don't let them get close to him, or his men, when he's on a job. But he likes them." He turned to Molly. "His horse's name is Sundance, after the ceremony and the Kid."

"Chess, eh," Spacecase said. "Figures, with a name like Bishop. Didn't he ride with Villa some? And he must'a known the James boys."

"As I recall," Harlin continued, "he got along O.K. with Frank. But him and Jesse didn't hit it off for some reason. He rode with Villa. But I don't know if it was to run the Spaniards back to Spain like we done the British in 76, or for the looting and pillaging. Most likely both."

They worked on several possible plans through much of the night, until Spacecase suggested they wrap it up and get some sleep. "We know he claims to be a businessman. It may be as simple as finding out what he wants and getting it for him. That we can do tomorrow."

They all curled up in blankets, with Fairly and Brother doing most of the guard duty. The next morning they had breakfast together and refined their negotiation procedures with a diagram of the saloon on the breakfast table.

Then they rode into Spitville, took up positions in the saloon, and sent a kid over to the hotel to tell Bishop they would be ready to talk at noon.

When the three gunmen walked through the swinging doors at twelve, on the dot, the place was crowded with some fifty or sixty people. Most hoping to see some gunplay.

Bishop stood just inside the door and surveyed the room, his partners to either side just behind him with their rifles aimed at the ceiling. Then he stepped aside and waited as the bar patrons suddenly realized they had urgent business elsewhere. Some filtered out through the swinging gates, past Bishop and his men. The majority chose to exit through the side doors and the back, then hurried around to the front to peek through the windows.

In a couple of minutes, the place emptied right down to Loralei sitting at the bar knitting, Bert sitting on the piano bench reading a paper, Harlin at the bar sipping a sasparilla and also reading a paper, and Spacecase and Molly at a table against the back wall, the former playing with a deck of cards, Molly cleaning her toenails with a Bowie knife. Fairly and Brother were sitting on the floor in the corner by the stove.

The bartender, a fat old geek called Arnold, was polishing glasses. Bishop looked at him. He decided to take a break from his bar duties and go check his stock in the back room for a while.

Bishop looked around the room until he was satisfied there were no hidden guns anywhere. Except the ones under the knitting, the newspaper, the piano bench, and maybe propped behind the stove. He motioned for his own men to stay where they were, then approached Spacecase and Molly.

Spacecase kicked a chair back from the table and motioned for Bishop to have a seat. He shuffled the cards and they looked at each other, each sizing up the other. Bishop finally sat down and put both hands on the table top.

He appeared to be about fifty years old, with several small scars visible on his face from a bolo match he'd lost in Chili, many years before. He had a full beard, and his one good eye looked like an Apache tear set in ivory.

"You say you're a businessman, Mr. Bishop." Spacecase opened. "So what kind of deal did you have in mind, saying I was to point out these folks you're looking for?"

"I've got a grand riding on doing nothing more than hauling her back to Frisco." He nodded toward Molly with his head, paused to spit a gob into the spittoon beside the table, wiping his mouth with a red bandana after. "Another grand if I bring in the head of the gang in a pine box."

Spacecase nodded slowly, looked across the room at Loralei. Molly was starting to visibly steam up at the prospect of being treated like a piece of merchandise. Loralei, exhibiting her excellent sense of timing, wandered over from the bar and asked if anyone wanted anything to drink.

Bishop ordered a sasparilla, and Spacecase a glass of beer mixed with that stuff with the worm in it. Cactus juice. Loralei brought him a sasparilla too.

"I hope we can settle this peaceable," Spacecase said after Loralei had gone to get the drinks.

Bishop looked at him. "We can settle it any way you want," he replied. "Just so I don't get short-changed."

Spacecase drew an ace of spades from the deck he was holding, showed it to Bishop, flipped it back in the middle of the deck, shuffled twice, and suggested off-hand Bishop might want to "Cut for high card?"

The gunman hesitated, with the wariness of a man who has learned to be extra careful what he does with his gun hand.

"I'll do it for you," Spacecase said quietly in that short space of silence. He ran his fingers down the pack, and flipped over the ace of spades. "You win," he said.

Bishop's mouth registered a very brief smile.

Loralei brought the drinks and set them on the table, being careful not to get between Bishop and his men standing by the door. "That'll be two bucks, gents."

Spacecase took a folded ten dollar bill out of the deck of cards and handed it to her, saying, "Keep the change, mam."

She tucked it in her bosom and returned to her seat by the bar, closest to the two gunmen by the door.

Bishop looked at Spacecase. "Lots of gamblers carry derringers," he said.

Spacecase nodded. "That's what I hear. And they pay their debts double, just to keep a good credit balance with their friends." He gave the cards a quick fan and shuffle, then looked at Bishop. "Two thousand, eh." He shuffled the cards again, said, "If you help me settle this up, we can get a lot more than that out of the stingy old bastard."

Bishop took a sip of his sasparilla, looked quickly and directly at Molly. "Who you helping?"

She nodded at Spacecase. "Him."

He looked back to Spacecase. "I'll think it over," he said. Then he stood, nodded a silent thanks for the drink, and walked quickly out the door, his backup men folding behind him like steel shutters slapping closed.

Spacecase sat around the bar for the rest of the afternoon, playing cards. Everyone wanted to know who Patch Bishop was gunning for, but Spacecase kept quiet. He told them it wasn't anyone they knew, anyway, and not someone from around these parts. He did mention that the gunslingers were here to do some business, and that they were interested in returning some horses that might have been rustled from a judge out on the coast.

Several of the locals wanted to play cards, so Spacecase was getting into a game when Fairly and Brother came in the back door. They'd been keeping watch on the hotel, from the building across the street. "One of Bishop's men is on his way over, and he's not packing, far as I could see," they reported.

The gunman came through the swinging doors as Fairly took up his position by the stove, looked around the now-crowded bar until he located Spacecase, then strode up to his table. "Bishop says you got a deal. We can talk about the fine points over at the hotel."

"Molly will want to be in on this too," Spacecase replied as he dealt out another hand of five-card draw poker. "Give me an hour to round her up."

The gunslinger looked at his pocket watch, nodded, and left.

Bert was playing the piano, a Colt .45 on a shelf just under the keyboard. Harlin was still sitting at the bar, his .44 cap-and-ball under the newspaper spread out on the bar top. Fairly's rifle was propped just out of sight behind the stove.

Spacecase hadn't felt too insecure, knowing he had plenty of firepower if the negotiations broke down. But retiring to the gunman's hotel to work out the details would be another matter entirely. He needed some time to think it over.

Loralei and Molly were out in the back stable with the horses, discussing business, and what that might mean to a professional murderer. Brother went out to fetch them.

Spacecase finished the hand he was playing, losing a few dollars to the men at the table, and excused himself.

The band retired to the back room to do some planning.

"I'm inclined to believe that Bishop is a man of his word," Harlin said, when they were all gathered, "but he only gets paid if he delivers a body to the judge."

"We'll have to cover that angle for him, then," Spacecase replied. "We need a dead body that looks like me." Then he added, "Actually, we only need a head."

"I can provide the head," Loralei said. "My people have some experience in making masks, and Molly knows about painting make-up on to give a life-like, er, rather death-like appearance."

"That leaves us the problem of reclaiming our investment," Spacecase said. "I guess we'd better discuss this with Bishop, then."

Bert suggested a parlay would be better done in the lobby of the hotel, where they could all be present. "We can't afford any slip-ups, and we need to know everybody's roles in this little drama."

"And we have to do it right," Molly said. "I don't want to ever go back to California again, unless its my own choice."

Bishop was already sitting in the lobby, resting in an easy chair reading a paper when Spacecase walked in. The others filed into the lobby behind him. The other two gunmen were not in sight, although they could be behind any of the doors to the various downstairs rooms. Or watching from the upper staircase. Or in the dining room having dinner.

Bishop folded his paper and nodded toward another easy chair beside him. "We'll talk this deal in private," he said. "Your people can wait in the dining room with my partners."

Spacecase hesitated, then looked to the others. They were willing to trust him, but he didn't want to leave Molly out of the negotiations. She was intimately involved, after all. "Molly has to stay," he said.

Bishop looked at Molly. "You say you're in this on his side," he said quietly. "Prove it."

Molly looked from Bishop to Spacecase, then back. She nodded once and turned and strode into the dining room. The rest followed, but Fairly said quietly to Brother, "Stay here," and nodded toward Spacecase. Brother padded over and plunked himself down at Spacecase's feet.

Bishop looked thoughtfully at the wolf, then nodded his willingness to make an exception.

The first thing Molly and the rest noted in the dining room were the two gunmen sitting at a table against the back wall eating steaks. Neither acknowledged the group. A waiter appeared to seat them and take their orders.

In the lobby Spacecase was saying, "We can provide you with a pine box and a head that looks like me. And Molly will go back to the judge's house."

Bishop nodded, took a silver spike out of his coat pocket and picked a bit of meat out from between his teeth.

Spacecase continued. "We're figuring on teaching the old man a lesson, after we get you paid off. Nothing physical. We just want to take some of his money away from him. If you'd help with that little chore, we can make it worth your while."

Bishop nodded again, with the assurance of a man who was not afraid of any man, judge or outlaw, and who didn't particularly enjoy doing someone else's dirty work, especially if the job has been misrepresented.

As a matter of fact, Bishop knew he was in the wrong camp the minute he'd looked down the barrel of Molly's .45. Having your queen in a protected position is important enough. Getting her where she can attack from a protected position almost always guarantees a victory.

He could have easily, and cheerfully, killed Spacecase and as many of the others as tried to interfere, hog-tied Molly and hauled her all the way back to the coast. But why do all that work if he could get them to ride back there on their own?

He could fulfill his contract to Judge Wrangle after they got back, or anywhere en route, so he didn't have anything to lose. He was holding the Wanted poster, which gave him the right to shoot Spacecase any time he chose.

"Maybe you should tell me how you intend to even up the score with Wrangle."

Spacecase smiled. "I'll keep that a secret until I let you know the part you'll be playing. At which time I'll fill you in completely on all phases of the operation. We can decide how to divvy up the loot at the same time. We work on an equal share basis."

"We'll be leaving day after tomorrow, then, for the coast." Bishop unfolded the paper and began to read, indicating the interview was over.

Spacecase joined the others for dinner.

12. The Wasp's New Stinger...

Automobile: n. A contraption designed to give one the illusion of freedom in exchange for the enjoyment of travel...

It was a good trip back across the desert and into the foothills of the coastal mountains. They stopped in at Tombstone Arizona, then rode down into the desert to visit some with Loralei's people, and make up a mask.

The Apaches packed mud to Spacecase's face to get a mold, baked it until it was hard, cooled it and smeared the inside with grease. Then they poured some more soft mud into the mold, working it until it was exactly the size and shape of his face and head. With some of his hair glued on to the top and the upper lip, and the proper dyes and paints rubbed on the right places, it came out looking exactly like a dead Buzzard O'Toole. After it was finished everyone stood around admiring it and commenting on how good the likeness was.

Bishop and his men were standoffish at first, riding a little way behind the others. But around the campfires at night, they all got to know each other a little. Harlin had been in the same regiment as Bishop's older brother, in the Yankee army, it turned out. They had grown up in neighboring states, Kentucky and Tennessee.

By the time they finally got over the divide of the coastal range, they were all on first name basis. In fact, the stories and lies they were telling each other were getting so outrageous that none of them were looking forward to breaking up the band.

The day before they reached the Eldorado, they made up a pine box that was big enough for the head,' using New Mexico boards they'd brought from Taos for the top and sides. They stuffed a bunch of pine needles and burlap into the box, tossed a couple of dead fish in under the burlap for atmosphere, then sat around and waited until the whole thing smelled just right.

They carefully lowered the head in, then packed in some snow from the last glacier they passed in the mountains, and tacked the lid on. With the box in a burlap bag tied to Bishop's saddle horn, he and his men, with Molly dutifully in tow, rode on down to the judge's house in Topika Springs.

Molly acted repentant, and the judge sent her to her room, took a quick look at the head in the box, and sent a buckboard for Mrs. Crumpet to come identify it.

"How come it's so well preserved?" he asked Bishop as they waited.

"We had the thing embalmed," Bishop replied evenly, "but them undertakers didn't look too competent, so we had them do it twice. Then we packed it in ice or snow when we could get some."

"Hum. Good thinking," the judge replied. "I hope Crumpet gets here soon. This thing is beginning to stink."

Mrs. Crumpet rode into the yard within fifteen minutes. She was in such a hurry to identify that head that she left the buckboard and driver, and rode the horse in bareback. She didn't seem to notice the smell

Jim Erkiletian

that mushroomed from the casket when the men lifted the lid, just studied the face for a minute and nodded.

"That's him, all right. I'd recognize that danged scalawag anywheres."

She pulled her hat off, mumbled a short prayer, then stuck it back on her head, looked at Bishop and the judge. "That's one halfbreed won't be stealing no more peaches." Looking back at the head she commented, "Mighty nice job them embalmers did, ain't it."

The judge thanked her for her trouble, closed the lid of the little casket and sent Mrs. Crumpet home so she could send him back his buckboard and driver. Bishop's men hauled the casket back out to their own horses and remounted while Bishop discussed money with the judge.

"That's a thousand for the girl, and another for the head," the judge said as he took his cheques from the drawer of the rolltop desk in his study.

Bishop nodded. "Plus fifty for the double embalming, and if you want us to dispose of the head, that'll be another fifty."

"That's a hell of a lot for embalming," the judge muttered. "But I sure don't want that thing in my house any longer than necessary."

He made the check out for $2100, signed it and handed it to Bishop.

The bounty hunter tucked it into his pocket and showed the judge the Wanted poster. "I guess you won't be needing to make up any more of these." He crumpled it and threw it in the fireplace.

The judge nodded.

Bishop rode into town to cash the check while his men rode out to the cemetery to dispose of the casket. They paid the caretaker to look the other way and dumped the box into a freshly dug grave that was easily deep enough for two bodies. The grave digger, of course, reported that he'd seen some men put something in the grave.

The judge told him to forget about it.

Bishop rode back up to the Eldorado later that evening, where Spacecase came out on the veranda to talk with him.

"So Wrangle bought the story," Spacecase asked. "and you and your men got paid O.K.?"

"Yep, and you're officially dead. So don't get in any trouble around here," Bishop replied. "You have my card. Let me know when the next act is scheduled." He untied a burlap sack from his saddle horn, tossed it to Spacecase. "Here. This might come in handy. It don't seem right to bury a work of art."

Spacecase looked inside to see his head leering back at him.

"Thanks," he said.

The next day Spacecase and the others rode down to San Diego. It was beginning to swing, with U.S. Navy personnel, Mexicans from Tiajuana and south, and quite a bunch of grifters and swingers from all over the continent collecting there.

Bert didn't have any trouble finding a piano. And Spacecase didn't have any trouble finding poker games. They were everywhere.

On the ride out from Taos, Spacecase had put together a game with Bert, Molly, Harlin and, after some cajoling, Bishop and his men. The stakes weren't high, nickel ante with dime raises, but he asked Fairly to watch and, most important, smell the game.

Half-an-hour into that game, Fairly knew he could smell out a winning hand as easily as a dog can smell fear and anger.

After Spacecase taught Fairly the game, they discovered an added bonus. The boy could tell which player was bluffing almost as easily as he could tell who was holding high cards.

"You see," Fairly explained, "when a man draws a real good hand, he smells, uh, different, just as soon as he sees the cards. But in a bluff, he doesn't smell up right away, not until after the bets start falling."

"So either way, there's time for you to signal me."

"Right," Fairly assured him. "I can scratch my nose for a bluff, my neck for a high hand. Or something like that."

"Great," Spacecase replied. "Now we just have to figure out how to get you in the room during a high-stakes game."

Fairly traded his rifle for a shoeshine kit, and a studded collar for Brother so people would think he was just a big dog. It worked for the most part, although occasionally someone would recognize the wolf. Brother seemed to realize he was in strange surroundings, so was willing to put up with this humiliation.

Apparently no one recognized the wolf in Fairly by that time. He had learned to pass as human very well.

Loralei was able to make some money singing in San Diego that month. In fact, there was a hall where no gambling went on at all, where people came to listen to entertainment. They signed her up to sing with a little band for accompaniment. It didn't pay a great amount, but it was more than she had made at the Eldorado.

My Uncle Joseph had been born in Apache country, so he was along on a papoose carrier. The band swapped looking after him quite a bit. Loralei was already carrying my mom in her belly, so she was taking care of herself and keeping a low profile.

Spacecase, meanwhile, was setting up the main players of the area to a big game, where he could have Fairly in his corner.

He was also spending a fair amount of time with whatever Irish immigrants he could find. There were quite a few. He studied their accents, and pumped them for information about their home country. During that two months he learned to talk English exactly like a cross between an Irish dandy and a British fop.

The game Spacecase set up, along toward the end of the second month, enticed in some of the biggest winners of cash money, and poorest poker players, in the San Diego area. It went all night, and ended with Spacecase dividing up over $12,000 between himself and the rest of his people.

He'd started with a different game every night, just to get to know the players in the area. He didn't win big in any one game, playing only to break even, losing now and then on purpose to certain players. One big-money player, he noticed, had a loss of concentration whenever a woman walked by. Another was into munching peanuts steady, except when he was holding high cards. And so forth.

Fairly, meanwhile, became known as a shoeshine boy who specialized in poker games. He'd come around and ask each man at the table if he could do their shoes, treating Spacecase like any other stranger.

Spacecase was able to control the games well enough to let whoever he chose win real big. Meanwhile, he just held his own and shuffled the money around until he had met the ones he wanted for his big game.

Then, in the second week of August, he proposed to each carefully chosen player that they get together for a marathon session on the last weekend of the month, with no limits on the bets or the raises. Each man was interested. They had in common that each had been able to pile up some pretty big winnings in games with Spacecase over the previous few weeks. They were ripe for the pickings.

Spacecase brought Molly down from San Francisco for the big game. The judge didn't object to her taking a holiday trip, to visit friends. He knew she wouldn't leave her horses behind for long.

She and Loralei were good at distracting the players who had a weakness for women, at opportune times. Other than that, with Fairly able to let Spacecase know when someone pulled an especially good hand, the game went off without a hitch. Like pulling cliches from a dime novel.

Needless to say he was no longer Buzzard O'Toole, halfbreed gambler, but Erasmus Y. O'Toole III, Esq., a lawyer on holiday from England. His newfound gambling friends called him Ari.

It was a little over two months after the distasteful episode with that smelly head that Judge Wrangle looked out from his morning breakfast to see and hear a Stanley Steamer automobile chuff-chuffing and hissing into his front drive. It was driven by a black man in chauffeur garb.

The well-dressed young man stepping out, looking around, and taking off his kid gloves, looked vaguely familiar.

Minerva answered the door, and returned to the breakfast nook with the embossed card of Erasmus Y. O'Toole III, Esq., of O'Toole, O'Toole, Robertson, Smythe & O'Toole, Barristers and Solicitors, #46 Hammond-on-Clyde, London, England.

"I guess you better show him in," Wrangle said, slightly annoyed. His first thought was that it might be some long lost relative. But on the other hand, he didn't think he had any relatives who were lawyers. And what did some smartass English lawyer want way out here anyway? "I'll see him in the study."

When Judge Wrangle entered the study, he noticed right away the resemblance between Spacecase and the head he had seen just two months before. But before he could introduce himself and ask what this was all about, Spacecase began talking.

"I'll come right to the point, sir," he said. "It regards my younger brother, Buzzard O'Toole, I think he called himself. He was last seen in this part of the country, and I thought you might have some word of him, as you are well known in these parts."

"Indeed," the judge answered, looking thoughtful. "Uh, would you like a drink, Mr. O'Toole. Or a cup of coffee?"

Molly chose this moment to make her entrance. Harlin had intercepted her on one of the riding trails the day before, and briefed her on her new role.

"Yes, thank you," Spacecase said, ignoring Molly. "Tea would be nice."

"I'll get it father," Molly said. Spacecase had his back to her, so she pretended to ignore him, went to fetch the tea. Spacecase continued. "We are afraid, that is, my family and I have reason to believe young Buzzard may have met with a bad end." He leaned forward conspiratorially, whispered, "You see, he had a wild streak that made him sort of the black sheep of the family, so to speak."

Then he leaned back and continued his story in a more conversational manner. "Just between us gentlemen, sir, my family and I wish to avoid any hint of scandal, or any embarrassment that could result from my brother's, ah, indiscretions." He looked around, again leaned forward, "In fact, we would be willing to pay quite handsomely to see any mention of this regrettable affair expunged from the records, so to speak."

Molly entered with a tray with some cookies and two cups of hot coffee. As she placed it on the table, she noticed Spacecase, or rather Erasmus III, for the first time. She gasped and almost dropped the tray.

The judge quickly said, "Uh Molly, daughter, this here is Mr. Erasmus O'Toole, the brother of that outlaw who kidnapped you last year."

"Kidnapped!" Spacecase rose quickly and took her hand carefully between his palms. "My dear, it must have been horrible."

Molly bowed her head, said, "Indeed it was a difficult situation for me, Mr. O'Toole. He was a liar and cheat, and treated me poorly. My father was able to make me see the error of my ways, and sent some men to rescue me."

"My dear," Spacecase continued quickly, "I am not without means. Perhaps there is some way by which I can make up to you the injustice you have suffered. We will discuss this further."

He rose to leave, extended his hand to Wrangle. "I have business in San Francisco. But with your permission I will call on you day-after-tomorrow to discuss what restitution is in order. Would nine in the morning be too early?"

"No, no, that would be fine," the judge said, rising to see him to the door. He was beginning to think that he may be able to get his $2100 back, which would be just the right definition of karma to appeal to someone like Judge Wrangle.

13. Crows on the Scarecrow...

Magic; n. 1. The science of creating illusions.
2. The science of another culture or time.

"Those ravens and whiskey jacks in the north are the ones who teach us teamwork. Crows too, but in a different way."

He was starting to get hot again. We were somewhere in the Rocky Mountain line. I listened.

"The jacks will team up to fool a wolf. One will get in close to his bone, pretend like he wants to steal some. The other waits 'til the wolf chases off after the first one. Then he darts in and pecks up as much as he can until the wolf comes back and starts chasing him. That gives his partner a chance. Takes the wolf a long time to catch on to that one. And some wolves never figure it out. The ones who like chasing jacks."

"Crows do it different?" I asked.

"Crows and ravens do that too. But they sometimes fool each other, to get a bigger share. I've seen a crow go after a rock or stick that looked like it might be good to eat. Then when another crow decides to take it away from him, he'll jump over and gobble down the worm he'd been eyeballing in the first place."

"Like magic," I said.

He stopped rambling and looked at me. I did a trick my father used to do, that made it look like I was pulling the top joint of my thumb off my hand.

He paid me back the next day with an illusion that looked like his eyeball had fallen out of his head into his water glass, and left a big bloody socket behind.

He did it with a little brown marble set in ivory, and a round mirror set into his eye just over the lid. Some lipstick smeared around completed the image. Looked ugly as sin and twice as painful. You heard the splash, saw the eye sinking in the glass, and just had time to think it's a joke and bang, there's that bloody socket staring back at you. Figuratively speaking.

Nobody's saying we actually used that image for anything but entertaining each other. You can imagine how valuable it would be if there was occasion. Like some jerk with a big Caddy bangs into the fender of your brand new 54 Vette and wants to avoid the hassle of court. He might be willing to up the ante if he thinks he caused you to knock your eye out on the steering wheel spinner.

They played a similar sort of game with Judge Wrangle, but different in that they let the judge make up the plot as he went along. Meanwhile, they exercised their artistic license to revise the script and doctor the lines, playing out the roles as they developed.

If Buzzard O'Toole was indeed a child of royalty, he may be the black sheep of his family, but he was still royalty. Those stiff-necked cockney yahoos had a reputation for protecting their own. Wrangle knew he'd better cover his butt, just in case some unpleasantness should result from this visit.

He gave Minerva two messages to take to the telegraph office in Topika Springs. Mickey had moved up to operating the office in Portland, fortunately for Spacecase and the others.

One gram was addressed to Bishop in San Francisco, asking him to contact the judge pronto. The other was to the Pinkerton office in Denver asking for any information they had on the law firm of O'Toole and etc. of London, England.

The one to Bishop got to him quite soon. He was busy on a job at the time. Specifically, he was sitting by a pole out the road from the Topika Springs telegraph office, with an earphone against his ear, listening to the dots and dashes of Morse code blipping down the wire above his head.

The reply he prepared regarding the message to himself read, "Currently unavailable. Will contact on return." Short, and designed to keep the old boy sweating just a little.

The one addressed to himself was his cue to write down the next message. And to wait for the reply.

It wasn't long in coming. The Pinkertons had never heard of O'Toole, O'Toole, Robertson, Smythe & O'Toole of anywhere. Bishop smiled and disconnected the earphone wires, stuck it in his pocket, and whistled for his horse.

A few minutes later, down on the main street, he watched a kid come running out of the telegraph office with a bag over his shoulder. A little blond kid about ten years old, who pulled a bicycle out of the shed behind the shop, climbed aboard, and started pedaling up the road toward the Wrangle place.

"Too bad," Bishop muttered to Sundance. "Sometimes even little kids get in the way of a job." He patted his horse on the neck. "Be thankful you're a horse, buddy."

He turned and took the back trail out of Topika Springs, but in the same direction as the boy had gone.

As he pedaled over the wagon bridge, the delivery boy noticed another kid with a straw hat and fishing pole, sitting on the bank. It was that native boy who's been hanging around the telegraph office lately. Probably looking for a job, but the company don't hire Indians.

As he drew up even with him on the bridge, the kid left his pole and hat and fell into an easy jogging gait that kept him even with the bike. "Hi," he said.

"Hi," the delivery boy said cautiously.

Suddenly, without warning, there was a full-grown timber wolf loping along beside the two boys. He seemed to have dropped out of the sky.

"What the heck…?"

"My brother," Fairly said, indicating the wolf. "What's your name?"

"Aaron," the boy replied uncertainly.

"This is your lucky day, Aaron," Fairly said. "You get to make a lot of money."

"Yeah," Aaron replied. "I get twenty cents and maybe a nickel tip from the judge if I'm lucky. If I don't forget to call him sir."

Jim Erkiletian

"No, I mean you gonna make fifty dollars today," the native boy said. "Silver dollars and real money."

Then he ran on a little ahead of the bike, and off to the side of the road, the wolf loping easily beside him.

Aaron watched Fairly carefully. That kid sure is a good runner, he thought. Then he glanced back over his shoulder at the sound of hoofbeats on the dirt. He could see a rider coming up the trail at an easy gallop. A tall man in an oiled slicker and wide-brimmed hat. He pulled his bike over to the side and stopped, to let the rider by.

Bishop rode even with the boys, tipped his hat, and rode on a few meters. Then he expertly spun his mount sideways in the road, took a leather pouch from his pocket and tossed it on the ground directly beside the front wheel of the bicycle. Within arm's length of Aaron's right toe.

He dismounted, said "Steady Sundance," and walked back to the two boys, squatting down on his haunches directly in front of the bicycle.

Aaron was looking at the leather sack like it was a still-smoldering devil who'd just popped up out of the ground and asked him for his soul.

"Listen to him, Aaron," Fairly said, and jogged on ahead to the crossroad some twenty yards further up the trail.

Looking him in the eye with his single-eyed stare and a disarmingly friendly smile, Bishop said, "If you deliver that message, some good friends of mine, including two nice ladies, might get hurt...or even killed."

Windigr

The boy looked uncertainly at Bishop. "How do you know that?" he asked slowly.

"They're friends of mine," Bishop replied. "I have to protect my friends, and I'd like you to help me. I'll pay real good to get a quick peek at that telegram. And you won't get caught because the only ones who will know are you and me."

Aaron looked at Bishop, then at Fairly standing just off the road at the crossroad. He was where he could see anyone coming from any direction. The wolf was nowhere in sight. "You're outlaws, ain't cha," he said with a kind of wonder in his voice.

"A businessman, Aaron," Bishop replied quietly. "I pay for what I take, as you can see. And even if I was an outlaw, I wouldn't steal from a kid."

Aaron looked down the road again. Fairly was leaning against a tree, relaxed looking. There was a sheath knife hanging from his hip. Funny he hadn't noticed it before. Would a kid outlaw steal from a kid?

He reached down and picked up the leather pouch, reached inside and pulled out a silver dollar, looked at it. There was folding money in there too. "You just want to look at this telegram?" he asked, looking back at Bishop. "Can you do that without breaking the seal?"

"Yep," Bishop replied. "I can tell what I need to know by looking at it through this here candle." He took a candle from his pocket and lit a match to it, shielding it from the wind. "But we got to hurry."

Aaron quickly pulled the telegram from his bag and handed it to Bishop who palmed it and did a quick turn around long enough to get the telegram in his pocket and substitute another gram he'd made up that morning at his hotel. It read: "O'TOOLES ETC A MOST RESPECTED HOUSE OF LAW BRITISH EMPIRE STOP PRESENTLY UNAVAILABLE PRIVATE CASES STOP DEALING WITH SOME OF HER MAJESTYS MORE PRESSING SCOTTISH PROBLEMS STOP.

The boy accepted the telegram, glanced at it, and stuffed it back in his bag. "You get to see what's in it?" he asked.

"Yup," Bishop replied. Then he turned and walked to his horse, swung aboard, and turned back onto the trail.

"Remember, Aaron. Don't tell anyone about this little deal. We would both be in trouble if you did." He set off at a gallop back down the road toward town.

Aaron sat looking at Fairly for a minute. Then he stuffed the bag of coins in his pocket, looking around like he was expecting to see a big hand come out of the clouds and snatch it away from him. He pumped up on his bike again. As he crossed the crossroad, the native boy again fell into a trot beside him.

"Where'd this money come from," Aaron asked. "robbing a train or something?"

"Nah," Fairly replied. "It come from a game we did in San Diego. Like those spin-the-wheel gambling games you seen at the fair, but more complicated."

"My mom don't let me go around that part of the fair," Aaron said.

"Your mom's smart. Them games is all rigged."

They traveled a bit in silence. Then Aaron said, "I, uh, never thought before that there might be kid outlaws."

"Learn something new every day."

"What's it like?"

Fairly spit into the woods at the edge of the road. "Not bad, I guess. Kind of exciting sometimes. And good money. Sometimes." He paused, continued, "I reckon I'd trade it all right now if I could have a mom alive and kicking, like you got."

"Your ma's dead, eh. How long?"

Fairly looked at the big wolf loping along beside them. "My first ma when I was too young to remember. My other ma about five years ago." He thumped Brother on the shoulder, causing the wolf to skip a stride. "She was his ma, too."

At the drive leading up to Wrangle's house, Fairly and Brother stopped. Aaron stopped too.

"I been thinking about this here money," Aaron said. "How am I gonna spend it without folks getting suspicious?"

"I'd take the coins," Fairly said, "put them in a metal box and bury it where you're the only one knows where it's at. And I'd get a money belt for the cash."

Aaron nodded.

"See you around," Fairly said. He and the wolf faded into the forest like so much smoke dispersing on a windy day.

Aaron pedaled up to the house with the bogus telegram.

"A man can be that easily seduced into a life of crime and further debauchery," Spacecase said, tamping in a pipeful of Missouri marijuana.

"That stuff you smoke is illegal," I said, for no apparent reason.

He scrutinized the pipe with the look of a semi-imaginary third eye squinting from between his bushy eyebrows. "Used to be legal, up until about five years ago. Then, with prohibition repealed, the state had all these unemployed revenue agents with no booze-runners to help keep up the graft payments."

I thought it over. "But doesn't it do something to you?"

"Yep," he said. "Makes you feel good." After a few minutes he said. "It works good for a bunch of things, like migraine headaches, pink-eye, or what they call glaucoma. Women use it for easing menstrual cramps and having babies. But mostly it's just for fun."

I thought that over a while. "Isn't it habit forming. Make you into a drug fiend if you do it too much."

He looked at me, again using that third eye. And his other two as well, of course. "I reckon people will keep doing whatever makes them feel good. Which could make it into a habit. But I don't know anybody who really needs to smoke this stuff. Or who gets sick if they can't get any of it. It grows wild all over the Midwest, so there must be lots of dope fiends around."

He looked back into the bowl of the smoldering pipe. "On the other hand," he smiled, "I'm glad I don't have pink-eye in a country where they tell us what we can't put in our own bodies."

He talked for a bit about an outfit in Canada he'd worked for that mixed maple sugar half-and-half with hasheesh oil and sold it all over America. "We couldn't fill our back orders, we had so many buyers. And was that stuff ever good. Especially to go see a picture show, like with Charlie Chaplin slipping out from under some irate looking boss or pretty girl's mad father. The main danger to that stuff is you might bust a gut from laughing too hard."

He blew a couple of notes on his harp. Then a jig in six-eight time that he used to warm up. An owl answered him, after a few minutes.

He and that owl played some lowdown blues for quite a few hours that night. I fell asleep against that weird lullaby, hoots and hoo-hoo-hooos played counterpoint to long, low wails from the blues harp.

The owl came back several nights in a row, and we met up with some of his relatives in other parts of the country over those years. It's because of those nights, falling asleep to that owl-and-harmonica duet, I can see so well in the dark. That and lots of raw carrots.

It wasn't only to keep the revenuers in business those marijuana laws were instituted, I learned later. It was all the big plastic and oil companies taking out the competition. Just like they did the Stanley Steamer, so people would have to buy gasoline powered cars.

The Stanley brothers got one of their steam cars up to over a hundred miles an hour out on the Bonneville salt flats. It only used about half as much gasoline as the first gas-run cars, and could climb mountain trails that wore out the best appaloosa horses. The Stanleys built a big hotel in Estes Park, Colorado, way up in the high Rockie Mountains above Denver, and trucked in all the supplies and tourists with whole trains of their steamers.

They were noisy, huffing and puffing excess steam out the relief valves. And it took a while to build up a head of steam so you could get moving. A little research and experimenting would likely have taken care of those problems. The main problem with steam machines, for the oil barons, was they just didn't use enough gasoline.

They weren't able to get the railroads to convert from steam trains to diesel right away, so transportation by rail was fairly inexpensive right down to the 1950s. But that's another story.

"It doesn't pay," Spacecase said, "to be on the wrong side in one of those big power shuffles. But then who wants to be on the right side with a bunch of thugs dictating your business, then puttin' on airs like they are better than you just because they are able to steal more money from more people."

"You had one of those steam cars," I said. "What happened to it?"

"Finally gave out in the Yukon, back up on the old canal road. Boiler froze up and split during a particularly bad winter because we didn't get it drained in time. And it was getting harder and harder to get parts for that thing."

"Too bad," I said. "Wonder what it would be worth today?"

"Lots," he said. "To a collector. Me and Bert were riding with the Benson Creek boys, staying about half-a-step ahead of the mounties. There was quite a pile of gold still being taken out of the Yukon back then, and a better price to be had for it in San Francisco or Chicago than up there. But we had to get it across the border, and the T-men were hot on our tails most of the time."

"Horse don't use no gas at all," I observed.

He nodded.

After the yanks turfed out the Brits in 1776, they set up their Department of the Treasury with two major assignments. The first, and most important, was to protect the American dollar. The T-men managed to do a real good job of it too, infiltrating all the major banking houses and money institutions and feeding info back to the U.S. Congress. About the only ones they couldn't get to were the backwoods farm people who ran corn liquor stills on the side, and who had the trust of their neighbors.

The second responsibility of the Treasury Department, and somewhat less important, was to protect the American president. It's a job they've been less successful with over the years, considering the record. But it didn't hurt their applications for funding any. Every president from George Washington on down slid as much money and power their way as he could manage to steal from the American people.

They're real cagey, those revenue agents. You hear lots about the FBI and the military spy organizations, not to mention every local and state police outfit that accidentally turns up at a crime in progress. But them

Jim Erkiletian

T-men keep a low profile. You'd likely get in bad trouble for blowing their cover, if you did happen to stumble on one of their operations.

When the big plastics and oil company owners first decided to cut down on the hemp industry, they gave that to the Treasury guys as well. They made out that the farmers hadn't been paying their marijuana taxes, and turned the T-men loose on them, instead of the local cops. If some farmer was stupid enough to actually pay his marijuana tax, they'd just send in the local constabulary to bust him for drugs. They had the whole country, and half the rest of the world, on the run by the late thirties.

Marijuana came back in during the second War to End War. It was still necessary for making strong, light cordage, everything from boot stitching through parachute webbing to the big ropes that they use to tie up battleships. The government paid farmers all over the states, especially in Kentucky and Missouri, to grow it. Even put out a movie in 1942 explaining how to plant and harvest it, called Hemp for Victory.

People don't get sick from smoking marijuana, or from withdrawal like they do with alcohol or tobacco. Or most of the drugs you get from the doctors like codeine and morphine and cocaine. There are some addictive drugs floating around, but they're easy to spot because the user gets terrible sick if he can't get a regular supply. Or if he takes too much at one sitting. And the effects are not pretty to watch.

Having some non-addictive drugs illegal, and lots of the addictive ones legal, tends to muddy up the water for anyone trying to understand the world. But then it also serves to make people aware of some of the basic hypocrisy in the system.

Scientists working for the government found out about ninety-six percent of heroine users had tried smoking hemp before getting wired to their opium-derived drug of choice. They conveniently didn't mention that 100 percent of those smackheads had tried tobacco before getting addicted. And over ninety-nine percent had tried alcohol. Both of which are addictive and legal.

Try to convince the big shots who make their money from those drugs their fortunes come from causing people to get sick and die. The response you get will probably be in uniform, and swinging a big night stick at your head.

14. The Singer Sleeps and the Ghost Floats…

Writing: n/v. A system of symbols used to illustrate a system of symbols.

Molly was writing some of her best stuff during that two-month stretch of imprisonment. Including one of her best poems, "Between the Lines", the one Loralei got asked to sing over and over, sometimes four or five times in a single night. Some of the older people around Vancouver remember it.

> *It is not you and is not me*
> *that tells us what will be*
> *that gives us reason to go on*
> *against the swollen river's strong*
> *unhappy pressure bearing down*
> *to death beneath the sea…*
>
> *You're over there, I'm over here*
> *across a gulf of circumstance*
> *the twisting dance invites us here*
> *but not to touch or see or hear*
> *beyond the circumscribed unchance…*
>
> *But if you get my meaning clear*
> *its not what happens there or here*
> *that gives our tortured, lonely lives*

the meaning that, like razor knives
allows a sense to sense its way
to something that can kill the fear...

You are you and I am me, of that
there is no doubt or loss
but what scene's seen of bright chaos
and meaning's mean meanderings
is not what's there or here
but what's there in between.

At least that's Spacecase's version. I hope I get to hear Molly's original version some time. It must have been a real hummdinger.

Loralei sang it slow and soft, like ocean waves flowing in and out on a sandy beach, building in intensity, but not volume, in the middle of each stanza. Grizzled old prospectors, mule skinners and river pirates from all up and down the coast would be sitting teary-eyed, quiet as a band of Shoshone hunters, with Spacecase blowing soft wailing blues and Bert chording tight lost-down-the-river piano in behind her.

Harlin would often sit that one out just to listen. When he was in the mood, and not too many people in the bar, he could put in little triplet-trills on his banjo that sent the hairs right up on the back of your neck. Spooky stuff that set your mind trying to look over its own shoulder, and back, so as to stare itself in the face.

Like dancing the Virginia Reel with about twenty-nine partners, and getting to go last. Or riding a tilt-a-whirl at the fair. Both of which can be dangerous to the heart if you're with someone you like. Loralei, Spacecase, and Molly rode one of them machines together. It was in San Francisco, just before the marriage.

That must have been a good wedding, with Loralei giving away the groom and playing bridesmaid at the same time. She wasn't worried. She already knew he was her's forever, so she didn't mind sharing him as long as it was with Molly.

Besides, she'd married Buzzard. Erasmus didn't turn her on like Buzzard did.

Erasmus came back to see Judge Wrangle and Molly at the appointed time, chuffing up the drive in the Steamer.

Bert, all decked out in his chauffeur's uniform, looked mighty interesting to Minerva. She tripped around the side of the house and invited him in to the kitchen for a cup of coffee and some fresh tea buns. He made it a point to tell her what nice buns she had as often as possible after that.

He was able to learn some interesting things about the Wrangle household, thanks to Minerva's interest in him. Like where the guns were kept and what the old man's schedule was. Which houses of prostitution he frequented when he went down to San Francisco, and so forth. Those matchbox covers from the Harmony House, for instance, that she had found in his coat pocket, were the preliminaries of an interesting story.

Minerva had never met a real born African under eighty-years-old before, so she was interested and intrigued. As Bert was pumping Minerva for information, Erasmus was sipping tea with Molly and the judge in the study. After the appropriate small talk, he happened to let slip that, "A Mr. Bishop, of San Francisco, may have seen my brother shortly before he was killed."

"Really," the judge said slowly.

Erasmus remained silent for an appropriate space of time. It seemed quite a long time to the judge. He commented on what nice weather they seemed to be having, and how nice the tea smelled, and some other irrelevancies. Then he asked, offhand, "Perhaps you can tell me, sir. What would be the procedure for having the body of my brother exhumed?"

"Exhumed?" Molly asked. "Why whatever for, Mr. O'Toole?"

The judge had paled a shade or two, they noticed.

"My family will wish the body returned to the family plot in Westminster," he replied. Then, turning toward her, taking her hand from her lap and holding it between his palms, he said, "I must reiterate my heartfelt desire to make up to you any inconvenience brought on by the unjust behavior of my brother toward yourself, Miss Wrangle."

"Oh, he wasn't that bad to me, really." she replied. "In his way, he even loved me, I believe. Would you care for another cup of tea, Mr. O'Toole."

The judge was thinking. Suddenly a plan plopped into his head. If he could distract this city slicker with the affections of his daughter, get in touch with Bishop before O'Toole had a chance to contact him, and tell him what to say, he'd be ahead of the game. If things got too complicated, he could just have Bishop take out this Erasmus as easily as he had Buzzard.

The judge excused himself, saying he had important business in the town. He told Erasmus that he would do anything to help, and would see what procedures were necessary for getting bodies dug back up. Then he went into the hallway.

Leaning back in the door a moment later, he asked Molly, "Would you come help me with my coat, dear?"

In the hallway he whispered to Molly, "You keep this O'Toole chap company, will you. Find out what you can about him."

"O.K. papa. Where are you going? Are we in some kind of trouble?"

"Of course not," the judge replied. "But I'm gonna make sure we don't get in any. You just find out what O'Toole wants, and keep him occupied.O.K.?"

"Sure," she said. "I quite like him. He's so refined and elegant. And he looks wealthy."

The judge strutted on out the door, saddled up and rode into Topika Springs to sit around his office and think, and give orders to the clerks and the mayor's secretary. On the way, he stopped in the telegraph office and sent another gram to Bishop, telling him to report to him at the city hall as soon as he got back, that it was urgent. And not to come to his house. Then he made up a bunch of regulations against exhumation of dead bodies.

"You wrote some stuff back then, too, didn't you Buzz?" I'd heard from my mother that Spacecase was sort of a song writer. Maybe that was only in the family, though.

"Yeah," he said. "But nothing like Molly's stuff." He paused to blow a few slow rifts on his mouth harp. "I must have written Friends about that time. We used to do it in D with an E minor instead of the G. I forget some of it, but the verses I do remember go like this,

> *When you're dining with pirates*
> *keep a bird on your shoulder*
> *for eyes in the back of your head.*
> *Keep out of the sun if you carry a gun*
> *And your mind behind what's being said.*
> *Get clear little dear that the price on my head*
> *Will be cashed in before very long*
> *You can love me and care, but don't ever dare*
> *Think you can own more of me than a song*
> *Aye yi yi yi...hey ye ye ye...*
>
> *An Outlaw's reward is a hot lead slug*
> *Delivered between the eyes*
> *Served up by the hand of self-righteousness*
> *Wearing a legal disguise*
> *Just tell me that after we're over this love*
> *As this feeling of ecstasy ends*
> *We won't be the worse, for having been close*
> *And someday will learn to be friends*
> *Aye yi yi yi...hey ye ye ye...*

Bishop waited in the little log cabin at the edge of the pasture until he saw the judge ride by. Then he rode on up to the house. Fairly was just arriving as well. Using the judge's best whiskey, they all drank a toast to a quick victory and, hopefully, a clean getaway after.

Of course nothing ever works out exactly as planned.

At this point they were thinking out how to handle the next phase. There were two possible scams that could operate. They could let Bishop kill off Erasmus, and bring in a renegade Pinkerton Bishop knew. That way Bishop would be able to pick up the money. He could charge lots for a lawyer-killing, and they could use some of their San Diego contacts to up the ante even farther. One disadvantage of that plan, it wouldn't give Molly a good reason to leave. At least not soon enough for her. She was champing at the bit.

The little time she'd spent in San Diego with the rest of her band had reminded her where she wanted to be. But she needed to get her horses out, too.

What they decided on was a marriage, between Erasmus and Molly, with Bishop covering the judges tracks for his part in the death of Buzzard. Bishop figured he could loosen up another three or four grand from Wrangle on that one alone.

For the next few years, every time Erasmus needed money, he knew he could ride down to Topika Springs and tap the judge for a few more dollars, just by talking about exhuming his brother's body. Until the judge tried to cash in his bonds, that is. By then it was too late, for Wrangle anyhow.

Molly fed the judge plenty of information that led him to believe those mining stocks were part of

Erasmus's inheritance, and not to be sold. But the poor boy was so lovestruck with daughter Molly, and so eager to please prospective father-in-law, he just had to help in some way by letting the judge have them at the original sale price, nothing like what they were worth today. Which was true, on the face of it.

It was the telegram that didn't tell the truth about the worth of those stocks.

"It's pretty near impossible to rip off an honest man," Spacecase claimed. "We never had much trouble with Wrangle on that score."

"What happened to Fairly?"

"What do you mean, what happened to him?"

"He must only be about thirty-five or so, by now. Maybe I can meet him."

"Not in this life, you won't. He bought it on the Great Divide in 1923, back-to-back, er, back-to-tail with Brother against three hundred United States cavalry. And a aeroplane."

"He's dead, you mean?" Little black holes were opening in my heart as I thought about it.

"Ranchers paid fifty dollars a pair for wolf ears. The U.S. government, rest its rotten soul, paid a twenty-five dollar bounty. Naturally they told their bluecoats to shoot any wolves they saw. Off the record, of course.

"As I heard it from one of the survivors, they took thirty-two soldier boys with them. Only got caught after the plane spotted them and pointed out their position before they shot it down.

"It started with the pilot spotting Brother and taking potshots at him. That brought a couple of troopers riding over to recover the pelt, or finish off the wolf. Fairly saw them attacking, waited until they were both in his sights and blew them both away with one bullet.

"The pilot saw what happened and circled back to tell the rest of the troopers. It turned into a running fight for several days. Every time one of the troopers got in range, Fairly'd put him down. Most veterans would have smartened up and written off their losses, but these poor jerks had a real estupido for a commanding officer. He was one of the first of the breed that hides behind the men on the line.

"There's a big bowl of desert on the Great Divide, up around the Wyoming-Colorado border. It's about fifty miles across, give or take. The pony soldiers eventually forced Fairly and Brother out into there and rode them down. He was out of bullets, and on the first charge, Brother lost a forepaw to a sabre. And Fairly lost his Bowie knife throwing it into the side of the soldier that was leading the charge. So the cavalry just backed off and shot them full of lead from all sides.

"That's the way I heard it from an old soldier a few years back. He wasn't proud of what he'd done, but willing to talk about it when he had enough beer in him."

"In the war between the Yankees and Confederates, the generals would lead the charges," I said.

"The Civil War," he said. "Yep. Not a very appropriate name for a war. But in that respect it wasn't too bad. The generals still had to do some fighting back then. Not as many generals get killed as used to. Too bad.

"Anyway, the Lakota found what was left of Fairly. Some of the men who rode with Sitting Bull, but stayed behind when he moved to Canada. They were on their way back from a big powwow up there."

"Lakota?" I asked.

"The horse people from the Midwest, the torso of the Bear. Especially the Black Hills. Some people called them Sioux. They were saddened beyond words at what the soldiers had done to the boy for protecting his brother and his land. Leaders from all over the Great Bear (or Turtle) met the next year at Council Bluffs and argued for six days and nights as to which tribe had the right to carry Fairly's banner in their house.

"I think it was Black Elk's people who carried it, in the end. That was back when Neihardt was riding with them. Before him and Black Elk started writing about those days. Maybe forty or more years after those same people, with their Arapaho and Pawnee brothers, had beat the shit out of Custer's butchers at the Wishy Wash Creek. What Custer called the Little Big Horn River."

A marriage between Molly and Erasmus wasn't even close to strange or abnormal, in the eyes of the rest of the band. Back in Spitville, the year before, Molly had decided to take a ride up to Colorado Springs with some of her horses to do some trading at their yearly horse show and rodeo.

Bert had a steady gig in Taos at the time, and Harlin was somewhere out in the desert with a mule and some prospecting gear. Fairly was still there, but he was out with the Navaho kids, and busy on some kind of wolf business a lot of the time. Loralei suggested Buzzard maybe should ride up with Molly.

Molly had planned on going alone, but she was willing to reconsider. There were some real dangers on the trail. She wasn't worried so much for herself, being real fast and accurate with a bull whip, knife and .45. But she was concerned for her horses. Two people were much better than one for crossing rivers and keeping track of a herd.

Spacecase and Molly became extra good friends on that ride upcountry. They were cold the first night, camping in the desert, until dawn when the back-to-back turned into front-to-front almost at the same time. She was a little before him in turning. In her sleep, maybe. That's what she claimed, anyway.

There was a flashback for both of them that reestablished a connection that went right back to McWorter's hayloft. Only the breasts were considerably larger, now, and they felt so much better than they had before, from both sides.

"Its not as if we haven't been this road before," he said.

"Only we didn't get to ride very far last time," she said back, looking him steady in the eyes.

By the time they got to Salt Lake, they were exploring so far down that road that neither one of them wanted to ever go backward on it. Figuratively speaking, of course.

Spacecase also learned a little more about Molly's father, on that trip. He said something about the old vulture and was surprised to see tears spring into Molly's eyes. She'd referred to her father as an old vulture, horse thief and sidewinder so many times that he was taken aback.

He put his arms around her and held her close, let her cry a bit. "So maybe he's a vulture, but he did look after you and Mickey pretty good, eh?" he said.

She dried her eyes and started playing with the fire. "He changed after my mother died," she said. "I felt sorry for him, even though I was just little."

"How'd she die?"

Molly sighed, looked at him from under the brim of her leather hat. "I don't know for sure. I was led to believe she was some kind of witch dabbling around in the black arts, and got caught in her own noose."

"That's what your pa told you anyway, eh?"

"Yeah," she looked back to the fire. "But I've always wondered if he didn't kill her in a fit of jealousy.

She leaned her head on his shoulder and absently poked at the fire with a willow stick. Neither of them said anything for a time. Finally she said, "There was a man, a very gentle and kind Pawnee warrior. I remember the way she used to look at him when he'd come riding up to the camp we had out there. He helped us a lot. Taught us to survive out there."

"Hum. And your pa found out?"

"I don't know. There was a lot of drinking and swearing and even some fighting. But most of the bad stuff is just a black nothing. And I was looking after my little brother, some of that time. Then one day she was gone."

They made love very slowly that evening, under the stars with a chorus of coyotes playing way out in the desert. They were really getting to like each other.

When they got back to Spitville the next month, the first thing Spacecase noticed was the little necklace of blue turquoise beads Loralei was wearing around her neck. He wasn't surprised.

Later that night around the fire the four of them, Molly, Spacecase, Loralei and Bert, discussed the future. And the past.

Spacecase commented on the necklaces Molly and Loralei were wearing. He said they looked like a good idea to him.

"Samburu custom," Bert explained. "A warrior has to make about forty or fifty of these for his girlfriends. Plus a goat for each girl's mother."

"Seems like you're way behind with only two to your credit," Spacecase observed.

"That's two you know about," Bert answered with an enigmatic smile.

"It must get kind of expensive," Molly said.

"Maybe. A man doesn't really notice. He's too busy breeding his goats and herding his cows and camels. Pretty soon he's got a warm woman within walking distance of just about everywhere in his country. Unless she has somebody else's spear stuck in front of her door that day."

"And the girl's mother has a good herd of goats," Loralei said.

"To keep her busy and away from the house while daughter and boyfriend, uh, get to know each other," Bert continued. "And the girl has a bunch of necklaces to keep track of each one of the men in her life. Pretty soon she'll decide which one she wants to settle down with. But she don't decide too early on account of he might not survive."

"Pretty rough life?" Spacecase asked.

"Right again. Lots and lots of ways you can die out there. Snakes. Scorpions. Lions and hyenas. Rustlers sneaking in to steal your livestock. One of your pals accidentally making a mistake with his spear."

"Sounds a lot like Yaqui country," Loralei said.

"Then again, I suppose it's the most beautiful and comfortable country in the world, eh," Spacecase said, with a kind of twinkle in his eye.

"Uh, yeah," Bert admitted. "I've heard tell the Eskimo folks live in the most harsh country in the world. Everybody thinks it's the worst, all ice and snow and polar bears. Everybody except the Eskimo, that is. He knows it's the most beautiful and comfortable place in the world."

Spacecase had met Inuit people in the Yukon. "That's exactly right," he confirmed. "In fact, I've met Inuit who asked me how we're able to survive in towns and cities. It don't look very inviting to them."

"Maybe," Molly said. "But having enough grass to feed a couple of horses makes a difference to me."

"You'd get to liking dogs if you was up in the arctic," Spacecase said, although he didn't sound too convinced. Molly without her horses would be like molasses without pancakes, or maybe nudity without sex. "Come to think of it, though, there are wild horses in the Yukon. At least one herd. Hairy little brutes who've learned to hoof out caribou moss in winter."

"They probably think it's the most beautiful place in the world, too" Molly said.

The two twosomes evolved into a careful and considerate foursome, with Harlin and Fairly and Brother quite naturally falling into the roles of other aspects of family. The horses liked Molly the most, but they too were a functioning part of the alloy that forged itself together out there under the desert sun. Cactus flowers and red sandstone makes different little girls than sugar and spice, and different boys than snips and snails and puppy tails.

Lots of music came wailing through the big cracks in the log walls of their shack, which they never bothered to chink up properly because they liked the extra light. Besides the old folk songs they had all learned as kids, there were the labor songs, and the antiwar protest songs, and a whole slew of new love and bitter tears songs. When they couldn't remember the words just right, they made up their own versions which, when they sang them for an audience in Spitville or even in the occasional Denver or Taos or Carson City bar, usually met with a better response than the original versions.

If it made them laugh when they sang it, they knew it was a good tune or rewrite. If they weren't sure, they'd ride into Taos or up to the pueblo and sing it for other people, just to find out. By the time Bishop showed up, they had a couple of hundred songs in their repitoire.

Bert had suffered a little at first from the lack of a proper piano. But he and Harlin had cooked up what they called a lumberjack piano. It was sixty strings in little groups of three, different weights steel fishing line, stretched across a short wooden box. It was shaped like a triangle with the point cut off, and fit right on Burt's lap. He played it with wooden hammers, thumping the strings directly instead of pushing little white or black keys, and when he got going, made the rafters of their shack ring like wooden bells.

Molly learned to play it some, and took a liking to clacking spoons together for a rhythm section now and then when they got into something fast and fun, with dance possibilities. Eventually they would have become too big for Spitville, anyway. So in a way, Bishop's coming had rescued the whole bunch at just the right time.

"You see, none of us was trying to make anyone into anything that they didn't want to be. We all just got on as best we could, and never paid any attention to the so-called proper way of doing things."

We were camping on a bar, had been hitching a ride on a fishing boat down from Prince Rupert to Vancouver. He had decided to get off at Kingcome, on the mainland across from the north end of Vancouver

Island, to visit some friends up at the village. The Dawson's and Moon's, I think. We'd been sitting out on the deck watching a pod of orcas heading up Simoon Sound. It must have been early spring.

He showed me an old faded brown photograph, turning yellow at the edges, of Loralei and Uncle Joseph, a toddler trying to get out of the picture. My Aunt Sarah was just visible in a papoose carrier, peering over grandma's shoulder.

I remembered a picture of myself sitting in a papoose carrier, hanging from a tree limb. "I guess mom had one of those baby packers," I said.

"Yep. Loralei made it for her. But she didn't like carrying you in it. Convenient, but too Indian looking."

He looked at the photo for a few minutes, reflecting, then said, "Loralei actually traded that one off some Armenian refugees we met in Vancouver. Funny how people as far apart as Armenians and Algonquins both figured out that little kids like to be sitting up where they can look around, even way before they learn to talk or crawl."

"How come mom was always trying to be white?" I asked.

"I don't know," he replied matter-of-factly. "She wasn't always. Sometimes she dolled herself up to look like a real Tlingit maiden, when she was feeling like it. And she was a sweetheart those times. But other times she just wanted to fade back to white. In a way she was lucky. Most people don't have a choice. Or don't think they do, anyways."

"So what are you, Buzz?"

"What do you mean, what am I?"

"You white or native?"

He frowned kind of like a big bear trying to decide whether or not to knock you into next week. "I was born and raised right here on the back of the Great Bear. I'm native."

"But you're half white."

"Well, now, I reckon if I want to be Erasmus O'Toole, in order to make a living, or even just for the fun of it, I can be a product of the empire."

"But that part's just an act, then?" I suggested.

"While I'm doing it, it's real enough," he said. "I guess I'd have to say I'm both. And a whole lot more besides. Shoot, them trolls and ogres you heard about in the tales was just European windigrs. It's all connected on some level, after all."

"Is the windigr real, though."

"Shore is. And if you find that out for certain, it may be the last piece of definite knowledge you ever acquire."

The fire died away to nothing, and it was cold out there. I slept better that night than I had since leaving home. I'm not sure why.

We walked up to the village the next day, and he explained how he understood the differences between natives and whites.

"When I was traveling around with Bert and the rest, all over B.C. and the Yukon, there was a lot of talk about the brand spanking new Theory of Relativity that Albert Einstein had just put together to explain the universe. Now at the same time there was a guy name of Ben Whorf living out with the Hopi people in Arizona who was trying to learn their language. The Hopi, you remember, were surrounded by Navaho, who were surrounded by Apache. So they had kept their language and customs even after the Aztecs had conquered most of the other people way up into the north of the Great Bear.

"Ben finally got a handle on the Hopi way of talking when he figured out that most of the words they use are verbs. Action verbs, at that. Now Whorf reasoned that the Hopi must have a different way of looking at the world from people who use nouns and participles and whatever else concoctions in the other languages he knew about. And he also figured out they must see the world a whole lot different than he did.

"So he made some educated guesses, and he spent some time explaining Einstein's theory to some of his Hopi friends. After he'd got through telling them about it, they looked at each other like they thought he was a little daft.

"The chiefs explained to Ben that, yes, the theory was essentially correct, as far as it went. They also made it clear that there were some elements of the theory that would need to be reexamined by Mr. Einstein. He used a metaphor to explain.

"You see, when a man goes out to hunt a deer, he may be the best hunter of his tribe, and he may know the land and the deer as well as it's possible to know them. Using his knowledge, he will go to the most likely place where a deer may be found. Yet even the best hunter knows the deer also thinks and moves and serves its own people. And each of the trees and plants and other animals, even the Great Bear and the world, and all the other worlds, are also moving. Even given the best of circumstances, when the man gets to the best place to find a deer, there may not be any deer at that place.

"In a universe of relativity, as the Hopi knew, no one person would be able to know all the variables, especially if his thinking was stuck in a cause-effect, linear language. Like Aztec or German or English. It was the Hopi chiefs that explained to Dr. Einstein, who was considered by the whiteman's culture to be the smartest man of the century, the one biggest flaw in his theory. If everything is relative, mathematics can't work. Not in what we consider the way it is supposed to work anyway.

"When Heisenberg discovered the so-called uncertainty principle in quantum physics a few years later, it made for some interesting fireworks. Neither relativity nor uncertainty could be explained in terms of each other. In some ways they are positively contradictory. And yet each one is extremely accurate in explaining the universe. Sort of like finding an alligator and a snow leopard living happily together in your living room, both of them waiting to eat you up.

"Ben suggested that probability might work. Instead of equal's and pluses and minuses, we'd have to start using maybes and most probables. Which is exactly what the deer hunter uses when he goes looking for dinner. All he knows for sure is the most probable place to look for his deer. And no matter how often he flips a coin, it still won't tell him a deer is at that particular spot.

"Beside that, it fit more closely with the branch of science your great-uncle Erascible O'Toole helped found with Murphy. A branch that most reputable scientists considered outright immoral, if not criminal. In spite of its being more accurate than the mainstream.

"Now you can imagine how that set with the white chiefs of the day. Ignorant savages claiming to know more how the universe works than scientists and scholars with thousands of years of written knowledge, passed down from generation to generation. Of course they had no way of knowing that the understanding of the chiefs goes back for literally hundreds-of-thousands of years, in an unbroken oral tradition. They had their own scientists and wise men and women, naturally, and they had passed the word on just as promptly as the moccasin telegraph does today. With a whole lot less confusion and deadenders."

"What's a deadender?" I asked. Sounded like a slow grounder to first base or something.

"I mean something that is investigated for hundreds of years and turns out to be false or mistaken. Like the Egyptian who thought all the planets and stars revolve around the earth, and worked out all the combinations of orbits you'd need to support that idea.

"But the really interesting thing to me is how the chiefs took to Einstein's relativity theory. They were flabbergasted that someone from the rigid, straight line way of thinking of the whites could have come up with something that was so close to a proper understanding of how the universe works.

"In fact, their estimation, in the eyes of the chiefs, took quite a jump. The whites couldn't be all bad if they were able to get that close to the real world, suffering under the horrible handicaps they had inherited, through no fault of their own, from their culture. Maybe, with a little work, they could learn to understand the natural world and how we all fit after all.

"Most whites, as understood from a native point of view, are kind of pathetic and lost. But they're also dangerous, like a wounded bear or cougar stuck inside a cave with you might be, thrashing around and trying to kill you, and not knowing how or why he's got a bullet lodged in his brain because he never did anything to you.

"Stuck in a world outside of nature and cut off from the world, kind of like a baby taken from its mother and thrown into a well. Seeing mostly just the rock walls of the inside of the well, with a little glimpse of sky now and again if they happen to look up, to make them wonder. And they think that's the whole world."

"Natives see more," I said, with a question riding on my lips.

He pondered that a while as he thought about it. Finally he said, "Some natives."

He rolled up a piece of newspaper and slid it up the sleeve of his coat. That was one of the more useful tricks I learned from him, how to take a newspaper roll and fit it into the legs and sleeves of your pants and shirt. Great insulation. You can alter the number of pages, depending on how cold it is out, and where you are. If it's raining, they soak up water, which provides even better insulation. Somebody is going to make a fortune some day, using that principle to make a raincoat that uses the natural insulation of water heated to body temperature.

"Like the theory of evolution," he continued. "Any native knows, just from observing the world and how it fits together, that some animals are selected out. The sick and the old and the little ones who aren't ready to grow into healthy adults have to be taken away somehow. With the buffalo, that means a cougar or wolf has to select out those guys and have them for dinner. That makes the herd stay healthy, doesn't get too old or sick or unfit.

"Now it took the whiteman's culture thousands of years to come to understand that simple fact of the natural world. There is still quite a bunch of argument around that number, even today. And it's led to trials and tribulations about whether or not we are related to monkeys, or descended from monkeys, or a bunch of other deadenders.

"The simple fact that all life, and all the animals including us humans, is kinfolk, got all confused somewhere along the line. Maybe it was knowledge that was lost to the whites. Or maybe they just didn't want to understand it. I don't know.

"It's the sort of understanding that each and every native kid, who listens to the elders and learns to watch the world around with open eyes and mind, comes onto naturally. But such a simple and direct, and completely obvious fact as that was turned into some kind of sacrilegious nonsense by white people. All anyone has to do is look at the five fingers on their own hand, and the fingers on the paw of their pet cat, and see the obvious. He's got claws, we got nails. He's got five fingers on each paw and so do we. Somewhere back down the line we are related to that cat, just as sure as I'm looking around the O'Toole nose on my face at the O'Toole nose on your face. Except that you and me is a lot closer related than we are to that cat."

"You make it sound like white people are kind of simple," I said.

"Maybe I'm telling it wrong," he replied. "Nobody and nothing is simple. But there ain't no need to dump a bunch of extra baggage on top of the real world, that's for sure. The whiteman's schools set you down in rows to put us outside of our home, outside the real world, and make a big artificial world for us. Then he wonders why it doesn't keep him warm at night and he can't live in it.

"They lost their place in the world, as soon as they saw themselves as better than the world. Outside the scheme of things. Building castles in the air is all right. But if you move into it, you're not going to be very comfortable. Eventually you're going to fall, and the longer you been living in that floating castle, the worse it's going to be when you finally do fall."

"Seems like the whiteman has pretty well taken over the Great Bear," I observed.

Jim Erkiletian

"Maybe they've taken over some of North America," he replied. "And I'll grant you they've cut some of his hair and dug some holes in his hide. But they haven't taken over the Great Bear. Not by a long shot. The Great Bear's hiding from the invaders. And he's hiding so well that even though he's right under our noses, they can't see him."

We passed the ranch, owned by some homesteaders who'd settled there in the 1800s, over on the opposite side of the river. A family that lives pretty much as the natives do, letting their cattle run wild, rounding up the survivors in the spring.

Later, as we came up to the village, the first thing I noticed was dugout canoes resting on the bank above the tide line. And some half-built dugouts further up on the shore. The houses were mostly built on stilts, to keep them from washing away when the floods come in the spring. A couple of hunters were bringing in a deer, waved to us and went on about their business. They knew we were coming, and who we were, by that time, even though we hadn't seen anyone on the way up.

There was a potlatch going on, at the time. Kingcome had been an important potlatch centre during the years when the ceremony had been outlawed by the Canadian government. Not that natives are into breaking the law, but the laws around the potlatch are a few thousand years older than the Canadian government. They have precedence.

"They have a very efficient way to settle disputes, grandson," Spacecase said. "Namely, don't let them get started in the first place."

The longhouse was just across the soccer field from the church. The preacher there at that time was smart enough to know he was a guest in Indian country, so was acting with some amount of decorum and trying to learn.

We were sort of uninvited guests, but as soon as we arrived the word went out that two new people were here. The potlatch was revised accordingly. One of the family members of the Moon clan made a special trip over to invite us to eat with them and enjoy the show that evening. They had even appointed an interpreter to explain all the general dances, and the speech, although grandpa seemed to understand pretty much of what was going on.

I couldn't understand the jokes, though. And there must have been quite a few of them, because those folks were laughing during most of the speech. But I learned later that although the speaker was talking for the couple who were getting married, he was also explaining which streams his people were going to use for harvesting salmon in the next year.

I lost track of the proceedings sometime after a big eagle walked into the longhouse and looked around, hopped up on a log and, with a couple of flaps of his wings, jumped out the smoke hole. He looked kind of lost, like maybe the drums had stunned him or something.

We left earlier than the rest of the people. Grandpa thanked the host and his family, explained we had been on the ocean and hadn't had much sleep for a while.

Jim Erkiletian

Some other kids woke me in the morning, invited me for a walk up the beach. They showed me the mountain in the background, told me it was named Noisy Mountain, because of all the groaning and moaning it does all spring. It has two peaks, and a big crack down the middle that gets stuck full of ice and snow. When it melts out in the spring, the mountain makes some horrible scary sounds, and big snow slides sometimes come rocketing down the slopes.

Between their scattered chunks of English and my really poor bits of Kwagwilth, I figured out the mountain had rattled the dickens out of an invasion party a few years before, had sent them packing before they had a chance to do any damage. You'd be smart to run the other way if you were invading a country where the spirits were strong enough to make a mountain shake and growl and throw rocks at you.

We only stayed in Kingcome Village for a couple more days. I wanted to stay longer, was just getting to know some of the other kids. And dogs and crows and the big gray tomcat that lived with the Dawsons. But Spacecase had heard another clue about that medicine bundle, that it was only a few months down the moccasin trail ahead of us.

Saying our goodbyes took nearly as long as saying our hellos had taken, but we were back on the trail the next day.

"Where we heading this time," I wondered out loud. Not that it really mattered to me any more. I'd become more used to being on the road by that time than staying in any one place. The itch to get going again was starting up in me almost as soon as we set our packs down.

"That old medicine bundle is trying to find us just as hard as we're trying to find it," he replied. "You feel it yet?"

I stopped and thought a minute. A brown bird, an owl I think, flapped through the trees across the river, disappearing into the dark rain forest between two huge cedars. Rain was starting to drizzle through the gray morning.

There was something we needed to the south, green and smiling with a kind of important basic knowledge. It was sitting there like a big bullfrog, with a certain and incomplete understanding. Waiting.

"I think it's that way," I said, pointing toward the mountains to the south.

"Right the first time," he said with a smile, turned and walked on down the spruce needle covered trail with his long strides.

I ran to catch up. "What if I'm wrong?" I asked. "Maybe it went some other way, or somebody has it and is trying to fool us into thinking it went this way."

"Can't happen," he replied, still walking. "Besides, the world is round, remember? Nobody hides a medicine bundle from its rightful owner. Not for long."

15. Peter Pan Meets Robin Hood…

Life: n/v. The cycle of organism survival whereby all animals and plants eat each other. ie: Men eat chickens, chickens eat worms, worms eat men.

"There are some parts of a man that should never grow up," Spacecase said. "But which parts, is the question."

The take was all in. Wrangle had some worthless bonds, and no way of checking them that wasn't covered. Telegrams to the head office in London were routed to Bishop's hotel in San Francisco. When Wrangle eventually tried to cash them, in 1929, he discovered the bottom had dropped out the day before.

He tried to make up the deficit with some Florida real estate he'd purchased on speculation. Most of it turned out to be underneath the Everglades swamp. He made some of his money back, but the straw that broke the camel's wind mushroomed into the rest of the stock market, with unfortunate consequences for other investors.

Until then, however, as far as Judge Wrangle could tell those bonds were increasing in value and making money for him, right through the decade.

Back in 1917, though, Molly was legally married to Erasmus, so Wrangle had no legal claim on her. The band was packing up to ride north the next day. They all would take turns driving the car, the team and wagon, or riding herd on the horses.

Spacecase had heard Bierce was dead, that the Mexican revolution was winding down to a more quiet level as the people gained a little more independence from Spain and Europe. Starting to elect their own oppressors, like Americans and Canadians had been trying to do.

"It was that wild streak combined with the feeling I was an artist," he explained. "As we were leaving, I realized there was one last chore left undone. Besides, it was Halloween again, in 1917, I think."

Spacecase was only about twenty-six years old, anyhow. Still slightly damper than he knew behind the ears. He considered himself creative, at cards and juggling, between the sheets thanks to some fine teachers, and at putting together deals in general. It managed to find its way to his head eventually, as all intoxicants do.

With the head of Buzzard in the gunny sack, he rode out the old trail to Mrs. Crumpet's house.

Mrs. Crumpet was spending her evening giving out sweets to the neighbourhood kids, as usual. What Spacecase didn't know was she kept her shotgun propped just inside the door. And a big bulldog on a leash right beside her left foot. She wasn't necessarily expecting any such foolishness as she had experienced in the past. But she was damn sure she was prepared, just in case.

He was smart enough to case the place first, before doing anything foolish. He saw she had a lantern on the porch, and would peek out the window to see who was on her porch before opening the door. Just to be on the safe side.

As before, he waited until there were no kids within hearing distance in any direction. Then he quickly ambled over to the porch, knocked a couple of times on the screen door, turned his back toward the window and bent over as he'd done before. This time with the head of Buzzard O'Toole staring out blankly from between his legs.

He unfastened his belt. Just as her face appeared in the window, he pulled his pants down and quickly back up.

He heard her yell Yaaawwhh and the dog start barking just as a small end-table came smashing through the glass window pane. The bulldog came roaring through right after, snarling and yelping and looking for someone to bite.

Spacecase hadn't counted on that dog being that close so fast. He hiked the head like a football, right toward the dog's snarling snout, and commenced to running as hard as he could go for his horse. The bulldog, with his rear toes still on the sill, dodged right, taking the head with his left shoulder like a hard-driving fullback. It bounced off a flower pot and sailed back through the window, taking out a sliver of glass hanging from the upper corner.

He heard "Gaawdddammmit" roar out from the interior of the house as Mrs. Crumpet observed what must be the head of Buzzard O'Toole come flying in through the broken window. The peach thief had come back to haunt her as the Halloween flasher. Spacecase distinctly remembers to this day the sound of the echo of that murderous rage-infested scream, ricochet-hopping back off the mountains ahead of him as he tried to outrun the bulldog.

Mrs. Crumpet didn't lose any time getting to her shotgun. Very quickly she realized it was too much of a coincidence that the ghost of Buzzard O'Toole would take that particular form to haunt her. She rightly put one and one together and concluded the scalawag was alive and well, well enough to be out playing Halloween tricks on defenseless old ladies. It was a condition she determined to remedy straightaway.

When she got out on the porch, she heard the horse galloping away down the road, with the bulldog yapping and snapping at its heels. She knew she was right.

He was too far away and it was too dark for her to get a good easy shot at him. But she knew the trail like Harlin knew the strings of his banjo, well enough to judge from the sound of the commotion just about where to aim. The scatter of the shot from the old double-barreled twelve-gauge guaranteed a pretty good chance of dusting his ass with at least a few beads of hot lead. She just had to be careful to aim high enough so as not to injure the horse. Mrs. Crumpet had a soft spot for horses.

As she was tightening her fingers on the two triggers, her ears picked up the sound of a second horse coming up the trail at an easy canter. She couldn't tell who the second rider might be. She had some moments of indecision as she heard both horses stop, and somebody, a man's voice that sounded vaguely familiar, calling her dog by his name.

There was some talk between the riders in the distance. The dog had stopped barking, for some reason. She strained to hear what was being said, with both hammers cocked back on the shotgun and her fingers still on the triggers.

Some low-down sinister laughter echoed back to her from the night. Then the clip-clop of a rider coming on toward her, walking his horse, as another rider could be heard galloping into the distance.

The rider coming into view, with the moonlit mist swirling around him, looked like the devil's right-hand hit man, at the very least. But just for a minute. Then it resolved into her old husband, Harlin, riding up with his banjo strapped on the side of Dixie. The bulldog was trotting along beside the horse, half-dragging a moose femur with some chunks of meat attached.

"Hello, Matilda," he said. "Put that dang shotgun away. I come back to stay a spell."

"Harlin, where have you been these two years? And what makes you think you're welcome!" The shotgun was pointed at the ground by this time. Mrs. Crumpet would never risk accidentally shooting Dixie.

"Hell, I don't know," he said, dismounting. "I just figured you might like to have a man around for a while." He tossed the stirrup up on the saddle, loosened the girth straps. "Besides, I got the rest of the mortgage money for our place here."

"The first thing you can do," she said, carefully lowering the hammers of her shotgun, "is fix the window that scalawag friend of yours busted." She turned on her heel and stalked back inside the house.

Fortunately she did not report her newfound allegations to Judge Wrangle, the main reason being it was the judge who held the mortgage on the Crumpet place. She assumed, quite rightly, that he wouldn't take kindly to being paid out with his own money, so to speak. He might even turn out to be some peeved at her for misidentifying that head. So she kept mum.

Harlin was able to dispose of the head properly and for good in his fireplace that night. A beautiful piece of Apache craftsmanship lost to posterity, in order to protect Spacecase's ornery butt.

Judge Wrangle got some of his money back when Mrs. Crumpet brought him the banknote the next month. She gave him to understand a long lost relative of hers had died and left her some money. She figured it wasn't that big a lie, since she was planning on killing Harlin eventually, anyway.

Spacecase, Bert, Molly, Loralei, with Fairly and Brother, and a crawling Uncle Joseph and my ma in a papoose board, moved on up to Canada, settling in Vancouver for a few years. That was where his nickname changed from Ari/Erasmus to Rounder, and where he met one of his best partners in free-wheeling flim-flamming.

She called herself Lana Gwage when they first met up with her, up the Fraser River in a town called New Westminster. Her grand-daughter was the writer I teamed up with back in the 50s for a while, Lynn Gwist. We lay down some good copy for the St. Louis

Post back then, before our careers took off in separate directions.

The judge managed to visit them now and again, in the big house where they lived in West Vancouver, British Columbia. It was back up against the Salish land on the north side of the Indian Arm. Beautiful place, blue-green ocean framed by huge deep green cedars and fir, although the big industries were hard at work polluting and messing up the shoreline all along both sides of the inlet.

"That's one reason whites and natives don't get along so well. Each thinks the other is dirty. Different ideas of what constitutes dirt."

"Dirt's just dirt, no matter who you are," I said.

"I suppose so," he replied. "But I've heard lumber operators complain about native workers who hadn't taken a bath in a few days, then turn right around and order men to dump whole barrels of waste oil into the ocean, sometimes right into the middle of good clam and oyster beds."

When Judge Wrangle went for a visit, the band went into a movie mode, where they each adopted an appropriate role. It was like a game, in some ways, and good practice for all their careers. They treated the judge like a sort of senile producer-director on the set who had to be humored.

Bert became the driver-chauffeur, and manservant of the place. He didn't actually have to do anything different, except avoid touching either of the women in the judge's presence. Something he wouldn't have done anyway, in the judge's presence. He played the role awkwardly, however, because he couldn't help ribbing the judge now and again with double entendres.

The first time Wrangle journeyed to Vancouver for a visit, Spacecase/Ari couldn't go to the station to pick him up. He had some kind of game arranged that required split-second timing. And he knew it wouldn't hurt to convince the judge he was hard at work running his law firm's Canadian office, which he had made up special for the occasion, located in a Howe Street building complete with Lana as secretary. Occasionally some local in need of legal services would happen in, to be steered to actual law firms after being high-graded for information that might provide some kind of edge.

Molly and Bert drove the steamer down to the wharf, and Molly sat in back with the judge on the return trip. She was a little nervous at first, but she got over it pretty fast when Bert started making conversation.

"Yes suh, massah Wrangle. Mah deah mammy, rest her soul, lived mos' her life in San Francisco, right near where y'all is from. I don't reckon y'all know San Francisco."

"Uh, well, I do know it a little," Wrangle replied.

"You don't say. Why she worked for a good many years in the Harmony House as a cook, until just last year. I don't suppose you ever knew her?"

"Why no. I don't think…What was the name of that place?"

"A wonderful cook, my mammy. Proud of her trade. Not like some, you know, who'd put the occasional dog turd in the rich folk's soup."

Jim Erkiletian

"Er, what house did you say that was?"

"Harmony, suh. A house of ill repute, some say, although I wouldn't know."

"Uh, yes, I mean I wouldn't know about those places."

"She died of terminal clap…"

By this point Molly had managed to insinuate her parasol between the seats of the steamer to give Bert a good solid poke in the butt. He and the judge discussed the weather, the scenery and automobiles for the rest of the trip.

Loralei did the part of the housekeeper-nanny to a T. She ordered everyone else around like they were her property, something she never did any other time. The others were so surprised at her getting so bossy so fast, they had to really concentrate on the movie in order to keep from busting out laughing.

She was looking after Uncle Joseph, who was crawling all over and getting into things when he wasn't strapped into a papoose carrier she'd picked up from those Armenians.

Molly was carrying my Aunt Sarah, and the judge was suddenly aware that he was going to be a grandfather. Uncle Joseph softened him up by calling him gampa, and he was starting to become very generous in his old age. The band weren't wasting any time working out elaborate ways to skunk him any more. It wasn't necessary.

Spacecase and Molly had no trouble playing the happy newlyweds, successful and well-to-do. After the judge went to bed, they sat around the kitchen with Bert and Loralei, laughing about the day's shenanigans and figuring out what to do the next day. There were trips to the zoo, and the Stanley's old place across the inlet. And the beaches.

The judge counted those visits as some of his best times, lying back in a skiff fishing while watching the boats come and go. Vancouver was the backdrop, growing into a thriving seaport catering to guests hailing from all over the Pacific rim, and through the Panama Canal in both directions.

Molly and Bert were spending most of their nights together, as were Loralei and Spacecase. When the judge was visiting, they'd switch around to make it look good. Since they were doing some of that anyway, it didn't result in any kind of hardship. It became even less of a problem after the kids were old enough to get around. They'd entertain the old man in the mornings, with Loralei cooking breakfast for him while Molly looked after the kids.

Judge Wrangle never did figure out, or even care after a few years, which kids were his grandchildren, and which weren't.

Like all good things, and all good people who respect the edges of their world, it couldn't last forever. Nothing does, except maybe the universe. And we know, if we have a realistic sense of our own self, what a minute part of that us humans are. Our whole planet and entire solar system is smaller than a grain of sand on the beach.

Still, we can't help wishing and hoping a single person's dreams might be bigger than the whole kit-

and-kaboodle, and then some. Possible and probable are no farther apart than the last millimeter of space between the lead slug and the centre of your forehead. A whole universe exists between the clap of the trapdoor and the snap of the slack of the rope around your neck, as the fiction writer, Crane, noted.

We may never find out everything. But we won't find out even a little tiny fraction while we're stuck here in this gravity hole, glued to our planet like flies stuck in a molasses barrel. And the little we can know from here seems like so much, it's good to be reminded every once in a while just how minute a part of the whole thing it really is.

"Enjoy it," Loralei would say occasionally. "Happiness is an Apache tear, turning black in the sunlight. Hold it close to your eye and turn, turn until you can see through it clearly."

"Probably a good thing that things change. Otherwise we'd be stuck in a system that probably wouldn't tolerate people like us."

"You philosophizing again?" I asked him.

"Why not," he replied. "I got seniority here."

He was right about that by about fifty years. "The way you tell it, there just ain't no point in even trying to change things. The bad guys are so much bigger and got so much power on their side, the best we can do is keep running around trying not to get squashed."

"Well, now, I never said there aren't some things we can do to give the tiger's tail a good solid tug now and again. In fact, it may be healthy to do that whenever you can."

"And spend the rest of the time running around trying to not get chewed," I said. I was feeling ornery that day.

"Might get him to change direction some," he said. "Maybe that's all we need, sometimes."

I fired a shot at a stump in the distance. Missed. "Even if I had a truckload of TNT, what good would it do? People is only people. It don't do no good to blow anybody up anyways."

He scratched his chin and neck and looked at the big cedar trees stretching up into the sky across the valley. Then down at the big clearcut swath of dead stumps and washed-out gray landscape that the logging crew had left behind. For their children. And grandchildren.

"Probably so," he said. He squinted down the barrel of the little Remington tube-loading .22 semi-automatic he'd given me to learn to shoot. We'd borrowed it from one of the men at Cutville. It was a honey, dead accurate at over a hundred metres. He squeezed off a round that snapped a dead root from the overturned stump I'd just missed.

"Wish we had this little baby when I learned to see bullets."

I assumed he was changing the subject. "What do you mean see bullets?"

"Me and Bert taught each other to see bullets, back in the Yukon in the twenties. The Yukon had sent a machine-gun regiment to Europe in the Big War to End War. Most decorated bunch of fops in the whole war, them guys. On either side."

He passed the rifle to me. I took aim and popped a branch off another dead stump that was a little closer. "You mean bullets flying through the air?"

"Yeah. Fired from a gun."

"So how'd you learn to see bullets?"

"Terry Black, one of John's boys, and a fair-to-middling poker player, had got ahold of one of them Gattling guns that old man Boyle had experimented with before he outfitted the Yukon regiment. We set it up so it was firing down a long valley, into a big sandbag. Then one of us rode down and sat beside the bag, I guess it must'a been a good four hundred yards, and watched the bullets come whizzing through the air as the other one turned the crank on the gun."

I handed the rifle back to him. "What did they look like?"

"You can't see nothing right away. Just hear the thump of the bullets whopping into the bag. After a while, maybe a hundred rounds or so, you can spot a sort of blue light circle spreading out from the slug as it smacks into the air molecules. As the bullet gets closer, the circle of light gets bigger and just before it hits the bag you can see the hole in the centre where the bullet nose is. After a while you can follow the arc of the light against the dark background rocks. Or the sky."

He fired again, kicking up some dust in the distance, handed the rifle back to me.

"How the heck did you ever figure out to do that?" I asked, taking aim at the original stump. I had the range now, and heard the bullet smack into the wood. I gave him back the rifle.

"I'd been talking to some of the guys who'd come back from Europe with their hides more-or-less intact. Some of them were real scattered, always jittery and funny acting. But they'd survived a kind of hell, and I learned a lot from them. A couple of them guys told me they'd dodged incoming bullets, was the only reason they was alive. One said he'd dodged a bullet at night. So me and Bert decided to test out the theory." He fired a shot into a knot on the stump we had decided needed to be emasculated.

"So if you was way down there and I took a pot shot at you," I asked, "you'd be able to see the bullet coming?" I still wasn't convinced.

"If I was looking up this direction I could, yes," he said. "You maybe could too. Men can do lots more things than we think we can. And pretty near anything we take a notion to do, given enough time." He handed the rifle back to me.

"So," I thought I had him. "How do we go about making the world better, seeing as how it's owned and controlled by a bunch of gangsters and crooks. Only thing I can see is to try to get to be a bigger crook, and then where are you?" I drew a bead on the poor defenseless old stump again.

He waited until I'd fired, then said, "Sounds like the snake that tried to eat his own tail. You'd be worse off than now, turning yourself into a crook to catch crooks. That's how the cops do it, so now we got more cops, and a whole lot more crooks, than ever before."

He took the rifle, pulled back the bolt and looked in the empty chamber. He'd been counting the bullets.

"But I have seen a well-oiled writing machine clog up the grinding cogwheels of the system more than once."

I took a sip from my canteen.

He put the safety catch on and slipped the rifle into the scabbard, stood up and stretched, said, "If you stuck a ballpoint pen in the barrel of this here twenty-two, it would blow your ear off if you was stupid enough to pull the trigger."

I don't know quite what he meant by that. But I was able to see what he was getting at, even then.

16. Tunnels on Rails…

Funny; n/pn, Anything that causes one to laugh that happens to someone else.

It wasn't long after we left Kingcome, Spacecase and I found ourselves on a southbound freight, or rattler as the bo's call them. Probably because they're constantly rattling your teeth when you're riding on one. Or maybe because they look and sound like a big snake from a distance, and will kill you with about the same degree of compassion if you get careless around them. We'd decided to ride the rails from British Columbia down into Oregon.

It must have been late October or November. The air mass coming off the Pacific Ocean blew clean and warm from the Japan current. Otherwise it probably would have been even colder than it was. No wetter though.

Most lumber mills were up and running. It hadn't been cold enough that year to close them yet. They didn't seem to put out as much stink as they do today. Rather, they spewed a different kind of stink. Maybe because back then they were in the business of cutting lumber and mashing up pulp, instead of making and using poisonous chemicals.

We managed to find an empty car with the door open, moving slow enough for us to sling our gear up and grab a handhold. There were some old pieces of skids and pallet-boards in one end, and the forks of a fork lift in the other.

We made ourselves as comfortable as possible in the forward end. Spacecase pulled one of his harps out of his vest pocket, tamped it on his sleeve, and blew a chorus of the Hobo's Lullaby. After, he reckoned as how Woody Guthrie never wrote that verse about the "nice warm boxcar."

We weren't too uncomfortable. We'd picked up some good blankets and extra socks and shirts in Seattle the day before. Lots of layers of thin clothes are better than one layer of thick clothes in that country. Plus you got the added advantage of extra pockets to carry stuff. We settled in for the ride.

Later that evening Spacecase shook me awake and said we were coming up on one of the last free towns in the world. He called it Cutville, but I've heard it referred to by a variety of other names over the years.

It's on the side of a mountain, cut back into the hill on the inside of the railroad bed, totally inaccessible except by rail. A jumbled bunch of shacks made from old pieces of plywood and packing crates, anything a hobo could manage to toss off a car. It housed some thirty or forty men and women. It was a true hobo village, built by and for the knights of the road, and is the hometown of the King of the Hoboes. The king wasn't there on that particular trip, although I met up with him in the Detroit yards some years later.

We tossed our packs down as the train started to pick up speed for the downhill run beyond the cut, and lit running. Someone grabbed my arm and swung me up away from the side of the roadbed. I heard Spacecase laughing and talking with someone who turned out to be a former partner of his, Bill Heywood. They called him Little Bill Heywood, to distinguish him from Big Bill, the wobbly organizer.

Heywood was six-foot-six and broad as an ox. Made me wonder what Big Bill looked like. He and Spacecase hadn't seen each other for years, so there was some reminiscing to do.

The man who had plucked me off the side of the car was Casey the Preacher, an Okey kid who had decided to be one of the characters in John Steinbeck's Grapes of Wrath. We all dusted ourselves off, introduced each other, and wandered across the cut to the shacks.

Some of those shacks were pretty nice, with glass windows and some pretty good carpentry, considering the materials at hand. One even had little window boxes with flowers and a sort of front porch with a swing.

We made our way to one of the end houses, where Bill said Claxton was staying.

Claxton turned out to be a clean-cut old bo with a tweed coat and string tie who had a pot of stew boiling and offered us some as we filed in the door. Spacecase donated a big head of lettuce and some potatoes he'd been carrying since Seattle, and we all sat down to bowls of whatever had been thrown in the pot.

It was here in this shantytown, many years earlier, that Bill and Spacecase had heard Joe Hill was sitting in a Utah jail waiting to face a firing squad. For murder.

Naturally they talked about it.

Jim Erkiletian

Joe Hill was a song writer and union organizer, riding the rails all over the country singing about the OBU, or One Big Union, as we called it in Canada. In the states it was the Wobblies or Industrial Workers of the World. Like the rest of the hoboes and union organizers of the day, he'd been pretty much an anarcho-syndicalist, and according to Bill and Spacecase, one hell of a poker player.

In one game they recalled, Hill had lost all his money. He'd sat out a round, watching the other men play, and made up a song about being poor, broke and homeless, but with the great good luck to have such fine and true friends that he never had to fear going hungry. It was a song all the men in the group could relate to.

The last verse, which he sang almost tearfully, emphasized how important it was to share all your good luck with your friends. The players listened to the song, as Joe sang it through a second time. Then they took up a collection and staked Joe to one last round.

Of course he managed to win back what he'd lost and went on to take everyone else's money, such as it was, before the agreed upon quitting time rolled around. That was the only story I ever heard where Spacecase lost a game.

"Joe and I made it policy never to take money from poor folks," he said. "In fact, we never took from each other, after that one game."

"Take from the rich and give to the poor," I suggested.

He smiled a toothy grin. "I guess," he said, "and not any more than you can carry at one time."

Bill and Spacecase, on hearing Hill was busted to the hoosegow, had jumped the next rattler for Utah. Some 40,000 other people had the same idea, when they heard Joe was in trouble, so there was quite a bunch of rowdies drifting into Salt Lake City that month. Most of them were bent on springing Joe from the city jail, one way or another.

The Utah state militia was out in force, though, and nobody wanted to tangle with them. They're the only state militia that ever took on the United States Army and won. If the people had decided to fight, it could have turned into a bloodbath. With no winners, just lots of dead and dying workers on both sides. Like the Great War to End War had turned out.

"Those Mormon farm boys who made up the militia weren't putting up with any nonsense, either. They'd been told we were all communists and atheists, aiming to rape their girlfriends. And their church had taught them not to think much beyond filling the larder and aiming their rifles. But then, as Bill observed, "What can you expect from a religion founded by a guy who had visions after working a twenty-hour shift in his papa's ginseng packing plant."

Most of the folks gathered at Salt Lake City didn't really think the state would kill Joe, anyway. Joe had a bullet wound to prove self-defense. There were no witnesses to the fight except a lady who Joe refused to name, being true to the code of gentlemanly conduct of the day. It would have been an open and shut case in any other place in the USA.

Unfortunately, the word had gone out from the mining companys' headquarters that Joe was an undesirable. The rich guys were calling in the favors they'd built up, the loans they made to the politicians so they could get themselves elected even though they weren't any too popular with the people. Most people didn't know that at the time. Just suspected.

Even knowing that, it was obvious to most people that the whole thing was trumped-up. They figured it was just as obvious to the governor, and like in the dime novels the pardon would come galloping in just in the nick of time. Just after the firing squad hears Aim and before Fire!

The copper mine bosses owned the governor and everybody knew that too. But general feeling was the good old democratic USA took precedence, and justice would prevail. It was after Joe went down that people came to realize survival is a problem of defending ourselves from the American dollar. And the blokes who figure the bottom line is more important than either justice or human lives are on the other side.

"Of all the dangerous addictions the USA has to offer," Spacecase said, "the dollar is by far the biggest killer, and the hardest to kick if it gets you. You end up strung-out, wired, and no matter how much you get, you always need more the next time. Whole cities full of people will sell their land, their trees, their souls, for those pieces of paper. They'll work themselves into an early grave trying for more. And will kill their relatives and friends, not to mention foreigners, to get their fix."

Or murder their own poets.

Joe, in the Salt Lake City jail, was doing what he could to go out with style and make his death mean something. He told Debs and Hayes and the others he sure didn't want any massacre on his conscience. He thought a pardon was on the way too. But he'd already told his jailers he preferred the firing squad to either the electric chair or hanging, because he was a soldier of the class war. In fact, Joe was actually a warrior, but didn't know it at the time.

Little Bill was wanted on some kind of warrant in Utah, but Spacecase was clean so he managed to get into the jail and see Joe the night before the execution by faking a Swedish accent and claiming to be a long-lost relative. He was there when Joe told the authorities his last request, to have his carcass moved across the nearest state line so's he wouldn't have to be "caught dead in Utah."

Spacecase watched the ladies cry when Joe's last will was read out to the gathering outside the prison. Lee Hayes did the reading. Then Gene Debs said a few words. Most of the people couldn't believe that the state of Utah would want the death of a popular guy like Joe on its collective conscience. Even the Rockefellers must be human enough to like a good song now and then.

Joe's Last Will became sort of a gospel's creed to the men and women who rode the rails, and Spacecase remembered it even then, word for word.

Jim Erkiletian

> *"My will is easy to decide*
> *For I have nothing to divide*
> *My kin don't need to fuss and moan*
> *Moss does not cling to a rolling stone.*
> *My body, ah, if I could choose*
> *I would to ashes it reduce*
> *And let the merry breezes blow*
> *The dust to where some flowers grow.*
> *Perhaps some fading flower then*
> *Would come to life and bloom again*
> *This is my last and final will*
> *Good luck to all of you...*
> *Joe Hill..."*

"I never felt the same about Mormons after that," Bill said. "Before they was just harmless buffoons. Now they took on a different light. Harmful buffoons."

After Joe was shot down the next morning, his body was turned over to the people out in front of the jailhouse. Spacecase and a few others, under the guns of the Utah militia, loaded it onto a wagon and, in a truly dismal mood, set out for the Wyoming state line.

All those other people came along, and the wagon procession stretched for quite a few miles back as they made their way through the mountains. Forty-thousand people, on foot or riding horses and wagons. Nobody talking much. Stunned, you might say, from the sudden realization that things were going to get a lot worse before they could get any better, for working people anyway.

"There's something about losing a poet that causes your insides to knot up and your world to turn an ugly shade of greybrown."

As soon as they reached the border, they rolled Joe off the wagon onto a pile of brush and wood and set the whole thing on fire. Then they packaged up fifty little envelopes with Joe's ashes and sent them to all the offices of the Industrial Workers of the World with instructions to toss them in the air on Joe's birthday. Which they did in most of the forty-eight states, Canada and Australia.

Three of those packets, though, were sent to the Wobblie head office in Chicago, which was raided by the police a couple of weeks before Joe's birthday. The files, with Joe's ashes in there someplace, maybe under A for ashes or H for Hill, were hauled down to police headquarters to be examined by the authorities. They were never returned.

Like one old wob observed, most of Joe is free, and presumably fertilizing daisies like he wanted, but a little bit of him is still in the hands of the cops.

After some more talk, scheming on the man and general road rap, Bill picked up an old guitar that had seen better years. Claxton thumped a string bass made from a little tea crate and a broomstick, and Spacecase blew a few notes on his harmonica so they could get tuned together. Casey took off and came running back with a long-neck five-string banjo, which he tuned up real quick. Hoboes came drifting in from all over the camp when they heard the sound of music.

Jim Erkiletian

The night got warmer and a couple of guys started dancing around, doe-si-doeing around each other, tipping their hats and swinging by the elbows. Claxton kept a steady beat on that bass while stomping both feet at the same time. Quite a feat considering he had to hold the bass down with one foot at the same time.

Pretty soon the whole place was vibrating so much that we didn't even notice the difference when the midnight freight rumbled by outside. Guys and gals were leaning in the windows and telling jokes and stories and whooping it up in grand style that night.

Those were the days before folk music got to be so popular, or got popularized by Baez, Lightfoot, Peter, Paul & Mary, Dylan, Sylvia and Ian Tyson. Before all those college kids started picking up on it. Funny that it was the old songs they were singing, about bad love affairs, racism and bad politics and the feeling of being down to your last piece of moldy sausage and some sheriff busts you and takes it and feeds it to his dog. When things are so bad that the very last and only thing you got left in this world is your ability to sit back, reflect, and bust out laughing.

No wonder people think hoboes are strange.

Later we bedded down in one of the shacks that was vacant. They called it Herb's place. Casey said he'd heard Herb was doing thirty days on a vagrancy bust in Texas, so he figured it would be vacant for a couple more weeks at least, considering the traveling time and all.

The sun was coming up over the other side of the mountain when I finally got to sleep. There was a girl there about my own age. Her name was Lynda. I was hoping to see her some more the next day. And I did. But that's another story.

At Cutville the world balances back out. It's up in the chest of the Great Bear, (or Great Turtle, or North America, depending on where you grew up). It's shaggy and thick up there, and one good place to earn your ideas, to try them out on some of the smartest characters in the world. It's a window into a style of living and thinking that doesn't allow material supports, either to grasp onto when you're going down for the third time, or to hold the roof up over your head.

That old medicine bundle was getting closer and closer. In fact, I was starting to feel it now, right inside my body. One heck of a pile of power in one of them things.

The next morning Spacecase and I went exploring back up the mountain. There was a bald eagle sitting on a spar near the top of the hill. He watched us climbing up toward him, then lost interest when he saw we weren't packing.

"Most of what you learned in the boy scouts is what our native ancestors did to educate each other. But the birds and animals you see in the bush are mostly by themselves. Alone. You can't really understand them unless you see them all together in their groups. Families."

The next year, up on the Chilcat River in Alaska, Spacecase showed me the biggest flock of bald eagles in the world. Five thousand eagles, all collected in one place. They come down there to fish during salmon season. Nobody seems to know why they come to that particular place in such numbers. There are other rivers all up the coast that have big salmon runs. Spacecase said that place has considerable power for an eagle. I believe him.

Last I heard there were only about four thousand in that Alaskan flock. Strange that the land that claims the eagle as its symbol has almost succeeded in killing them all.

"You ever see an eagle family move?" he asked.

I told him I hadn't.

"I did a few times, first time out on Blackfish Sound in B.C. When I first heard those eagles, I thought I'd sneak up on them, so I got up real early and started sneaking around the bay. They spotted me before I'd gone a hundred yards, naturally, and one of them scouted me out, flew right over my head and checked me for firearms with one eye at a time.

"Those eagles had a good spot, nesting in trees that are protected, just behind snags that stick out over the water. They could hop right out of the nest and be in a position to see any fish swimming around in the sound.

"Sometimes porpoises or seals would round up a bunch of fish and herd them right into the bay, just below those eagles' nest. As they tighten the circle, the fish swim in smaller circles making a little ball that the seals could whip in and grab a chomp, one at a time. Teamwork. And the eagles could swoop in and grab the ones that tried to get out of the water.

"I'd been camping there about a month, long enough that they'd gotten used to seeing me and knew I wasn't going to bother them, when I heard a bunch of squawking and carrying on over there. I thought maybe the nest was coming apart, or a big cougar was maybe climbing up their tree or something. There were hoots and whistles and a whole bunch of sounds I didn't even know eagles could make.

"I guess they were discussing the move, because the next day I saw them take off for better hunting grounds, further up the channel. First the three young adults, just old enough to have their white head feathers, took out in different directions, landing on spars that allowed them to see as far as you can see in all directions, up and down and across the channel.

"Then the oldest one flew across the bay, a big fat guy that was just huffing and puffing. But he was a good flier, caught the updraft just right as it flowed against the cliff face. When he landed, he was perched on a spar that was just a little higher than all three of the scouts.

"Then came the females with the youngsters. First one white-headed mamma, then the little brown ones who didn't have white heads yet, and another adult following behind. And another white-headed adult bringing up the rear."

"So they all move together," I remarked. I still wasn't too sure what he was getting at. "Like a wolf pack?"

"Sure thing," he replied. "Like a pack of wolves, or a pod of whales, or a bunch of beavers. Most animals live in families. Even cats and bears, some of the time."

17. Swinging in the Family Tree…

Evolution: n/v. Spare change.

One of the reasons Bert and Spacecase made such a good team was they had learned some of the same lessons from different teachers. Riding up from San Diego in the steamer, they'd talked a lot about family. And how wolves and baboons organized themselves to take on the world in its own terms, and in their own terms as well.

"The wolf families that live around where I grew up were our teachers for how to be good providers and look after kids and women. And how to work together hunting," Spacecase noted. "They look after each other, and do what the pack leader tells them. Not so as to restrict each other or boss each other around, so much as because that's the way things are, for a wolf. Pack leader knows best."

"It was some the same for me," Bert replied. "We shared the world with quite a few other, uh, families. Baboons range through the same country we do. A tribe of baboons is one formidable bunch of smart and ornery dudes. They'll round up a leopard and kill it, if it eats their kids. You make the mistake of getting inside their space, you have to get on the good side of the head male or you get ripped apart fast."

"I never heard tell of wolves actually attacking anyone," Spacecase replied. "Not from anyone who'd be expected to tell the truth, anyway. I guess they could chomp you up real quick, though, if they took a notion."

"Baboons camp in the same places we do," Bert continued. "They're kind of a nuisance if you're looking to get a good night's sleep. Cause they like to socialize and they're noisy about it. But they let us know if there's lions or leopards in the vicinity. The antelope like to be around them for that reason, too, so there's usually plenty of game."

"Wolves are real quiet, except when they're having dinner. They're noisy eaters, though. And they howl to each other, sometimes. They let us know if there's caribou nearby, when you learn how to tell what they"'re saying."

Wolves and baboons may be our closest relatives, as far as making families go. But when it comes to sharing food, neither baboons or wolves have much in common with us.

"That's what baboons can't figure out about us," Bert said. "How we can do things pretty much independent of each other. They have to have a real rigid structure, with a boss baboon to tell them all what to do."

The native people of the Northwest Coast of British Columbia, Alaska and Washington state maintain a great number of clan houses, represented by nearly every animal. The totem poles provide solid images, give tangible proof that you can touch and see, that we are all related and interdependent.

The Wolf, the Eagle, the Orca, the Raven: each has a special place in the lifeblood, survival and mythology of the People. Each has crucial importance in the continued spiritual existence and evolution of the Great Bear. The elders teach us to pay special attention to each of those relatives. We learn to live proper, healthy, and long lives if we observe them correctly. We will die if we fail to understand the lessons they teach us. Or our children will die early deaths, sick and alone.

It's no accident each of these animals lives out its life at the very top of our food chain.

"We had to keep our family intact, when those kids started coming. And we all knew it. So we worked out the best deals we could, there in Vancouver. But the pressures are the same, to break the family up. That's the ultimate goal of the church, the government, and especially the industries. If they can get us divided up, they can pick us off one at a time."

Vancouver was good to grandpa and his family (or troop or pack or whatever). But there were some major heavy times coming down in the early twenties. Lots of city folk, good people, but with no work except what the big companies could provide. And it was mind-deadening work, on assembly lines or cleaning up garbage. Or shoveling around dangerous stuff like sulfur or asbestos. Or tanning hides with acids and lye.

Mining was the big money occupation in B.C., and it was all run out of San Francisco. But logging was starting to get important in a big way.

MacMillan, one of the big operators, was trying to log carefully, to preserve the forests for the future. But he was the exception that proved the rule. Nearly all the rest were just trying to cut as many trees as they could, measuring their life's worth by how much dollars they could pile into their bank accounts. Gambling they would end up dead of overwork before a tree fell on them.

Some people got mean, either because they couldn't make as much money as they thought they should be making, or because they had nothing meaningful to do except some kind of dead end back-breaking labour to make somebody else rich. It was discouraging times for most people, despite what the papers said. Especially poor people, because it looked like everyone else around you was getting rich, while you struggled to keep what you had. Everything from school to the advertisers made you feel like you weren't worth as much as your neighbours.

Hollywood movies and newspapers, especially the Hurst papers that had lied the Americans into making war on Cuba in the 1800s, portrayed a life-style that most people didn't have, and wouldn't want anyway if they thought about it. It kept on telling them they should want it, a new car and house every year or so and twenty young boyfriends or girlfriends. And that they were not worth much if they didn't get lots of stuff.

A surprising number of people bought that line of bull, partly because they had never had more than what they needed, anyway. Most folks were cut off from the land, which was almost all owned by big ranchers and companies.

Jim Erkiletian

Some people started getting mean, in some cases, and good, energetic people, honest and hard working, were going backward two steps for every one step forward. Whatever was pushing them back was a whole lot bigger than them, and there wasn't any way to talk to it. Like a big machine that had gone out of control and no one knew how to stop it.

All they were getting for their trouble, and spending their lives for, was money. And the largest number weren't even getting that.

Spacecase and the band could have lived off the judge for those years. But none of them wanted to get lazy. Or decadent and dependent. Or lose the edge they had spent so many years honing and polishing.

Molly was the first to become aware of the problem. Her writing was starting to get angry and self-indulgent. She was spending some time with Pauline Johnson, paddling around the inlets and riding on Vancouver Island. Lots of real vigorous influences. Emily Carr was painting the backdrops. But the road was getting narrow and the city was killing off what was left of the country along Indian Arm.

Problems were coming down the skid road, the forests eaten by the lumber and paper mills, human flotsam drifting in, or left behind, defeated and used up. People were sick and tired, and not eating right. The shoreline was getting more polluted and smelly every day. A sadistic and cruel type of criminal, called gangsters, were beginning to grow in the festering sores called slums in the cities, sliding up out of the woodwork, and taking over some of the gambling and other recreational activities. A friendly game could get dangerous if the right people weren't paid off ahead of time.

One week in August, in 1921, they all decided at once that it was time to pull up stakes and head for the country. It was Bert who made it clear to the rest of them.

Molly was talking about her writing, how it didn't seem to be going anywhere. Loralei said something about the kids getting in trouble with some of the neighbourhood white kids from the waterfront. Spacecase and Bert were both just in from a fishing trip where they'd caught nothing but a string of dogfish sharks, one right after the other. Not too bad, marinated like the Japanese do them, but nothing like the big salmon they'd been trying for.

Spacecase said he thought the whole system was turning into one big party, that people didn't seem to realize the world had changed, and some important things had gone by the wayside. Like freedom and compassion.

Fairly was the most optimistic. "Heck," he said, "things could be a whole lot worse. It looks like all the big countries are patching up their differences and getting along, what with the new League of Nations. Even if the USA ain't playing ball, they will eventually."

Molly said that he was "Partly right. But the U.S.A. and Russia look to be on a collision course, and the Germans don't like the look of that peace treaty, considering it puts the whole blame for the war on them."

Loralei agreed, said "War won't end until both sides admit they did wrong, no matter what the reasons, no matter what the excuses."

"People haven't grown up enough for that yet," Spacecase said.

Bert listened to the rest of them talk for a while. Then he said, "My people have a saying. Something like whether the elephants are fighting or making love, the results for the ants are pretty much the same."

Four days later they were on the road, headed north. Some of the Salish fisher people who lived next to them had been invited to take over the rambling old house and grounds, with instructions to keep the trees, except what you need for firewood or building onto your own houses and boats.

They never went back.

It was quite a trip into the starting-to-freeze-up Canadian North. Most people would have waited until spring, to catch the summer months for traveling, and to give some leeway to prepare for the next winter. Not this bunch. They didn't want to hang around any longer than necessary, for one thing. For another, any one of them might be offered a good job or get into some particularly interesting deal that would need time to play out. Best to leave right away and get on down the road.

Fairly and Brother took the scout position, generally keeping a couple of hours ahead of the rest, looking for good camping spots and figuring out which trails went the right direction, which ones dead ended or turned into creek beds. He was able to meet people and discuss which roads were best. Or put up posters for the show's they gave in the towns along the way to make traveling money and friends.

They had a good herd of twelve horses, including four Clydesdales, a couple of milk cows and a calf. For riding, they had a covered wagon built on the chassis of a three-ton truck,with lots of room inside for the kids. Four kids. By then my mom and Uncle Will had been born.

The Stanley Steamer was bringing up the rear. They must have looked like one crazy bunch of gypsies, following the logging roads and trails into that cold and heavily forested bush country. Lots of old prospectors and loggers remember them coming through.

There wasn't any particular road into the far north in those days, but there were enough trails and partly-completed roads so they could always figure out some way to get through to the next place. Sometimes they had to double back for a few hundred miles, but they weren't on any particular schedule. It took them a couple of years to make Whitehorse. Whenever they got bogged down they'd just stay for the rest of the winter or summer, whichever it happened to be, and head on out again when they could travel, either on the frozen rivers or on the roads and trails.

The kids loved it. Uncle Joseph and Aunt Sarah were big enough to be helping with chores, and Uncle Will and mom were enjoying the whole trip from their papoose carriers, swinging along in the wagon just behind whoever happened to be driving Major and Tom, the team of Clydesdales that did most of the pulling.

It was a pretty self-sufficient bunch that headed out that fall. Some of the land had been clearcut logged, but not enough to make a difference. Any native kid knows he can eat pretty well, even in the middle of winter, if he has some old-growth forest to draw from. They had lots.

When the money ran out, they had show business.

They'd hit some little mining town or native village that hadn't had a real kick-up-your-heels dance in years, find out who the best fiddle or guitar player was in those parts, and get together a shindig of some kind. They made lots of friends and a fair amount of money.

"Not that much money, though," Spacecase said. "It don't make for good relations to take lots of money from those little towns where a dollar goes a long way."

"A dollar goes quite a ways right here," I said. "We could get us some candy or something."

"No," he said. "I mean a dollar will keep revolving in those little towns and will help everybody out. Hell, one dollar will pay the barber, who pays the butcher, who pays the cleaning lady, who pays the bartender who goes to get a haircut the next day. And it will keep going around and around like that until some banker comes along and steals it. I don't never want to be thought of like the kind of thief who will take that dollar out of circulation and loan it back to someone who also wants to steal it at interest. Besides, you never can tell when you're going to be back through that way."

The crew always had more than enough to eat, and stayed warm even on the nights when it dipped below minus forty. They stayed together and tight. And got somewhat bigger out there in that frozen forest.

"Roughing it teaches you make yourself as comfortable as possible," according to Spacecase. "Old man Bompas, the Yukon missionary, told the deacons in Chicago it's really the city folks who live the hard life. They didn't believe him, of course, and contributed that much more to his mission work because they thought he was being so noble and self-sacrificing by living out there all alone with the heathen Yukon Indians."

"Like Livingston, I guess," I said.

"Yep. Like Livingston."

I'd read about the great expedition to find Dr. Livingston, supposedly lost in darkest Africa. Bert had heard the real story through the grapevine of what really happened when Stanley found Livingston and uttered those famous words, Dr. Livingston, I presume?

Livingston's reply was seldom reported, if at all, except among the people tapped in to the moccasin telegraph. With an astonished Who the hell are you? Bugger off, you dumb jerk! Livingston had turned on his heel and stomped into his thatched-grass house mumbling a number of swear-words in Swahili and various other African languages.

Jim Erkiletian

Livingston hadn't wanted to return to the so-called benefits of civilization, but not for any idealistic reasons of helping the savages to become more civilized and modern. It was just too uncomfortable, living like a white man. And much, much too unhealthy.

"Your great-grandpa, my old man, was an O'Toole, from somewhere in England. But the actual father isn't who we grow up with in most tribes. It's really your mother's brothers who teach you how to do things. Or the father's brothers in some tribes."

Spacecase had just finished telling me that his father had probably gone back to England, then maybe India, and eventually had died in South Africa fighting Boors.

"You don't mind that he left you and your mom behind?" I asked.

"Heck, no. What's to mind? As long as the tribe stays intact, one person coming in or leaving doesn't hurt, more or less."

"You said the big companies and the government and the church broke up the tribes."

"Tried to. So they can get control and make each one of us have to buy their stuff or pay them taxes. Or worship their god and pay them donations. Instead of sharing."

"I don't know about the churches."

"They're the first ones," he said, "who try to break down the family. Right from the wolves on through the clans, from here to Scotland and back again."

"But they get people married," I objected.

"They don't consider people married unless they do it the church way," he replied. "Not too likely they would have said any kind words about the four of us, me, Loralei, Bert and Molly, going in and asking to be double-hitched, would they."

"Not likely," I agreed.

"The people of the Northwest used to have fights now and again. But most of the time they have parties, where they invite all the rival chiefs and their families. They dance and sing, and the host chief gives gifts and food to all the other people, even the kids."

I remembered the small carved eagle feather I'd been given at Kingcome, and the storyteller standing in front of the drummers talking to the rest of the people. I hadn't been able to understand what he was saying, only that it was a good and funny speech from the reaction of the other people. "Like at Kingcome," I said.

"Right," he said. "That chief was explaining what streams he was planning to fish the next year, and why he figured he and his people were entitled to the fish from that particular area. Like how many grandfathers back his people were in that part of the country, and how many mouths he has to feed in his own group."

"Sometimes there was fighting," I said. "The kids told me about invaders starting to attack, but Noisy Mountain scared the poop out of em."

"Sometimes," he agreed. "Young warriors being what they are. But never at or during a potlatch. Everybody was too busy having fun, inspecting their new gifts and stuffing their bellies. The boys and girls getting to know each other was a big part of it, too. All above board and proper with everybody's kinfolk sitting there watching.

"It worked out so everyone had enough to eat, and more, because everyone was trying to build up extra so they could throw the best potlatch for their neighbours. They compete to see who can share the most, instead of who can get the better of the other guy. Or who can get the most stuff.

"When the church missionaries saw this partying, they got right shook. Them folks were doing pagan rituals, with all that dancing and singing. And the kids weren't even in school, learning to sit in nice straight little rows with everybody at his or her own desk. They were sharing among themselves instead of giving to the church.

"The government, rest its rotten soul, saw pretty much the same thing. There didn't seem to be any way to tax people who used up all their surplus by sharing it with their neighbors. Even the poorest natives didn't need any of the trinkets the companies made. Instead of buying a plow for every farm, they'd get one plow and share it around, depending on who needed it.

"So the Canadian government outlawed the potlatch, sending in Northwest Mounted Police to break up the parties and arrest the people's leaders. Most places they just drove it underground, but some villages they managed to destroy a system that had been working up here for thousands of years. Kingcome, Bella Coola, a few others that were so far back in the

Windigo

woods the RCMP couldn't get in there easy. They got to be big potlatch centers for a few years.

"It was a system based on sharing, head-to-head up against a system that believed in competition, one based on tribal traditions and circles, up against one based on corporations and straight up-and-down lines. Warriors facing soldiers across a thin line of misunderstanding. And deceitfulness."

"It don't make a lot of difference to the ant," I said "if he gets stomped by a tomahawk or a sabre."

He eyed me like a big wolf again, nodded thoughtfully for what seemed like a long time, finally said, "You been listening. But the misunderstanding boils right down to the nitty-gritty when you look at the natural world, the trees and land and animals.

"When a warrior decides to swing his tomahawk, it's him who decides, nobody else. When a soldier decides to swing his sabre its because he's been told to by some other soldier. And he better not swing it unless he's told to by his commanding officer. Mutiny, in any army, is punishable by death.

"Juan Matus, a Yaqui medicine man's apprentice I knew in Juarez back in the thirties, said it best. A warrior is impeccable, cause he knows he's got to take the blame, and the whole blame, for whatever he does. Soldiers don't, so long as they follow orders. But the main bone of contention, between the whiteman's world and the native's, is that way of looking at nature. The warrior has to fit in with nature. And he does it by sharing and by living together with the whole thing."

"Like Coyote," I said. He'd once told me a Cree tale, about Coyote challenging Old Man to a race, after faking a broken leg, then beating it back to Old Man's food cache and making off with the goodies. Old Man lost the cache because he was greedy, unwilling to share.

"Like Coyote," he said. "But all those soldiers got to tell them about the natural world around us is the Three Little Pigs, each one of them building their own separate little house. The guy who builds the strongest house, out of bricks so to wall the natural world out the best, don't get ate by the wolf."

"But the soldier has to fit in too," I said. "Everybody has to fit with nature. We're all part of nature."

"That's not what the soldier thinks. He figures he's better than nature, somehow. And he thinks he's in control, working together with his mates. So he tries to manipulate the world, never realizing that it's himself that's being manipulated and controlled."

"They beat Fairly, though," I said. I was still kind of disturbed about those soldiers shooting someone I considered grandpa's most interesting friend.

"Correction, Yeuzor," he replied. "They blew him on into whatever happens after this life. They never beat him. They only beat themselves."

"Still," I was unconvinced. "He's dead."

He took his pipe out of his pocket and leaned forward, cleaning out the residue from past smokes with his knife. "Didn't you ever take any physics or chemistry in school?"

"Sure," I replied.

"Didn't they teach you nothing is ever created or destroyed, that everything always comes out equal in terms of matter and energy, eventually?"

"Something like that," I agreed. "But a dead man is still a dead man."

"And he's still here, somewheres, every particle and sub-particle and whatever of energy that went to make him up. Right?"

"I guess so," I agreed reluctantly.

"In fact, he may be all spread out and part of everything, now, instead of stuck inside a narrow little body, in one particular place.

"Now that soldier, all huddled together with his little group, never had the opportunity to understand his place in the general scheme of things. He's so scared of nature, of getting eaten by wolves or whatever, and of dying, he never learns how good it feels to live. Maybe he's the one we should be feeling sorry for."

My grandparents made it to Prince Rupert, a little fish packing and lumber town on the coast, late in 1922. It wasn't that big a town, but the people there thought it would grow, because it was ideal for a deep-sea port. Lots of room for even the biggest steamships to tie up there. The best site between Vancouver, B.C. and Anchorage, Alaska for supplying the interior of the continent. Right in the neck of the Great Bear. They were able to winter there, one of the rainiest places on the coast, to continue on north the next spring. On a barge pulled by an ocean-going tug.

Jim Erkiletian

There is a way back. It goes through the lessons we learned in the 1930s, and the ones we should have learned from our native ancestors.

This Great Bear, and the other Great Bears and Turtles and Lions and Jaguars across the seas can show us where we went wrong. The really meaningful life of a human can discover itself, given half a chance and a bunch of determination.

For a couple million years people lived in harmony, sharing the abundant goods of the land and sea. For a few thousand years they decided they had the right to take more than all the other creatures. Like worms on a corpse, they eat it until there isn't enough left to look after everyone.

People will eventually realize they can't go on growing forever. There is a limit to how much the land can produce. When people get over that limit, they got two choices. They can steal off somebody else. Or they can drop back to living smart, in tune with the rest of the animals and plants.

That old medicine bundle might be the answer. The cure. But it wasn't the same as just taking a pill to cure a cold. In fact, taking a pill wouldn't work at all. Medicine is different from pills.

I was beginning to see that.

When he was working with the Buffalo Bill Wild West Show in England, grandpa introduced Sitting Bull, also with the show in 1904 when it toured England, to Charles Darwin and Karl Marx. With Annie Oakley as the catalyst.

They'd put on a special showing for Queen Victoria complete with burning wagons and narrowly rescued maidens, great riding and large amounts of staged gunplay, and had a couple of days off. Annie wanted to take in an English pub. Sitting Bull wanted to see the university library at Oxford. Spacecase was delegated by Cody to ride herd on the two of them, to make sure they got back in time for the next show.

Annie, in spite of being the big star of the show, was tagging along after Bull like she'd been love-struck for the first time in her life. Which she was.

Here was a woman who had never been out of control of her rifles, her contracts, her life or her men. And suddenly here's this elderly Lakota who commands about ten times her charisma and about a hundred times her confidence, and doesn't care about stardom. Or about her.

Bull was in the business for two reasons. He wanted to see that his men were treated fairly and that they worked out scenarios where nobody got hurt. He was one of the earliest show-biz special-effects men. He'd had some practice designing battlefields where his own men and women suffered minimal casualties while inflicting heavy losses on the other side. So he was a natural. And Annie was smitten. That he already had a couple of wives back home, which would have ordinarily made homespun Annie weary, only served to intrigue. The more so when she found out his wives were twin sisters, some forty years younger than Bull.

"Made my back hurt," he explained to Spacecase. "Won't let me sleep on my side. Jealous."

Jim Erkiletian

At Oxford, Bull asked the librarian for some of the works of Erasmus Darwin, Charles's grandfather. Erasmus had laid out the idea humans and apes are related, he'd written it in a series of poems which got fairly popular among the nobility. It bought him a reputation as the old geezer who thought humans and apes are related. They were calling it Darwinism in England 30 years before Charles wrote his first words.

"What the heck are we doing out here?" Annie wanted to know when they arrived at the university.

"We come to talk with apeman," Bull explained, then strode into the library like it was his personal property. Which maybe it was at that moment.

The librarian sent word to Charles, who kept an office on the grounds, that there were people inquiring about his grandfather's poems. For the first time in some years. He investigated, found Bull to his liking, Annie quite delightful, and Spacecase rather a boor. Perhaps he could foist the latter off on that German expatriate, Mark or Manx or some such. Philosopher of economics or some bully thing.

Annie didn't talk much, but it was obvious she was far more interested in Bull than in any of the other men no matter how important and brilliant they talked. Naturally this fact didn't enter the consciousness of either Marx or Darwin, and didn't prevent them from attempting to impress her with their erudition and confidence. And caused Spacecase to reflect on the futility of understanding sexual selection on the basis of the male perspective only.

They ended up in a pub near the school with bitter brown ale in tankards before them and old thick tables with carvings in their tops.

Sitting Bull considered. "Lakota kill buffalo. Take big bulls, the ones who have many wives. Little bulls get more nookie after big bulls gone, until new bull take over. Herd gets strong new blood."

Darwin nodded, took a pull on his pipe. "I have an idea called evolution of species through natural selection. The herd changes when the big bulls are gone. But what is selected for?"

"Selection for differences. Strongest little bulls get available nookie. Cows get more strong babies."

Darwin nodded. Marx took a drink from his mug, leaned over the table and asked, "But see here sir, you are killing the strongest ones?"

Sitting Bull nodded, stroked his chin. "Herd don't get stronger because head bull keep all cows for himself." He drew a quick arrow with his finger in the mist on the table top, inscribed a circle around it. "Wolf kill sick and injured and old buffalo."

"The wolf?" Darwin asked. "But that must make the herd stronger?"

Sitting bull nodded, dabbed his finger in the centre of the circle several times. "Sometimes wolf get killed trying to kill healthy buffalo."

"By Jove. Survival of the fittest for the wolves, and the buffalo too." Darwin was excited enough to slop some of his ale on the table.

"Sometimes Lakota die in hunt, too. Buffalo stampede, horse stumble, rifle explode backwards, commanchero shoot for bounty. Many ways to die on the prairie."

"Commancheros?" Darwin asked.

"Mostly war veterans from the losing side," Spacecase said. "Hunt Indians for their scalps, which bring around $25 from the ranchers and some army generals.

"But see here," Marx said. "These commancheros, scalp hunters and such, they are workers, victims of the class war."

"Dead Lakota warrior is worse victim. But Lakota must be plenty strong people, after so much natural selection."

Marx and Darwin nodded thoughtfully, took simultaneous sips from their mugs.

Spacecase laughed. "You guys might have forgotten how the libido influences the selection process."

This change of direction didn't result in any great insights from the assembled crew. It did result in the intellectuals noticing Annie for the first time as a non-participating member of the conversation. And in a couple more flower bouquets sent backstage after the next show for Annie to add to her collection. But nothing from Sitting Bull except a grandfatherly affection that Annie would have traded for all her fame in a minute. A new feeling for her.

18. Snakebite Kits and Salmon Skins...

Radical: n. 1. A political free agent.
2. A chemical free agent that cannot remain so for long.

"But what about the windigr?" I asked. "It must be supernatural."

"Supernatural?" Then he drawled it out real slow. "SU-per-NAT-ur-awl. Nope, it ain't. It's natural, like everything else. Ain't nothing supernatural, far as I know, except in the comic books."

"Anyway," I said, "there don't seem to be any way to protect yourself from something like that."

"The windigr," he mused, lying back on the chunk of quarter-inch plywood he'd wedged in between the wall and floor of the car. It gave him just enough bounce to make for an easier ride. I was resting on both of our bedrolls and packs, getting into the rhythm of the rails clackata-clacking underneath, trying to forget the wind blowing through the cracks around the doors.

"You know," he continued after a time, "the most scared I ever been was the time I was attacked by that beaver up the McLintok River. Dang near killed me, or worse."

"What's worse than getting killed?" I said.

He pondered for a minute, said, "Almost made me pee my pants."

I considered that for a time, said, "Beaver, eh. What'd he do, try to gnaw on your head?"

He looked over at me with a stern and serious down-the-middle-of-the-nose look, then broke into a laugh. A short one. "Good guess," he said, "but no cee-gar. It was 1909 or there abouts. I was seventeen. I'd been working with John Joe most of the summer, hauling logs with a team of horses. There was a man who knew his business. He could bang a silver dollar out of the air with a muzzle-loading rifle, just as easy as tossing a piece of candy in the air and catching it in your mouth. And with a six-shooter he could do six dollars.

"He had some people to see in Tagish, dropped me off at the mouth of the McLintok to look around for moose. Said he'd try to get back that way in a week or so.

"Along about ten o'clock, with the sun just below the horizon keeping a long twilight like it does in the summer up there, I heard this horrible cronching sound from way up the river. Sounded like dry skulls being crunched together and pulverized in a mortar and pestle. Or maybe a river god grinding his teeth in anticipation of having you for dinner.

"I'd seen lots of beavers, over the years, but never heard one chewing on a tree before. Out there where it's real quiet, so quiet you can hear for miles, and there's no one and nothing around, it set the hair right up on the back of my neck.

"Up the river an old forest fire burn had left a bunch of snags standing. When the wind was blowing through there, those burned trees sometimes scraped together and made noises that sounded like voices of our ancestors calling to each other over the gulf between life and death. But that cronching was something entirely different.

"I got lots of wood in close to my fire and kept listening. But I didn't hear anything for quiet a while. That pretty long space when I couldn't hear anything lasted maybe fifteen-twenty minutes. Just long enough for the sky to slide from twilight into an inky-blue darkness. And the forest all around to close in from all sides like a big infinity hole.

"Just when I was starting to think I hadn't really heard that cronch-cronchin', or whatever the bugaboo it was had gone away, there it come again!

"And it was closer!!

"Well, I don't need to tell you the second time I heard that racket I nearly jumped out of my boots. I thought about making a move, but didn't want to get away from the fire very far. My rifle was handy, an old Kentucky muzzle-loader, the kind with the octagonal barrel. I rested it across my knees, primed, with a full charge and a slug tamped in. But I was some spooked.

"The wind was blowing from up the valley, carrying my scent away down toward the lake. Whatever it was wouldn't know I was there til it was real close. I sure wasn't planning on doing anything to draw attention to myself with that big croncher out there in the blackness closing in on me.

"All kinds of monsters chased themselves through my head, each one bigger and nastier critters than the one before. I took a leak real quick, not as far from the fire as I usually go, looking back and forth over my shoulders and into the dark as far as I could see. You ever try to take a pee under them conditions?

I said, "Sort of, a few times. It ain't easy."

"That went on for over an hour," he continued. "Seemed like five hours. Every fifteen minutes or so, just when I was beginning to relax and think it had gone away, that cronching again. Closer each time. My skin was champing at the bit to jump right out of itself by the fourth cronch.

"Finally it was right over the bank from my camp. Rustlin' in the dry leaves. I didn't know what to do, but figured I better make the first move. At least if it came for me, I'd be able to know where it was coming from. I'd never get to sleep with that gigantic beast roaming around in the woods. What if my fire died out while I was sleeping? As if I could sleep with the heebie-jeebies jitterbugging up and down my backbone.

"I had some dry spruce branches with the needles still on. They burn real bright, but only for a minute or two. I piled most of them on the fire, and moved back around away from the bank, so I could see what might be coming over the hill.

"There were a bunch of pebbles on the ground by the fire. I scooped up a big handful as the spruce needles started crackling. Then, with my rifle in one hand, I rared back and threw those little rocks in the general direction of the noise, patted the handle of the Bowie knife in my belt, aimed my rifle, and waited.

"Some of them rocks may have actually bonked him. But the main thing for me was to get him surprised enough to show himself, or run away. Preferably the latter.

"There was a few moments of silence after the pebbles stopped falling, then a rustle of dry leaves and, a minute later that slap of tail on the surface of the river that means danger or bugger off in beaver language.

"Man, was I ever eased, all of a sudden. All them apprehensions drifted away like a sparrow fart in a hurricane. And I was feeling pretty foolish at the same time, considering I'd let myself get all tight and clammy at a beaver, cruising the riverbank, checking out the trees along the way."

"So he didn't really attack you?" I said. "At least not so as to try and get his teeth into you or something."

"Nah. Not like the bears sometimes do."

"Bears only attack when they got cubs to protect," I observed. I'd learned that in scouts.

"So they say, so they say," he replied. "And that happened to me the next year, about the same place, over on the trail that runs from Tagish to Caribou Crossing. Up above Marsh Lake at the head of the Yukon River. I was together with Khash that time, hunting moose again. We did a lot of that in those days.

"We'd just come out at the top of a winding valley. You could see six different beaver families living along the creek bottom from the top of that ridge. Each had its own lodge house and lagoon. They'd put in a whole beaver city, with the creek right down under their control. Living the good life for beavers, for sure.

Jim Erkiletian

"Wind was in our faces. We were making some noise, talking to warn any bears we were in the neighbourhood. And trying to talk soft enough that we wouldn't scare off any moose or caribou. Only problem was, there was a low bank between us and the bears. And so much noise from the water pouring over the beaver's dam, them bears didn't hear us, or smell us coming.

"And there she was, a big momma grizzly, teaching her cubs to fish. Fishing for a bear means batting them out of the water with their paws. The top beaver's spillway was the best place to teach her cubs that trick. That's where the biggest fish are found, the ones that had made it past all those other beavers and jumped all the spillways on each dam.

"I saw them first, even though I was a little behind Khash. We were almost past them, when the momma stood up on her hind legs to check us out. One of the cubs was just visible beside her, to her right.

"I thought, Wow, that's a big bear. Then I had this terrible realization there wasn't anything between her and us but that low bank. And the only trees on that whole hill were little saplings with trunks about as big around as your pecker.

"A friend from Kingcome told me about somebody he knew climbing a little tree to get away from a bear, and bending the tree right back over. He ended up staring the bear in the face upside down. Said the bear just shook his head, turned around and walked away.

"Not this one though. She'd seen us, and we were way, way inside her territory. She had two cubs to protect, and no time to think out an escape plan.

"She went back down on all fours and disappeared around the edge of the bank. Circling, to come at us from some other direction and take us by surprise. Bears are smart that way. They think real fast, and they move even faster. I knew she was coming for us, but not exactly from where or when.

"I clapped Khash on the shoulder and said BEAR in his left ear, and took off running as hard as I could, looking for a big tree to climb. There weren't any for what was a long ways, so I stopped and looked back. Good thing for both of us I did. Khash was standing there, looking off down the valley. Thought I'd seen a moose.

"Me yelling in his ear like that, even though I'd said bear loud and clear, hadn't registered as any more than some big noise. Since he'd been thinking moose at the time, he thought that's what had got me so excited. He was standing there looking off down the valley, his rifle resting easy in the crook of his arm.

"The next year he actually killed a bear with his muzzle-loader. Quite a feat, if you know those guns. But he ate some of that bear and got real sick, so he's avoided bears ever since.

"Anyway, I hooked my thumb in the sling on my rifle and swung it off my shoulder, cocked the hammer back and fumbled for a cap. Along about that time the adrenaline hit my system and everything got bright and shiny. The breeze tickled the leaves and made that whole grove of alders crackle in the breeze and sparkle in the sunlight, all at the same time. Big mama nature took a sudden notion to shift on into another mood of existence. Like when they run movies in slow-motion, except I was inside looking out.

"Nothing happened for quite a spell. Then everything happened at once. That bear came charging over the hill, right dead on toward Khash, with the big hump on her back just bristling. She was moving like a locomotive, except she wasn't making a sound. It's really something to see a full-grown bear blasting through the woods, her big pads cushioning each step like giant pillows. Not a crisp of dried leaf or nothing. The wind bouncing through the leaves overhead was making more noise than she was.

"Khash looked down and saw her coming when she was still about twenty yards away. He yelled, Aha, you bugger! As he suddenly realized why I'd been so excited. He rolled his rifle off his shoulder with one hand, nipped a cap out of his shoulder bag with the other. By the time he had the hammer cocked and the cap stuck in, she was almost on top of him. And she was almost as tall as he was, even down on all fours. By the time he got his shot off he was looking her eyeball to eyeball. With no more than an arm's length from the end of his front sight to that bear's big black nose.

"I never seen anything quite so fast. In the time it took me to stick my own cap into my rifle, Khash had cocked, primed, aimed and fired. The explosion echoed off down the valley, cutting through the silence like a giant scythe. Like a boxcar load of TNT at a Sunday afternoon picnic in the park. The bear heaved on the brakes and stopped, with one front foot still in the air, claws close enough to Khash's midsection she could have slashed him in two with a sideways swipe.

"His slug may have hit her in that big hump of bone those bears have on their back. I guess we'll never know for sure. Unless we find her skeleton some day with a big chunk of lead stuck in it. I was in a low squatting position, just about down on one knee. If the bear knocked Khash down, I'd have to shoot from a low position to keep from hitting him. I was thinking I'd better get her in the head, because if she got mad and came at me, I wouldn't have time to reload for a second shot.

"My little Bowie knife felt about as useful as a toothpick in a sword fight, up against ten cutlasses and a couple maces. Assuming she'd make the tactical blunder of letting me get to use it, which she probably wouldn't.

"There was a moment of real spiritual enlightenment while I watched the bear and Khash looking each other in the eyes. I fumbled the primer cap into my rifle, still not too sure what to do next. Khash wasn't moving a muscle.

"The bear decided not to kill him, for some reason, and turned toward me, just as I was bringing the barrel into firing position. She shifted and spun like a ballet dancer, straight toward me. It was my turn.

"By the time I had a bead on her, though, she was going the other way, back down to the creek to round up her cubs and herd them off down the valley. I pulled my shot just over her head. Didn't want to make her mad.

"The explosion rocked me back a little, and when the smoke cleared away, there she was, stopped dead still. Looking back over her shoulder at me with the most godawful mean scowl on her face you ever seen. Those grizzlies have a long, curved snout. Her's was wrinkled right up with big deep creases, with all her teeth gleaming white against her gums. And if you care to know how many wrinkles there are on a mad momma grizzly's snout, there's seven. Four on the lower curved part, and three more up just below the eyes. And there's enough teeth and mouth just below them wrinkles to snap your skull like a walnut in a drill press.

"Her eyes stared steady into mine for what seemed like a long time. Then she decided not to kill me, for some reason, and headed back down the bank to look after her cubs. Khash, I could see out the corner of my eye, was ramming a charge into his rifle. He was already down on one knee just in case he had to shoot the bear from off the top of me. Good thinking, I thought, and flipped my powder horn around to the front so I could tip it into the barrel.

"Those bears didn't waste any time getting out of there. The last we saw them were three humping rear ends disappearing into the bush a couple hundred yards down the valley. Khash fired a charge in the air, just powder, no bullet, and I did the same. Just to let the bears know they better not mess with the thunder-benders ever again. Then we both sat down and reloaded.

"He didn't bother to tap in a primer cap, so I didn't either.

"I sure didn't expect to see no bear," he said with a kind of awe. Then he built a fire.

"He told me to bring over some green branches to heap on top when he'd got it going pretty good. I did, not really knowing why he wanted to do that. Smoke signals, maybe? I found out later, he'd noticed the wind blowing, just a little, down our back trail. That's why they hadn't smelled us coming. It was blowing between the trail and where the bears had run off. He knew bears avoid smoke, from their experience with forest fires. He was giving us a little insurance against running into those same bears again when we went back.

"I always thought that was pretty quick thinking for someone who'd just stood eye-to-eye with a mad grizzly not ten minutes before."

The boxcar gave a jolt as we rounded a hillside and caught a big buffet from the wind. I reflected on the idea of looking a big bear in the eye and snuggled down deeper into my blanket. "Sounds like a close call, all right."

"It was that," he said. "But one thing I can tell you about that little episode. That bear could'a taken both our heads off with one swipe of her front paw. Wouldn't even have worked up a sweat doing it, neither. And I knew it. But I wasn't really scared that time. I was too busy and too zinged on my own adrenaline to have time to get scared.

"Besides, scared was what I was when that danged beaver almost got me."

I slept well that night, considering how cold it got as we rattled on closer to Cache Creek. From there we would walk and hitchhike up the Fraser Canyon, through Prince George, eventually up to the very top of the continent where the rivers all run north into the Arctic Ocean instead of east or west.

Later that fall we made Whitehorse, and the next spring, Dawson City, the place that made the Yukon Territory a big time deal. Ghosted boom town site of the big gold rush of 1898.

Spacecase had been just a kid then, but he remembered the excitement and the interest well enough. Gold was something the most powerful and astute white people, and quite a few natives, would give you great amounts of their goods and services in exchange for. Good stuff if you can get it without having to give up anything. But that's not really how the universe works, as we learn with maturity and wisdom, and by listening to our elders.

Dawson City was the biggest town west of Chicago and north of San Francisco for about ten years, right around the turn of the century. Lots of Americans had trekked in there, looking to make the big strike, or just get in on an adventure. In 1898, young men didn't have a lot of choices. They could go fight Spaniards in Cuba. But anybody smart enough to see through the Hearst newspaper's line of bull stayed right away from that ignorant little assault-and-battery. One of many committed by the United States against our closest neighbours on this side of the world. Which is one of the reasons I'd rather be a Canadian flea than an American flea, given those two choices.

When I first saw it, Dawson City was a crumbling ghost town catering to a few wealthy families and the local natives. And the odd tourist. "You would have done all right, here, with a deck of cards," I told Spacecase.

"Hell, I'd have been a millionaire if I'd been here during the heyday, knowing what I know now. But I was just a kid back then. Still, I did all right. Especially after I teamed up with John, shooting tin cans and dollars out of the air."

"He must have been good."

"Like greased lightning bolts in the palm of your hand. He'd been potting birds with a bow-and-arrow from the time he was little. Hitting a silver dollar with a good rifle isn't all that much harder than potting a grouse on the wing. Easier in some ways. Grouse will flip and flop all over the place, riding the wind. But a dollar goes up and down. The trick is to wait until it's right at the top of its arc, where it's standing still for just a split-second before it starts to fall. Then aim just below it. Still, it was impressive."

There wasn't a whole lot to do in the Yukon in those days. Gold mining was all big business by then, with big steam-driven dredges digging their way up the river bottoms on the Klondyke and Bonanza, and all the little nearby creeks that showed any colour.

There was some gambling still going on. And some entertainment. Show people always manage to get by, and there was a real need for entertainment in that land. For the most part it was cold, cold country with a couple of months of below minus-forty degrees darkness right in the middle of winter.

"Bert was responsible for keeping the fire going one night, in the cabin we were staying in up the Klondyke. He wasn't too worried about it. Decided he'd rather get a good night's sleep, and could build up a real big fire in the morning. Chopping wood warms you up anyway.

"He jumped out of bed the next morning, all ready to get out and chop, and the shock of his feet hitting the icy floor caused him to spontaneous shit a big turd. I swear to god if that turd didn't freeze solid as a rock by the time it hit the floor with a thunk! We were all kind'a impressed. Bert's body was a normal ninety-eight point six degrees, after all. So it must have been cold out there."

They didn't go hungry, by any means. Setting up shop in new places and living with the land and sky was their style for those years. They'd been at home on the open road, with destinations decided by consensus, and, more often than not, which way the wind happened to be blowing that particular day. Dawson City looked like a good place to settle in for a few years. Maybe get the kids started on some proper schooling, whatever that might be.

Brother and Fairly left them the next year, to make the trip overland that had killed various expeditions of

Northwest Mounted Police and gold-seekers. The first Hudson Bay trader in that country, Joe Campbell, walked overland all the way to Minnesota after the Chilkats burned down his trading post for cutting in on their business. Fairly thought he'd like to try that, to see if it was as hard a trail as people said. He and Brother saw some good land, and met some good people, before they ran into that cavalry troop.

"He always was interested in exploring the Great Bear, even the tail and back legs eventually. Without getting too scatological, he even wanted to check out the asshole of the Great Bear, which, by a strange quirk of fate, happens to be precisely where Washington, D.C. is located today. He'd heard of the Seminoles, who had never surrendered their lands in the southeast, was planning on checking them out, eventually.

"So what happened to Bishop?" I asked. "I didn't know quite what to make of him at first, but I guess he was all right."

"All right for a cutthroat, I guess. Bishop died in his sleep in the early 30s, at the Harmony House in Frisco. The big depression was just getting started, not that it effected his business much. In fact, it probably made man hunting more profitable than ever. Maybe he got fat and lazy. I heard he was still riding Sundance, even the day he died."

"The depression," I said, "must've been hard times."

"Who said?"

"Well, mom, for one. And just about everyone talks about how bad it was."

He lay back against the wall. "Maybe," he said. "Your mom was just a baby back then. The people who suffered most were the ones tied into the system."

"There wasn't any work, I guess."

"Not much. I worked for one factory down in Oregon did all right. Ran three shifts steady, around the clock, right through the nineteen-thirties. Made glass sealer jars for people who do home canning."

"But most people were out of work," I said, "and lots were hungry."

"Yep, lots were. But there was some didn't even know there was a depression on. The ones who live back in the country and don't depend on the system to provide for them. They don't let their needs expand, or their wants to get the better of them, if they can help it. And they live around other folks who believe in helping each other and sharing, instead of trying to always get the better of the other guy."

"Like natives," I said.

"Some natives," he said back. "Might be the real enemy, the real cause for things like depressions and hard times, is what they call civilization."

"Aztec armies were eating and killing poor farming people all over the Great Bear, before the Spanish took over down there. They killed twenty-thousand captives in a big free-for-all bloodbath, a few years before Cortez invaded Mexico. Some of their games were kind of like football, except lots faster, and the losing team got cut up and ate for dinner by the winners. Or maybe vice-versa. Must have made for some real cliff-hanger end games."

I thought about missing a pop fly, or not touching third, under those conditions. "Cannibals?"

"Some say so," he continued. "Course it was the Spaniards who said they ate their enemies, so the records might not be correct on that one. Lots of missionaries found they could get better funding if they claimed the people they were trying to convert were cannibals.

"Cortez took Tinochtitlan, Mexico City we call it today, with just a few hundred men. After marching all the way through Mexico. The people out on the land could have fought him, but they didn't. Why help Montezuma when his armies were always rounding up their healthiest sons and daughters and sacrificing them? Not to mention making them pay taxes. They figured they didn't have much to lose, siding with the Spaniards."

"Did they?" I asked, "have much to lose, I mean."

I'd heard him say some pretty uncomplimentary things about Spanish conquistadors working natives to death in mines and on big plantations.

"Maybe. It was a gamble on their part, alright. The Spanish, over a couple hundred years, had massacred quite a bunch of their own people for religious reasons. Millions were tortured and burned at the stake or hanged in the inquisition. Most of them women. Cats, too."

"Cats?" That was a little hard for me to swallow.

"Yep, cats. Thought they was familiars of the devil. Along with wolves and most'a the rest of nature. They had a few big cat killings all through Europe in the middle ages. They'd already cut most'a their forests building monasteries and churches. Habitat was going down. Naturally, killing the cats gave the rats a chance to build up big populations.

"When there got to be too many rats for the food supply, they started dying off from the various rat diseases. Eventually they sprung one that gets people too. Black plague. Real horror show with big black boils all over your body, and slow strangulation as your throat swells closed.

"The wise women who knew about the plants and medicines weren't around to help, either. They got tortured and burnt alive if they did anything looked like witchcraft."

"Sounds pretty stupid," I said.

"It was. That's why so many Europeans started moving out, exploring and looking for new lands. They'd pretty well destroyed their own land base by the 1600s, went looking for somebody else's land to rape and pillage."

"But what about the windigr. You said it really exists."

"I does, all right. And you've heard tell of what they call the Yeti over in India, or the Bigfoot or Sasquatch here in Canada. But them's good windigrs, or at least they leave you alone as far as we can tell. I guess I'd hate like the dickens to have one mad at me."

"What would you do if one did get onto you?"

"What did I do? Well, I sat down and told him all about me, who my father and mother were, and named off all my kinfolk and told him on what part of the Great Bear they each lived."

I didn't really believe him, then. I know better now. But I was leading him on, for what I thought was the fun of it. "How come you told him that stuff?"

"Because then he knew I had a right to be here walking around in his territory and maybe using up some of his food and things. But even if he didn't want me here, at least he would know a little about me. Maybe I wouldn't taste so good, if he was eating someone he knew."

"And it worked?" I asked.

"He didn't bite my head off. Not yet, anyways."

"Not yet," I repeated.

19. Reversing the Tides…

Elements; (Clas.), n. Earth, air, fire and water. (Mod.), n. Solid, gas, energy and liquid.

During that trip, he asked me to tell him a story. We were camped on a spit of land along some river in the north. Somewhere in the throat of the Bear, I think, although I can't remember for sure.

I made up some bull that sounded pretty hokey, finally just degenerating into Goldilocks and the Three Bears.

He stopped me halfway through with "Hey, that don't sound right. Let me tell it proper. It's actually an Algonquian tale them Europeans must have copied.

"Once upon a time there was three bears and they were foraging around for food, because winter was coming on, and they needed to have enough extra to live through the cold months. They'd already gathered some, but they knew every bit helps. Bears like to have a good store of extra food, in case they wake up in the middle of winter and want a snack. Meanwhile a stingy little girl named of Little Ravenhair crawled into their den and started eating up the stuff they'd gathered for the winter. Her mother had told her over and over not to go in a bear's den, but she wouldn't listen.

"When the bears came back home, after sniffing around the cave some and commenting, Someone's been eating MY chunks of termite wood, and Someone's been wallowing in MY hole in the floor, they found her. She was sleeping in the baby bear's hollow spot. She'd made quite a pig of herself, eaten up all their winter stores, and she was fat as a tick, I tell you.

"While she was sleeping they decided how to deal with her. The baby bear said they should just keep her around until they got hungry, then they could eat her. The papa and momma bear decided that would be fair, but that she should be adopted into the tribe first so she could help them get more food for the winter.

"When she woke up the papa bear said, "Welcome to our tribe. Now get your butt to work gathering food so we don't need to dine on little girls this winter."

"She went out with the bears and foraged, and between the four of them they just managed to bring in enough to keep them all alive that winter. And they lived happily ever after, the three bears and their pet human, Little Ravenhair."

"I never heard that version before."

"Might say something about what we need. If it's a strong house to hide inside from the world of wolf eat wolf, only two pigs survive to the end of the story. If you want little girls to stay home and look after things, you got Goldilocks. If you don't want greed taking over your house, you have Ravenhair."

"Could be a problem, you got the wrong stories for the people you're with."

"Can be fun too. Learning the new stories. And trying the old ones out with different people." He turned toward the wall of the tent, was snoring within minutes. In most of the stories he said he learned from one or another tribe, the loser was always the greedy one.

Greed is taught. Or not taught.

Looping the loop with crows and hawks is bad enough. Doing barrel rolls with angels is even more fun. Giving Spacecase a license to fly was like giving a tiger a pillowcase full of catnip, then hanging around the inside of his cage with him and swapping tales.

There were guys like Mac Courtesy, Wiley Post, and women like Amelia Aerhart, flying all over the world in those days. Lindbergh proved you could make it across the Atlantic in a flying machine. And the pilots in the War to End War had made flying into a sport.

"Flying in those days was by the seat of your pants. Because we didn't know any other way, rather than because we'd learned how from someone else. Kind of exciting, when a good landing was one you could walk away from."

It was the sort of thing that appealed to Bert and Spacecase on many levels. You could get a bunch of gold across a border real easy in a flying machine. Or see if there were moose in the next valley. It was dangerous and made people look at you differently when they found out you fly. And there was the art of sculpting in three dimensions with the wind as your medium. The real pioneers of the twentieth century were heading up and out, not over to someone else's country to exploit and disrupt.

"Not that they were all bad, the immigrants. Some of those folks who headed for sunnier, or even colder climates, gave us some positively hummdinger good ideas. And are damned fun to be with. Joe Hill was from Sweden. Bert was African, originally.

"Most of the really good ideas of this century came from combinations the stay-at-homes couldn't understand, or handle. Charlie Darwin sailed right around the world before he started making up theories about life and how things change.

"He met some people in Tierra del Fuego, the Island of Fires at the tip of South America just off Antarctica. The Ona and Alakaluf. They live on land that's colder than some Eskimo country. But they didn't even wear clothes, most of the time. Didn't need to.

"Seeing the natives walking around naked, or the men paddling along in their little boats with their wives swimming along beside, had a strong effect on young Charles D. The women would dive for shellfish, bring them up for the men to roast over a little fire they'd carry on a round rock in the middle of their canoe. You can bet your sweet bippy those men loved their womenfolk. And the women must have loved their men right back. The water is awful frightfully cold down there.

"Only thing colder than the water is the air. Two of Magellan's men froze solid as rocks at their sentry posts, on the one night he camped there. They may be the first European bodies to rest in that particular ocean, although we wouldn't have any records of pirates who made it that far.

"Darwin noticed he had to sit up close to a big fire, huddled in three buffalo robes, and still couldn't keep his teeth from chattering. He could see natives standing way back from the fire, sweating like sausages on a spit. It was a lesson he never forgot. Humans, he realized, are one tough and successful animal. Adaptable.

"Comfort, and health too, he decided, must be pretty much relative. And humans are only one of the combinations born out of mother earth's and father sun's loving. It set him to wondering just how this particular animal had become so successful.

"It didn't take him long to notice something peculiar about animals and plants all over the world, even on the Galapagos Islands where there were only a few lizards and birds and bugs. Every living thing has more babies than can be fed. He got to wondering why, and put his wondering together with what his grandpa had said about change.

"Grandpa Erasmus Darwin said all life was evolving along together with all other life, with each one eating some of the others and taking care of all the others at the same time. Selecting the most fit to carry on the next generation while eating the left overs, so to speak. So Charles was one of the first Europeans to figure out all life is related and interwoven together in a big food web. From there he set to trying to figure out what was really going on, what was driving the engine of life all over the world.

"The folks on Tierra del Fuego didn't over-eat their country. They were balanced right in there with all the other animals and plants, happily chomping up whatever they could score in the way of energy and fat.

But one thing they all did was reproduce more of themselves than survived to adulthood, or to get to be breeding age.

"The Ona and Alakaluf lived pretty well. No natural enemies they couldn't handle. Yet they didn't over reproduce their environment. Humans may be the only animal ever evolved who could actually learn to live in harmony with nature. Which means they might be the only ones who could, if they took a notion, destroy it."

"So what's that got to do with flying," I said. If he was going to keep me awake nights rapping, I'd lots rather hear about flying airplanes than the dang natural world.

"Nothing and everything. You was telling me the other day about impossible things. I'm just setting the stage for letting you know that nothing is impossible if you get determined enough."

"O.K.," I said. "I'm interested in getting a million bucks…tomorrow."

"It'd take me more'n a week to get that kind of cash together," he replied.

"Next week then," I said. I was a quick little brat.

"I'll start in tomorrow," he said. "But only if you listen real close and do exactly what I tell you."

He seemed to mean it. There might be some kind of snowball's chance in the Mojave in August that he had a big buried treasure somewhere. I listened.

"The thing that went wrong, after the Great War to End War, was all those top-to-bottom outfits, set up like armies, all over the world. Each country was a little corporation, and a man had to have papers, a passport, and all manner of respectability to travel.

"A few guys at the top took it on themselves to decide what is proper work, and how much each job gets paid. It works out the folks who do the most work, like raising food and sewing clothes, get the lowest pay. The system's not only straight up-and-down, it's upside down to boot.

"In the tribes, the organization is round, like the earth and moon and sun. Everybody gets to decide for himself or herself what's most important to do, if it's carving a mask or hunting moose or making a drum or fixing the tailpipe or buying new sheets. And everybody has to take responsibility for their own screw-ups.

"Everybody works as much or as often as they want to. And everyone survives."

"What about on a boat," I said. "Like you got to have a captain if you're running a ship. There has to be some guy who can navigate and maybe someone to steer, so the other guys can get some sleep on long trips. If nobody wanted to steer one day, your boat might be onto the rocks."

"No doubt," he replied. "Today there's all kinds of welfare programs, work projects, loan programs and other government stuff to make life better. And plenty of work besides, with war building up across the oceans. But what people really want and need is freedom, or free enterprise as the Americans call it."

"What's that?" I'd heard the words before, usually spewing out some forked-tongue drunk or blowhard's mouth.

"That means the government sends out a contract each year to all the citizens, asks them what they want to do, instead of letting the bigwigs decide. Then they divide up all the tax money coming in and pay it back out to everybody in the country equal. That'd be free enterprise. Where everybody could decide what was best, and what was real work, instead of some jerks at the top who never did a real day's work in their lives deciding for us."

I couldn't find any big holes in his thinking. Some guy could decide to lay around on the beach all year and play with his balls. But then who am I to decide that isn't meaningful work? Hell, lots of guys doing that already, come to think about it.

"I'd feel better with real sailors on my boat."

"No doubt," he said. "Our people are real sailors. They wobbled all over the Pacific in dugouts. Atlantic, too. Way before Columbus."

"So how come they didn't discover the Europeans first, then?"

"They did," he replied. "They didn't bother to write it down, but the native Americans knew about the other people who lived across the sea. And told about them all over the Bear. They even traded some, with Portuguese fishers, Vikings, Chinese, Hawaiians. But they never saw any percentage in sending armies over there. Columbus gets the credit, but he's just the first one to write about what he thought he discovered.

"It's the children of the Great Bear, though, who're making this century. Whatever it is. Even today, them folks from the old countries are still trying to kill and slaughter each other, instead of trying to live together with their land, their animals and each other."

"But most of the people of the Great Bear are not natives."

"Not connected to one of the tribes, you mean."

"Right."

"That's true, Yeuzor. But they are natives, really, most of them. They just don't know it. Shoot, they got a whole education system and newspaper system telling us we're good little Europeans. The power people spend millions making sure we don't know about our Great Bear roots. But they can't bury us completely, no matter how hard they try."

I stuck my stick into the fire and twisted it around in the coals. "So how come even the chiefs and everybody says we got to go to school?" Even Kingcome had a school for the kids.

"That's the test for you," he replied. "It's because the world is small and you need to learn about all of it. And we know that when the chips are down and you feel the hot breath of the windigr on the back of your neck, you know where the real world lies, and how you fit together with it. And you'll know which way to jump if you're smart enough to ignore the propaganda from across the ocean."

"Mom didn't seem to know."

"Your mom forgot. You won't."

"Funny how the word band is a bunch of music makers playing together, and a bunch of people traveling together both," he observed. "And it's also a circle of metal to hold a bundle of stuff together, including the band you slip around your finger. Means you got somebody special you really care about, or who cares about you."

"Some words are more powerful than others, I guess."

It was early in 1943 he turned me loose on Lana. A message arrived by moccasin telegraph, passed along through the reserves and towns until it got to us in the northwest. Loralei wanted to see him, about their daughter and a funeral. Some things that needed to be done to help my mom's troubled soul along into the next stage of existence, or something. Something that had to be done within three years after the death.

I told him I didn't want to go. I decided I'd rather remember mom as she was, and see Loralei and the rest of them under different circumstances.

"Is there someplace you could drop me off, maybe pick me up later?"

To tell the truth, I was looking for a little settled living for a while. Kind of like when you spend a long time living on a little boat. It feels good to sleep on dry land once in a while.

"Maybe Lana's place," he said. "In Westminster, up the Fraser from Vancouver." So we caught some cars from Cache Creek down through the Fraser Canyon to Vancouver.

Jim Erkiletian

Lana turned out to be a real sweetheart of a lady, into supping tea every day with invited guests from just about every walk, run, trail and back alley of life. She took everybody seriously, and at face value. Including me.

She decided right away I should be in school, and that I should have a room in her big house I could call my own. She thought I might have some catching up to do, being out of school for so long, took on the formidable task of helping me get into building my reading and writing skills.

He gave me his A harmonica. And his knife with the sheath, on which he'd added some beads and a little carved thunderbird.

I never saw him again after that.

I could have, I guess, if I'd wanted to. But I got into school, and then got real busy, with making a buck here and there. Keeping out of trouble. Getting into trouble. Riding the rainbow trail as much as I could get away with, but somewhere along the way I fell off and got too self-indulgent. Made some good money, and sold out my soul doing it. Good thing I remembered him telling me that soul is the most resilient and durable part of a man, or I might not have made it this far.

Lana's granddaughter, Lynn, went traveling with me for a while, especially in the north. I decided on, and put together some adventures of my own that sometimes mushroomed into interesting times like the Chinese curse suggests you may live in. The last few years been hard, though. Times I wasn't too sure I was gonna make it.

Funny how you hit rock bottom and you manage to pull yourself up a notch or two and Thump, you take a tumble that lets you know that wasn't rock bottom at all, just a ledge on the way down you were lucky enough to land on for a while before the bottom gets kicked out from under your rock. Happens a couple of times and you begin to wonder how many ledges there are. They all seem like the bottom of the pit.

But I got a message this morning.

He was a little drunk, the trapper who sometimes stops by here running his line. It's his land I'm staying on. In amongst the usual small talk and gossip, he relayed the message he'd been carrying for me. It had come half-way across the Great Bear. Even half-cut he still had it word for word. Loralei and Spacecase want me to come down for a visit, in Colorado. It's about a medicine bundle he's finally got back. And a windigr he's got caged up in a big hole down there, feeding him a couple of beefalo a day, and can't afford to keep it up much longer. I'd have to hurry if I want to see him before they turn him loose.

There was a written note. "Fairly's back. I recall you wanted to meet him. He waltzed in yesterday with an Inca maiden named Rosalita who totes an AK-47 and is real protective of him. Leading twenty head of llama. Brother too, or rather his son and a couple of Andean she-wolves. Seems those bluecoats didn't get him after all. The chiefs held the funeral anyway, to throw them off the track, I guess. He's read some of your stuff and wants to meet you."

Jim Erkiletian

Guess I can leave this paper in the can. Might still be here when I get back.

There are ways to deal with windigrs, and there are ways to deal with the world. There are medicine bundles and there are ways of living, and dying, that heal, as well as destroy. The choice is yours. Ours.